MW00910037

WARRIORS AT 500 KNOTS

Intense stories of valiant crews flying the legendary F-4 Phantom II in the Vietnam air war.

Robert F. Kirk

authorHOUSE®

AuthorHouse™
1663 Liberty Drive
Bloomington, IN 47403
www.authorhouse.com
Phone: 1-800-839-8640

First published by AuthorHouse 4/25/2011

ISBN: 978-1-4567-5675-8 (sc)
ISBN: 978-1-4567-5676-5 (hc)
ISBN: 978-1-4567-6125-7 (e)

Library of Congress Control Number: 2011905192

Printed in the United States of America

Disclaimer: The call signs I have chosen to use in this work are limited to 1 (one) and 2 (two) for both F-4s and for forward air controllers. I am aware that this is not factual but have chosen to use them so that no identification will be made between real events or pilots and the short stories in this work. I thank the knowledgeable reader in overlooking this writer's choice. All characters in my work are fictitious and are constructed from characteristics of many individuals. Any resemblance to any individual living or dead is merely coincidental.

This book is dedicated to my wife Vicki,
my best friend, with love and infinite thanks.
Her support and help made this book possible.

I would also like to thank Fran, Paul and Niles for their help and support in this project.

I want to thank my father for teaching me the importance of integrity and my mother for teaching me the importance of faith. Psalms 91

I offer this book to my grandchildren so they can know what really happened.

Contents

Foreword

I flew two tours of duty in the areas encompassed by this book. One in the F-4 aircraft and one in an O-1 aircraft as a forward air controller, call sign "Red Marker." As I read the mission stories I was once again taken back to the 1965-1967 time frame, with all of the thrills, emotions, and fears that combat flying brings to the warrior's heart and mind.

I participated in missions very similar to the missions so vividly conveyed by Robert Kirk. I found all events described in this book to be accurate and forcefully depicted just as I remember them. The author is an excellent pilot and a master writer. The events that pilots experience in combat are the crucible that refine us and make us better men, better citizens, and better fathers of the generations to come. At no time did I feel that we were not acting in the best interest of the United States of America.

This book should be read by all who have an interest in the war in Southeast Asia, known as the "War in Vietnam."

Robert Kirk has done us all a favor by telling it "Like it was," in a time of great national confusion.

Colonel Paul Fisher, Jr. USAF (Ret)
O-1 FAC, F4C Fighter Pilot

If you want to find out some facts about Vietnam or the war effort, then Google it. If you want to live a mission, feel the humid jungle air, or feel the bombs fall off the F-4D during a bomb run then Robert Kirk's book is for you. You will hear the talk between controllers and alert crews as they scramble to go to combat. You will feel the sweat run down your neck, a 5-G turn off a jungle target, and the impact of the loss of a friend. You will taste the overcooked eggs and the great feeling of landing back in the States, done with the combat tour and moving on with your life.

This book is for you. You will love the short stories taking you right into combat the way it really happened. Robert's book is a one-of-kind read. Read and experience the war first-hand.

Lt. Colonel Niles Bughman USAF (Ret)
F-4D/E Fighter Pilot

Preface

This book is a work of fiction organized as a collection of short stories. However, the stories have origins in real events and with few exceptions the author was part of every story. The author served a year tour of duty in South Vietnam in 1969 and flew 197 combat missions in the F-4D Phantom II aircraft. These missions took him over South Vietnam, North Vietnam and Laos.

The author has wanted to write the stories in this book for the last forty-one years. However, it seemed that life just kept getting in the way. Still, he had reason and desire to record these events that were simple but powerful. That reason was to show the dedication to duty exemplified by American aircrews. For them assigned missions were to be completed no matter what the challenges attached to them. They displayed an exceptional dedication to duty.

As a young lieutenant sitting through mission briefings at Da Nang and Phu Cat there were times he would think: *This mission is going to be dangerous and the weather is horrible, or damn, we could get killed doing this. Are we going to that dangerous place again so soon?* During these times he learned a great deal from the men who were sitting around him. He knew these men had to be thinking the same thing, but they never said a word. They just got the mission done! It was never too hard, it was never too dangerous, they viewed each assigned mission as their duty. He never heard fellow officers whine or cry about a mission before it was completed and in the books. It was all about doing one's duty. This served as a very powerful model for the author. It set a pattern for living his life that has served him well. Just get it done!

It isn't suggested that the men didn't bitch and moan after the mission was over. They did! In the bar or in the gatherings of men packed into someone's room playing cards and drinking an assortment of beverages, all sorts of stories were told and complaints were expressed. The military, particularly the military leaders and the politicians in Washington were all given hell. It was expressed many times in jest that Mickey Mouse wore an Air Force watch! However, as soon as the missions came down the next day, it was all business, all duty.

The author was also impressed with the professionalism of the men with whom he served. In all his professional life since, he has never seen its equal. Professionalism was the norm from the airman basic, through the crew chief, chief master sergeant, and the officer ranks. When an aircraft was broken, it got fixed. When an F-4 was written up for some mechanical problem there was the expectation that it would be corrected before the next flight and be ready to fly. All were thankful to the maintainers of the aircraft who saw to it that pilots, who "broke" the airplanes, would have them ready and safe to fly the next mission.

The author also observed that throughout the ranks there was not only a dedication to duty but also to honor and country. It's hard to express the concepts involved in these three words. However, what is known is that the commitment and work ethic of those service men displayed this dedication to these three powerful words. The author suspects it has always been that way with the American fighting man whatever his or her assignment. The stories recorded throughout the wars and conflicts of this great nation echo the truth of this.

Somehow Vietnam received a distinction different than those of other conflicts. There were efforts made by some to try and make it less than honorable to serve there or that it needed to be stained by some contaminant of shame, guilt, loss or failure. The author wants to express his view that Vietnam shouldn't be stained with shame, loss or failure. It was about success gained through the blood and efforts of those who served, and lived or died. They worked through the media criticism and political ineptness to express again and again: duty, honor, country.

Every day the author experienced the real meaning of courage. He learned that courage isn't the absence of fear in dealing with the difficult events in one's life. It's meeting these fearful challenges head on and facing them anyway. It's the moving ahead in spite of our fears and not in their absence. Courage is doing one's duty even when fear is demanding that we cut and run. The author saw real courage every day from our servicemen in Vietnam.

The author wants to publicly express his thanks for all that was learned from these men, and for their great sacrifice to maintain the fragile wall that protects our freedom and stands between us and the destruction of our liberty.

Those who served in Vietnam took a beating, not just from the enemy without, they won the fight from that enemy, but from those within, who either couldn't or wouldn't comprehend how this honorable conflict contributed to our security.

It has been a long time, but the author wants to say to all our Vietnam veterans: Thank You and Welcome Home!

Duty, Honor, Country

"Duty, Honor, Country: Those three hallowed words reverently dictate what you ought to be, what you can be, what you will be. They are your rallying points: to build courage when courage seems to fail; to regain faith when there seems to be little cause for faith; to create hope when hope becomes forlorn. Unhappily, I possess neither that eloquence of diction, that poetry of imagination, nor that brilliance of metaphor to tell you all that they mean.

The unbelievers will say they are but words, but a slogan, but a flamboyant phase.

But these are some of the things they do. They build your basic character. They mold you for your future roles as the custodians of the nation's defense. They make you strong enough to know when you are weak, and brave enough to face yourself when you are afraid.

They teach you to be proud and unbending in honest failure, but humble and gentle in success; not to substitute words for action; not to seek the path of comfort, but to face the stress and spur of difficulty and challenge; to learn to stand up in the storm…

Their story is known to all of you. It is the story of the American man at arms. My estimate of him was formed on the battlefields many, many years ago, and has never changed. I regarded him then, as I regard him now, as one of the world's noblest figures; not only as one of the finest military characters, but also as one of the most stainless.

His name and fame are the birthright of every American citizen. In his youth and strength, his love and loyalty, he gave all that mortality can give. He needs no eulogy from me, or from any other man. He has written his own history and written it in red on the enemy's breast.

But when I think of his patience under adversity, of his courage under fire, and of his modesty in victory, I am filled with an emotion of admiration I cannot put into words. He belongs to history as furnishing one of the greatest examples of successful patriotism. He belongs to posterity as the instructor of future generations in the principles of liberty and freedom. He belongs to the present, to us, by his virtues and by his achievements.

In twenty campaigns, on a hundred battle fields, around a thousand campfires, I have witnessed that enduring fortitude, that patriotic self-abnegation, and that invincible determination which have carved his statue in the hearts of his people.

I do not know the dignity of their birth, but I do know the glory of their death. They died unquestioning, uncomplaining, with faith in their hearts, and on their lips the hope that we would go on to victory. Always for them: Duty, Honor, Country. Always their blood, and sweat, and tears, as they saw the way and the light.

And twenty years later, on the other side of the globe, against the filth of dirty foxholes, the stench of ghostly trenches, the slime of dripping dugouts, those boiling suns of the relentless heat, those torrential rains of devastating storms, the loneliness and utter desolation of jungle trails, the bitterness of long separation of those they loved and cherished, the deadly pestilence of tropical disease, the horror of stricken areas of war.

Their resolute and determined defense, their swift and sure attack, their indomitable purpose, their complete and decisive victory – always victory, always through the bloody haze of their last reverberating shot, the vision of gaunt, ghastly men, reverently following your password of Duty, Honor, Country.

Let civilian voices argue the merits or demerits of our processes of government. Whether our strength is being sapped by deficit financing indulged in too long, by federal paternalism grown too mighty, by power groups grown too arrogant, by politics grown too corrupt, by crime grown too rampant, by morals grown too low, by taxes grown too high, by extremists grown too violent; whether our personal liberties are as firm and complete as they should be.

These great national problems are not for your professional participation or military solution. Your guidepost stands out like a tenfold beacon in the night: Duty, Honor, Country.

This does not mean that you are warmongers. On the contrary the soldier above all other people prays for peace, for he must suffer and bear the deepest wounds and scars of war. But always in our ears ring the ominous wards of Plato, that wisest of all philosophers: "Only the dead have seen the end of war."

Selections from:
General Douglas MacArthur's Farewell Speech
Given to the Corps of Cadets at West Point
May 12, 1962
Used by permission
Executive Director
General Douglas MacArthur Foundation
Norfolk, Virginia

1

First In Country Flight

It was going to be a memorable night for Lieutenant John Peterson. It was going to be his first combat flight in the F-4D since arriving in Vietnam. He had arrived at Da Nang Air Base only a couple of days earlier and spent his time getting a BOQ room, processing all the needed paperwork and getting issued all the necessary flying equipment that he would be needing for his year long combat tour in Vietnam.

Lieutenant Peterson's arrival to Da Nang hadn't been an easy one. It took him the usual three months to complete his Combat Weapons School at Davis-Monthan Air Force Base in Tucson, Arizona and the six months of F-4D Phantom II flying training at George Air Force Base in Victorville, California. Then he had to complete three survival training schools before he would be ready to go to Vietnam.

The first survival school was the United States Air Force SERE School. SERE stands for Survival, Evasion, Resistance and Escape and the survival training school was at Fairchild Air Force Base, Spokane, Washington. This two-week school had one difficult task after another for the trainees to accomplish. It included the escape and evasion course where everyone got captured, no matter how good they were, or thought they were, at evading capture. Next the "prisoner of war" training began where the trainees went through an assortment of training experiences that made one main point very clear: never get captured!

The worst part of the training for Peterson was thc "little box."

During this experience, he was forced into a small wooden box. He was not sure about the exact size of the box, but it was small, very small. It was approximately 12 to 15 inches deep, 18 inches wide and 34 to 36 inches tall. Peterson's first thought, as three men attempted to cram him into the little box, was one of humor. He was blindfolded with a black hood over his head so he couldn't initially see what was going on. He thought: *They can't put me into this little box. I am over six feet tall and too big to get into it*. He was wrong, very wrong!

Peterson's emotions began to run wild as the three men forced his large frame into the small, narrow wooden box and then forced the strong wooden door closed against his back and hips. It didn't help that Peterson was a little claustrophobic and hated being in closed places. Very quickly the joints of his body began to ache and his muscles became tense and strained. His immediate fear was not being able to breathe.

Air, his mind screamed to him; *I can't breathe, I don't have enough oxygen*. Fear and panic began to take over his thoughts. *No*, he yelled in his mind, *I have to stay calm and keep my head.* He began to pray, *Dear God, please don't let me panic in here, please give me air and help me be calm.*

Then his nose felt a small tiny stream of air. Fresh air! It was coming from a small crack between the wooden boards that were used in the construction of the small boxes that lined the walls of the room. Peterson could hear other men in their boxes. Some screamed and bumped or flailed around trying to get out. Some cried and yelled because they couldn't stand the confinement. Peterson placed his nose against the crack in the wood planks that were providing him needed air and vital oxygen and breathed deeply.

Stay calm, he said to himself. *I have to stay calm, if I panic, it'll be all over.*

The trainees had been told that if they couldn't withstand the training then they'd be washed out of the program and they wouldn't fly in the Air Force. Peterson's greatest desire was to be able to fly in the Air Force. He'd proved that over and over again during Officer Training School, Pilot Training and in the F-4 Training Program. He was determined not to quit now.

I can breathe so I won't die in here, Peterson repeated over and over to himself.

I have to stay calm, I can breathe. This can't last long, Peterson continued.

However, it did continue. Peterson's legs and joints began to cramp with excruciating pain. He dared not try to move. It could get worse. His knees were high up in the box, at least as high as his head. His neck had been bent down to allow him to be stuffed into the box. The cramping got worse. The pins and needles pain came with the lack of blood supply to his muscles. His body was aflame with pain that came from joints cramping and muscles screaming from lack of blood circulation.

His thoughts continued; *I can breathe, I can stay alive. I have to keep my mind off of the pain. Think about something else, anything else.*

He continued to pray in increasing desperation, *God, please don't let me fail this test. Please give me strength to take the pain and not give up and quit. Thank you for the air. Thank you for the air, help me stay calm.*

It amazed Peterson how the small pencil-lead stream of cool air gave him so much strength and comfort. Without it he thought he would surely have given up or panicked in that little box.

Peterson lost all track of time while in the box. He didn't know if he was in there for 30 minutes, an hour or for half a day. When the door was opened by three men posing as Communist prison guards, he was overcome with thankfulness. Like a cork from a bottle his body popped backward from the small-enclosed area. Two men caught him, grabbing him under each arm, as his body left the box and fell toward the floor. His muscles were paralyzed. He couldn't move his arms or his legs. He could breathe more freely now and again that gave him comfort. The two men, without saying a word, dragged him into a dark small room about the size of two phone booths. They dropped him onto the floor and closed and locked the door behind him. He was to spend considerable time in the solitary confinement of this small room. He was out of the small box and he was very thankful for that.

The Fairchild Survival School had many other challenges that Peterson and all others had to complete successfully. However, for Peterson, none were like the "small box." He faced many personal demons that day in the box. Fear and pain came upon him like never before. Like most pilots Peterson had been a controller all his life, yet while in the box he was helpless except for his thoughts and his faith. He learned how important these were in times of trouble and need. This was especially true in times of total helplessness. This hard lesson served him well in the months to come.

Peterson became reasonably well settled at Da Nang. He was excited about his first combat mission. It was to be a night mission over Laos. He knew few details concerning the mission; however, he didn't like the weather that had settled in over Da Nang the last few hours. It was raining like hell and the clouds hung over the tops of the mountains just a few miles north of the base. The visibility would decrease then get a little better and then decrease again. At best it would increase to about two miles visibility and then go down to about a half a mile. Peterson wondered what the minimum weather would have to be before a mission would be canceled. So far, there had been no talk of it.

Peterson checked the status of his personal belongings before he left to go to the mission briefing. Flight crewmembers were required to leave their billfolds and all personal items in their quarters. No personal family pictures, letters, etc. could be taken on the mission. This was to prevent the personal items from being used as propaganda should the crewmember be shot down and captured. Under the Military Code of Conduct, if a crewmember was captured, he was to give the enemy only three items of information. These three items were the crewmember's name, rank and military serial number. No other information was to be provided to the enemy.

Peterson heard the call outside his door that the crew van was leaving to head to the squadron building. He grabbed his hat, opened the door and headed for the van. The weather was not getting any better and with the thick clouds it was hard to tell if the sun was even shining. It was getting dark even though it was only 1730.

Peterson arrived at the squadron building and immediately went into the mission planning room. He was a little early for the mission briefing because he wanted a little extra time to plan and make sure he was prepared for the mission.

The dark sky and the rain reminded Peterson of his second survival school training. It had been at Homestead Air Force Base, Florida and it was Sea Survival Training. It had been cold and rainy during his training there. The training was to prepare aircrew members for the eventuality of possible ejection from their aircraft over water. Aircrew members were taught to head for the water if their aircraft was damaged by enemy fire, because the United States Navy owned the waters around Vietnam. These waters were patrolled at all times and rescue teams were constantly standing alert to pick up downed airmen. However, ejecting over water had its own set of challenges, but with proper training the survival of crewmembers was improved by ejecting over water.

There were all sorts of tasks required in water training. These tasks included jumping off high towers into deep water and swimming under a parachute that had been hung over the water in a swimming pool, its nylon cord hanging under the water. This trained the aircrew members in the proper procedure to prevent getting tangled in their own chute when they hit the water. Training was provided on how to retrieve the pilot's survival kit from the seat after ejection from the F-4. The training included how to extract the small one-man life raft, inflate and crawl into it, without puncturing the raft. This was not an easy set of tasks to accomplish. Even with training, Peterson almost didn't survive the experience.

It was cold and raining on the day of Peterson's training at Homestead. The wind was blowing and the wind chill index made the temperature seem even colder. Peterson and his fellow airmen boarded a large sea craft and headed out into the ocean. The training began when they were out of sight of land. Each aircrew member put on a parachute harness with a survival kit attached to it. Two men were selected from the group and attached to a set of rails running off the stern of the craft. On separate command, each crewmember was dropped into the boiling current coming off the craft's propellers. The crewmember was to stay in the wake of the boat with one side of his parachute harness attached to a cable running from the craft. This was to simulate being drug by the parachute in the wind after ejection if a clean separation was not achieved.

It was soon Peterson's turn and down into the foaming water he went. Being pulled, rotating through the boat's wake up to the surface and then down under the water was frightening to Peterson. He disconnected as soon as possible from the cable that was pulling him through the water. He watched the craft pull away from him as he struggled to keep his head above water. He pulled on the cord that attached the survival kit to his parachute harness. The kit was heavy as he slowly lifted it toward the surface. While retrieving the survival kit, he had to constantly kick to keep his head above the waves. Finally he pulled the kit to him and fumbled to open it. He yanked the small rubber one-man dinghy out of the kit and pulled on the device to inflate it. Almost instantly the raft inflated. He then attempted to crawl into the small raft.

He'd been warned it would be difficult to climb into the small dinghy and to be careful not to puncture it with the sharp metal parts of his parachute harness. Peterson tried to pull himself out of the water and into the small craft. On his first try he wasn't successful. He gathered all the strength he had in his body and struggled again to attempt to pull himself into the raft. Up and into the dinghy he went as he pulled his shoulders over the end of the raft. Then he heard a terrible sound. It was the sound of air rushing out of the raft. *Damn it*, he thought. *I have torn a hole in this damn thing.* He was right. Within seconds he found himself back in the water and the raft had become only a heavy rubber weight.

What am I going to do now? He thought. In training the instructors had discussed how to repair the raft if it became punctured. However, that required a knife and he'd left his back in the BOQ room. Now his concern was to keep his head above the water and to come up with some kind of plan. Just then he saw a small boat coming toward him. He started waving his arms to get their attention. He had no way of knowing that they were coming to check on him and make sure he was okay. Quickly the boat came up to him and someone asked how he was doing.

"I punctured the damn raft and I don't have a knife to repair it," Peterson yelled to the men on the boat.

"I have a knife," one of the men told him. "Try not to lose it in the water."

The men brought the boat close to Peterson and handed him a small knife. Peterson opened the knife and pulled the deflated raft up out of the water and started looking for the puncture. He soon found it. It was a hole about a half an inch long. Peterson then started looking for the repair kit that was stored somewhere in a compartment on the raft. He found the compartment and the repair tool. It was two pieces of metal with rubber gaskets around each of their edges and a threaded steel shaft running through both sides with a wing nut on the end. The repair tool was too big to go through the puncture hole so Peterson had to cut the hole bigger so one end of the repair tool could go inside the raft and the other side would stay outside. The wing nut would then need to be tightened to make a tight seal. While bobbing up and down, Peterson took the knife and started the cut.

Don't drop the knife or the damn repair tool, he kept saying to himself.

Don't cut the hole too big or it won't seal, he continued.

No one could hear him talking to himself, but it helped him concentrate as he worked to repair the raft.

There, it's done, Peterson remarked to himself. *Now let's see if it will hold air.*

Peterson began blowing into the inflation tube on the raft. All the while he was struggling to stay afloat and keep his head above the waves.

How much air do these damn things hold? Peterson thought.

It seemed like it took an hour to blow the raft up. In reality it took only minutes.

When Peterson filled the raft with air he signaled to the circling craft that he was going to try and climb into the raft again.

"Be careful," one of the men yelled to him from the boat. "There is only one repair tool on the raft."

No pressure here, Peterson thought.

Peterson carefully pulled his body weight up and over the side of the raft making very sure that nothing metal touched the small dinghy. He was in. He turned around and positioned his large frame in the small craft as best he could. He had to pull his legs up to his chest to fit into the small raft.

"How are you? Is it holding air?" one of the men yelled to him from the boat.

"Yes, it seems to be holding," replied Peterson. "Here's your knife back. Thanks a lot for your help."

The boat pulled close enough for Peterson to hand the knife back to its owner.

"Thanks for not losing it in the water," replied the man.

The boat quickly moved away from Peterson and disappeared over the horizon.

The small one-man dinghy rolled with each wave. It rolled up and down and side to side.

The wind blew and with each dip of the dinghy Peterson was drenched with water. He rapidly became very cold from the water and the wind. There was not much he could do but to stay in the dinghy and wait for this exercise to come to an end.

Peterson began to get sick from all of the pitching and rolling motion. One moment he could see the horizon and then only water and waves around him. He'd never been much of a sailor and really didn't care for water.

Peterson became colder and colder. A science major in college, he knew that under these conditions he could suffer hypothermia. He glanced at his fingernails. They were a dark bluish, purple color.

Oh crap, he thought, *I'm going to die from exposure out here.*

That wasn't the first time he thought he might die from the training in survival school. He had to remind himself several times that this was only training.

He began to shiver uncontrollably from the water and the cold wind. Peterson had no idea how long he stayed in the raft. It could've been two hours or maybe three. However, eventually he saw the large craft that had dropped him into the ocean coming toward him. He had the idea of using the signal mirror that was in the survival kit. He quickly fumbled to get to the kit and open it. His hands were stiff and would hardly follow the commands coming from his brain. He finally found the mirror and pulled it from the kit. He knew how to use it and as quickly as he could he sent an SOS signal to the craft. Peterson didn't know if the boat saw his signal and came to his rescue or if it was already coming to pick him up, but the boat did come to him. He was quickly pulled from the water and covered with a dry blanket. He sat down on the deck of the craft shaking uncontrollably. He was cold, very cold.

I have to get down below out of this wind, he told himself.

He pulled himself up to his feet, all the while shivering uncontrollably with his teeth clicking against one another. He went to the steps leading down into the craft and soon found himself with others who had been in the water. They too were cold and miserable. There were hot showers available and Peterson wasted no time stripping off his flight suit and claiming a showerhead. At the top of the showerhead was a mirror and Peterson took a quick glance at his face. His lips were blue from the cold. He turned the temperature control as hot as he could stand and adjusted it to hit the top of his head. He continued to shiver as the hot water poured over his cold body.

After some time in the hot water, Peterson got out of the shower, grabbed a towel and dried himself off. He slipped on a dry flight suit, but continued to shiver. All that night, after getting back to the base, he shivered and just couldn't get warm in his BOQ room. Luckily the next morning's activities were canceled because of the cold, windy weather. All trainees were given their graduation certificates and taken to the airport to fly back to their duty stations.

When Peterson arrived back at his duty station he hadn't recovered from the survival training experience. He developed a high fever and his chills continued. He decided to go to the flight surgeon to obtain some medical help. The diagnosis was that Peterson had developed pneumonia. He would spend the next two weeks recovering from what could have been his last survival school.

"Hi John," greeted Captain Tom Curtis, "how the hell have you been?"

"Good, good," the startled Peterson answered. "And you, how have you been?

Peterson regained his focus on the mission's preparation. He'd been joined by the other crewmembers for the sortie. Captain Tom Curtis, Lead aircraft, would be his aircraft commander and the other crew included Captain Joe Yin and Lieutenant James Cook. They all were pouring over the vast amount of information on the target along with its exact location and military significance when an intelligence officer entered the room.

"Gentlemen, the mission has been changed because of the weather in the target area," explained the officer. "It's going to be a Sky Spot mission with Bongo controlling the weapons drop. Here are the Lat / Longs for the initial contact. You can talk to them on 242.2."

Peterson had no idea what was just said about the mission except the part about the weather. He knew that with low clouds and visibility less than two miles it would be impossible to see and attack a ground target in Laos.

"What's a Sky Spot?" asked Peterson.

"It's a method developed to deliver bombs on targets from high altitudes in bad weather," replied Captain Curtis. "It's like a GCA in the sky."

A Ground Controlled Approach or GCA, was a radar controlled landing approach that was used during bad weather to guide aircraft from high altitude down a final approach course, to the runway. It was so precise it could guide an aircraft to within less than a mile from the runway and a couple hundred feet above the ground. The pilot would then pick up the high intensity runway approach lights and make a safe landing even when the weather was extremely bad.

Captain Curtis and the other crewmembers sat down in the mission planning room and talked through the plan for the Sky Spot mission. The basic idea was that they'd take off from the base and climb separately through the bad weather and rejoin in formation when in the clear on top of the clouds. They'd fly together in formation to the target area and contact Bongo Approach for the mission details. If the bad weather extended up to their flight altitude they'd use the radar on the number two aircraft to get within visual range for a rejoin.

The two crews sat through their intelligence and weather briefings. The Intel briefing sounded good because there would be no ground fire that could reach them at their cruising altitude and they'd be dropping their bombs at that altitude under Bongo control. The weather however was another story. There was rain and thunderstorms forecast from takeoff all the way through the planned mission and the return to base. The only good news was that the visibility on their return might improve to two miles. The improvement in the visibility would help the F-4s find the runway for landing on their return.

Combat missions in Vietnam always had their risks. Taking off an aircraft with tons of bombs on board, flying hundreds of miles over enemy occupied territory, dropping the ordinance and returning to base were hazardous. However, by adding the night conditions and stormy weather into the mix the risk or possibility of something going wrong increased exponentially.

The change in the mission also delayed their planned takeoff time by thirty minutes. So, after all the new planning and briefings the crews had a few extra minutes before going to their aircraft. They decided to stay in the squadron area and drink a cup of hot coffee before going out into the cool, very wet, nighttime weather. Peterson poured himself a cup of coffee and put in his customary dab of powered milk. For some unexplained reason, the coffee in Vietnam was usually bad. It was either too weak or too strong but it was always bitter. However, none-the-less it was coffee, and most drank it willingly for the effects of the caffeine.

Peterson took his coffee over to a window and peered around the window coverings at the conditions outside. It was very dark and the rain was coming down in torrents. The wind was impacting the tropical vegetation with ferocity. Thoughts raced through his mind. *What would it be like ejecting from the aircraft in weather like this? What would it be like descending in a parachute through the heavy rain and wind, through the triple canopy jungle of Laos and then hitting the ground?*

Damn, he thought, *I'm not going there.*

Peterson's thoughts shifted to his jungle survival training that he'd completed only a few weeks earlier. Aircrew members were required to complete this one-week course at Clark Air Force Base in the Philippines. Peterson, with only a stopover for fuel in Japan, had flown, on a contracted military airline, from the States to Clark. He had told his wife and other family members good-bye and had flown out of the San Francisco International Airport. The good-byes to his family were hard but they were especially hard for him and his wife. They'd been married for only a year and the thoughts of being apart for the coming year were difficult. He remembered standing there in his military uniform, hugging his wife, and then turning around to walk through the crowded San Francisco airport to the plane. The crowd, though not openly hostile, was certainly not friendly. Peterson wasn't spit on or given calls of baby killer that had been reported by some veterans. The crowd only looked at him with indifference and with a sort of cold contempt. He remembered turning his head and taking one last glance at his wife as he entered the plane for departure. She was crying but standing bravely among the indifferent crowd. He remembered thinking as he took his seat in the departing airplane. *Well God, here we go. It's going to be a long year!*

Peterson had been excited about going to jungle survival school at Clark. As a boy he'd enjoyed the Tarzan movies and had become infatuated with the jungle and all of its promised adventures. The training that he received in the jungle survival course was excellent. The training stressed how to stay alive in a jungle environment including what to eat and what not to eat. It involved not only how to get food and water and travel in the jungle unnoticed, but also how to escape and evade the enemy. Part of the course included a two-night stay in the jungle. The first night was spent with one other crewmember. They were given a two hour head start and were told to go as far into the jungle as desired to hide from the enemy who would be hunting for them. After the two hours had elapsed and it became nightfall, the indigenous native warriors of the Philippines were sent out into the jungle to find the hiding crewmembers. Each crewmember had been given five poker chips that were to be given to any warriors that found them. Each warrior that found a crewmember was to be given one poker chip. The chip would then be exchanged for a pound of rice back at the base.

Peterson had been assigned a young F-100 pilot as the second member of his escape team. His name was Lieutenant Allen Beck and he and Peterson hit it off immediately. They quickly decided that they weren't going to be found by the enemy. They headed off into the jungle and traveled for at least an hour before finding their hiding place. It was a stand of very tall elephant grass that was positioned on the edge of a steep cliff that ran along a long jungle canyon wall. Peterson and Beck reasoned that no one would dare travel along this dangerous cliff area at night, especially just for a pound or two of rice. To help conceal their location they both ran and jumped over the outer portion of the elephant grass into its interior. They did this so as not to leave footprints that might give away their location. Together they pressed down a center section of the grass and made comfortable pads for their expected good night's sleep. The dark sky gave way to a black one. Peterson and Beck decided to pull out their C rations and have some semblance of dinner. They were both excited about the possibility of a successful night of evading the mock enemy that would be searching for them.

The first part of the night passed quickly and both Peterson and Beck fell into a light sleep. At about 2300 things began to change. They heard noises that woke them both. It was the sound of men traveling through the jungle and barking directions back and forth to each other.

"They'll never find us here," whispered Beck to Peterson.

"I think you're right," responded Peterson. "It's just too dangerous for them to come to the edge of this cliff at night."

The group of searching indigenous warriors came closer. They weren't speaking English so it was impossible for Peterson or Beck to understand what they were talking about. They were speaking in a relatively normal tone and it was clear that they hadn't discovered their location. Suddenly the pitch and volume of one of the searcher's voices went up. It was clear to both what had happened. One of the warriors had come across the edge of the cliff and it had scared him. He was loudly explaining the hazard and his near escape with death to his fellow searchers. It was clearly a humorous moment for Peterson and Beck. Both began to laugh quietly about what had happened. Their plan was working. Surely now that the cliff was identified all the searchers would leave this location and move to another less dangerous area to continue the search. Like many well thought out, foolproof plans, this one began to rapidly fall apart. Instead of the warriors stopping the exploration of this location, their search intensified. More warriors joined into the hunt and within minutes their hiding place had been discovered. A single warrior pulled the long grass back as he stuck his head into the little clearing made by the two men. He smiled and said "Chit! Chit!"

Both gave him one of their poker chips. He smiled again and pulled his head back from the grass and disappeared. Of course this man told his fellow searchers of their location. Within minutes all of their chips were gone but the visits continued all night long. Both men didn't sleep the rest of the night. Every few minutes another warrior would greet them with, "Chit? Chit?"

Peterson thought of the second night he had to spend in the jungle. This night the requirement was that each crewmember had to stay alone. Crewmembers had to go into the jungle, with only minimum survival gear, and establish some kind of sleeping location and stay there alone until dawn. At first this sounded like fun to Peterson. He had liked to camp out as a boy and he was beginning to really like the jungle. So after a dinner prepared by one of the indigenous warriors, that demonstrated how to cook and eat items found in the jungle, Peterson struck out to find his sleeping location for the night. He decided to get as far away from the base camp as possible. So he gathered his assigned survival materials and took off to find and prepare his camp for the night. He traveled a long distance, at least a half a mile from the base camp. He'd been given a piece of parachute canopy along with some parachute cord. He stretched the canopy between two trees and tied it together with the parachute cord thus making a small hammock. He was proud of his work and was glad that he didn't have to sleep on the ground. The week before, a crewmember in the jungle-training program had eaten a fruit bar for dinner and had decided to sleep on the jungle floor. While he slept a large jungle rat, who must have smelled the fruit bar on the crew-member's fingers, came up and bit off the end of a couple of his fingers. Being able to sleep off the ground seemed like a good idea to Peterson.

After setting up his campsite, Peterson made his way back through the jungle to the base camp. The trainees were to have some additional training on jungle survival that evening. Peterson arrived at camp a little early and sat down with the trainers and began to listen to their discussions. They were talking about the Communist guerillas that operated in the mountains around this training area. Peterson listened as they discussed how the guerillas searched for American servicemen that were training in the area. They talked about how servicemen had been captured and killed in the jungle by the Communists who roamed through the area. Peterson decided that staying a great distance away from the main camp wasn't a good idea. It was dark, but with the assistance of a bright moon, Peterson left the camp and rapidly moved through the jungle. He arrived at his sleeping site and began to break camp. He fumbled to get all of his gear together and started moving back toward the base camp. It was hard finding his way in the dark and every jungle sound had his imagination running wild. He was relieved when he saw the fires of the base camp about 100 yards away. He moved even closer to the base camp and looked for a spot where he could spend the night. He eventually found two trees the proper distance apart and hung his hammock. He got back to base camp just in time for the start of the evening training. He was relieved to be much closer to his buddies and help if he should need it. He was thankful that he didn't encounter any Communist guerillas that night.

The next day involved more training but it came to an end at 1200. The afternoon was utilized awarding certificates of completion, processing out and retreating to the BOQs to clean up. Peterson was scheduled to fly to Da Nang the next morning to begin his combat tour. The year combat tour didn't start until the crewmember's boots hit the ground in Vietnam. Peterson was anxious to get his tour started as soon as possible.

Peterson completed processing out and went to the BOQ room to pack his stuff for the trip to Da Nang the next day and then rest before dinner. About 1800 he went to the Officer's Club to have a good dinner since he had eaten very little during his stay in the jungle. He planned to eat dinner, get to sleep early that night, and be ready for his 0455 departure flight to Da Nang the next morning. He had a good dinner at the Officer's Club and visited with a few friends after dinner while at the Club. When it was time to leave, he went outside the Club to wait for transportation back to his room.

While he was waiting, he began to chat with a couple of Air Force officers who were also waiting for transportation. When he introduced himself during the conversation one of the officers remarked that he thought that the Red Cross had made an announcement at the Club for Peterson. He wasn't really sure about it but he suggested that Peterson call and check with the Red Cross when he got back to his quarters. Peterson wondered what this could be all about. He soon was to find out. When he arrived back at his room he tried to call the Red Cross. The phone service was terrible and it took him several tries to finally get through to an official. When he finally got through and informed the official who he was, he was told that they had an emergency message for him. Peterson asked what the message was. The official informed him that he didn't want to give him the message over the phone. Peterson insisted that he be given the message. He feared what it might be; all kinds of different tragic scenarios ran through his mind. He needed to know what had happened and he needed to know now. The official relented and agreed to read Peterson the message. It read:

"Lieutenant John Peterson,

It is with deep regret that we must inform you that your father has died unexpectedly after being admitted into a local hospital. Please contact your local Commander's Office ASAP for emergency orders back to CONUS. The Red Cross will assist you in any way possible during this emergency."

For several moments Peterson couldn't speak. The Red Cross Official asked several questions from Peterson but didn't get a reply. Thousands of thoughts raced through Peterson's mind. He couldn't sort through them. Of all of the terrible possibilities that he'd let fill his mind before the phone call, this one never entered his mind. Like most sons he just assumed that his dad would live forever. Peterson finally thanked the Red Cross Official and slowly hung up the phone. He went over to a chair and started to sit down. *No*, he thought. *I have to get going.*

Within minutes, he left his room taking the luggage that he had already packed for the flight to Da Nang. He didn't really know where to go for assistance, but soon found himself in an Officer of the Day's room. He told the officer on duty of the Red Cross message and the need for an emergency flight back to the States. The officer was very helpful and within a couple of hours, with the receipt of paperwork from the Red Cross, Peterson was scheduled on a military contract flight. He didn't sleep that night. He walked to the flight line terminal and sat on the wooden benches inside the terminal. He must have been in shock, as his thoughts continued to race randomly about his dad and mom and what must be happening back at home.

The military contract flight arrived on time and Peterson boarded it for his trip back to the States. He could remember very little about the flight except it seemed very long and dark. The sun didn't seem to shine any during the long, long flight. He hardly spoke to anyone on the flight, and his thoughts continually centered on his dad. He reflected on his childhood memories and how unknowing to him his dad had prepared him for this moment. He realized that the anchor of his life that his dad had provided was now severed and gone forever. It was now totally up to him to steer the ship of his life with only the memory of the training and love his dad had provided. At first this was a cold, chilling and scary thought. However, he soon realized that he had been provided the psychological and spiritual strength for this time of his life. He realized that his dad and mom had done a great job of preparing him for this moment. These thoughts provided him needed strength.

The next two weeks for Peterson were a fast blur. Being reunited with his wife, mother and other family members, and attending the services for his dad were events that he struggled through. He couldn't allow himself the opportunity to grieve for fear that some weakness or loss of focus might set in. He had to suppress all of his emotions and his loss. He had only days earlier fully set his mind, his strength, and the next year of his life, on being at war. He knew his buddies, those he had trained with, were already there risking their lives in the war effort. He felt guilty for not being there with them and he knew he had to get in country as soon as possible to join them in the fight. As soon as he thought his mother could take the news, Peterson told her he had to go back and he had to go back as soon as possible. It was painful for all. He and his wife flew to Los Angeles International Airport where he was scheduled for a direct flight to Da Nang. Once again the airport was an unfriendly environment. There were cold stares from passengers waiting for flights as they looked at him in his uniform. No one seemed grateful for what he was about to do. No one said anything kind or encouraging to him. His sacrifice, like so many Vietnam warriors, would be a private sacrifice. As Peterson and his wife walked to the airline gate there were a few derogatory comments made regarding him and his uniform. He never responded but walked steadily with determination through the crowds to the loading gate. This second time of departure from his wife was much worse than the first. He emotionally just couldn't say goodbye to her. As she stood bravely in front of him with tears in her eyes, he gave her one last hug and then turned and walked through the entry doors of the departing plane. It was the hardest thing he had ever done in his life.

"Peterson, Peterson," called Curtis. "Where the hell are you?"

"Sorry Sir," Peterson replied, "I was just thinking about some things."

"Well, you better get your ass in gear and hit the head one more time before we launch, there are no restrooms where we're going."

"Yes Sir, great idea," Peterson responded, "I'll be back in one."

Out the door and through the wind and rain, the two crews made their long, wet journey to their F-4s. It was a dreadful night to fly. The crewmembers, soaked through and through, went through their preflight checks and climbed into the cockpits and strapped on their F-4s. Soon the engines were running and Curtis called for permission from the tower to taxi to the runway.

"Da Nang Tower, Gunfighters 1 and 2 taxi," radioed Curtis to the tower.

"Gunfighter Flight," replied the tower. "Taxi runway three-five right."

"Roger, runway three-five right," responded Curtis.

The two fully armed F-4s taxied out of the safety of their dry concrete revetments into the dark, rainy night. The lights around the base reflected through the raindrops that collected and ran across the F-4's canopies. The rain made it very hard for the pilots to see anything clearly. The blue taxiway lights helped them keep their aircraft centered on the taxiway and headed for the end of the runway.

Once at the departure end of the runway the armament crews pulled the safety pins from the fuses of the eighteen 500-pound bombs that each of the F-4s carried. The armament crew chief held up the pins with their red flags to show the pilots that their bombs were armed. Curtis gave the crew chief thumbs up, and then called the tower.

"Da Nang Tower, Gunfighters 1 and 2 ready to launch runway three-five right."

"Gunfighters 1 and 2 cleared for takeoff runway three-five right," responded the tower.

"Cleared for takeoff, runway three-five right," radioed back Curtis.

Both F-4s taxied into position onto runway three-five right and began their takeoff checks. Soon Gunfighter 1 was ready and Curtis turned on, then off, his taxi light to signal to Gunfighter 2 he was ready for takeoff. Yin responded with a flash of his taxi light to signal that he was also ready for takeoff.

"Gunfighter 1 rolling," called Curtis over the radio.

Seconds later Gunfighter 2 responded.

"Gunfighter 2 on the roll."

Within seconds after bringing the gear up Gunfighter 1 entered the thick clouds with rain coming down hard on the aircraft. The red rotating anti-collision light flashed distracting signals within the clouds.

"That's disorienting as hell," remarked Curtis to Peterson over the intercom.

"I'm going to turn the damn anti-collision light off."

"Great," responded Peterson. "It's driving me crazy."

In clouds, flashing light from a rotating beacon can give the pilots vertigo and make it difficult to fly the aircraft. It was a good idea to turn it off under these conditions.

Gunfighter 2 joined on Gunfighter 1. Captain Yin kept his F-4 tucked in very close, within feet, to Gunfighter 1. They continued their climb to Angels Two-Seven-Zero or 27,000 feet. They remained in the soup all the way to level off. With no moon in a dark sky, and in the thick clouds, there was no outside reference for attitude flying. Captain Curtis had to rely completely on the F-4's flight instruments for attitude reference. Air Force pilots are trained to do this but it required a lot of extra work and increased the dangers of flying.

"Gunfighter 2, Gunfighter 1, change to Bongo frequency 242.2 now," radioed Curtis.

"Bongo on 242.2," replied Yin.

"Gunfighter 2, are you up?"

"Gunfighter 2 with you."

"Bongo Control," called Curtis, "Gunfighters 1 and 2 with you, each with eighteen Mark 82s. We are on the zero-four-eight degree radial, 62 DME off Channel 72, Angels Two-Seven-Zero."

"Gunfighter Flight, Squawk 2723 and Ident for radar contact," responded Bongo Approach.

"Squawk 2723 and Ident," responded Curtis.

The IFF (Identification, Friend or Foe) code was used to identify aircraft on radar. The ground control radar would send a signal to the aircraft's transponder and the transponder would reply with the code that was entered into it. Each aircraft under control by a ground facility could then be identified and controlled utilizing the code assigned to the aircraft.

"We have radar contact, zero-four-seven degree radial, 61 DME, off Channel 72, Angels Two-Seven-Zero," responded Bongo. "We'll give you heading and altitude instructions for a Sky Spot bomb drop. When you're in correct position we'll give you a command to release your bombs. We'll give the verbal command, "Pickle, Pickle." On the second "Pickle" you'll release your bombs. Both Gunfighter 1 and 2 will drop on the same signal. If I give the command at anytime to "abort" you'll safety your bomb switches and not drop your bombs. Do Gunfighters 1 and 2 both understand my instructions?"

"Gunfighter 1 Roger," radioed Curtis.

"Gunfighter 2 Roger," radioed Yin.

"Gunfighter Flight turn to a heading of one-eight-zero degrees and maintain Angels Two-Seven-Zero. You are 40 feet high. Maintain your current indicated airspeed. Please correct altitude and do not acknowledge further transmissions," radioed Bongo Control.

"Damn," radioed Peterson to Curtis over the intercom. "They can tell our altitude by 40 feet?"

"Yes, I guess so," responded Curtis. "I hope you're up to it tonight."

"What did you say?" replied Peterson.

"You're going to fly this mission. Tonight we're going to make a killer out of you. You have the aircraft," radioed Curtis over the intercom to Peterson.

It was like Curtis had plunged a dagger into Peterson's heart with the comment, "Tonight we're going to make a killer out of you."

He'd never thought of what he was going to be doing for a year as being a killer. Peterson was a religious man. He'd been a Christian since a young boy. He had conflicts about this war and about killing but they had always been academic. His sense of duty to country had always won his mental battles. But tonight, on his first mission it was no longer academic, not just a discussion, it was real and it was personal.

"I got the aircraft," responded Peterson.

No time to think this over, he thought. *I've got a job to do here and I have to fly this damn aircraft as best I can.*

Peterson's eyes focused sharply on his flight instruments. He looked at the attitude indicator, the vertical velocity indicator (VVI), altimeter and air speed indicators, then back to his attitude indicator. He knew he had to get his instrument scan up to speed in a hurry, a lot depended on it.

"Gunfighter Flight, heading one-eight-one degrees, 20 feet high, increase airspeed 5 knots," radioed Bongo Control.

Peterson's thumb reached up to the mike switch to acknowledge, then realized he was not to respond to their call. It was a strange feeling not to respond to air traffic control's (ATC) instructions. He then noticed his heading indicator was one-eight-four-degrees.

Damn it, he thought. *I'm not going to screw this thing up.*

He put gentle pressure on the control stick to the left and pushed a little on the left rudder pedal to correct his aircraft's heading back to one-eight-one-degrees. At the same time he pushed forward on the control stick very lightly to lose the 20 feet of altitude.

"Gunfighter Flight, correct left to one-seven-eight degrees. On altitude and airspeed," radioed Bongo Control.

They caught me off the damn heading, he thought. *But the altitude and airspeed are good.*

Peterson took a quick glance out the canopy and then back to his instruments. There was no light in the sky only thick, dark clouds. It was like flying through a bottle of black ink.

I have to keep focused on flying, he thought. *I have to be perfect tonight.*

"Gunfighter Flight," radioed Bongo Control, "two miles from target, check switches, turn right one degree, 20 feet low, airspeed 2 knots fast. Correcting nicely."

Focus, focus, Peterson thought as he made small corrections. He could feel the sweat created by the tension of the mission. He refused to be distracted by it or anything else. *Small corrections, small corrections,* Peterson whispered to himself.

"All switches are set," Curtis called to Peterson.

"Roger," answered Peterson, as he focused like a laser on his mission.

"Ten seconds to drop," radioed Bongo, "on altitude, on heading and airspeed."

Peterson focused on his instruments and froze their position.

"Ready, ready," radioed Bongo, "Pickle, Pickle."

Peterson's left thumb moved to the pickle button on his control stick and pressed the red button on the second Pickle command. Instantly the bombs began departing the F-4. Peterson glanced quickly to his right at Gunfighter 2. The Mark 82s were dropping off Gunfighter 2's aircraft as well.

"Gunfighter Flight," radioed Bongo Control, "good job tonight, the bombs are on their way to the target. Looks like a good strike. Cleared off frequency, have a safe flight home. See you next time."

"Roger," Peterson radioed to Bongo, "thanks for your help."

"Good job," Curtis remarked to Peterson over the intercom. "Now take us home."

"Thanks Sir," Peterson replied a little startled. "You want me to fly us home and fly the approach?"

"Can you do it?" Curtis asked.

"Yes Sir, I can," responded Peterson. "Will you take the aircraft for a moment, I need to take a breath."

"For a moment," replied Curtis, "then it's yours. I got the aircraft."

"You have the aircraft," responded Peterson.

Peterson reached over to his oxygen regulator and switched it to 100 percent oxygen and also hit the pressure-breathing switch. This delivered cool 100 percent oxygen under pressure to Peterson's oxygen mask. He took one deep breath while switching the inertial navigator control panel target window to Da Nang. The navigation needles responded by providing navigation directions to Da Nang. The cool flow of 100 percent oxygen gave Peterson the boost he needed.

"I have the aircraft Sir," Peterson called to Curtis over the intercom.

"You have the aircraft," responded Curtis.

"Gunfighter 2, Gunfighter 1, switch to Da Nang Approach," radioed Peterson, "We'll make a two ship approach for landing."

"Roger, switching to Da Nang Approach, I'll stay on your wing for landing," responded Yin.

After all, Peterson thought, *I've flown one Ground Controlled Approach tonight, and I can fly another one to land.*

Peterson completed the GCA approach and landed at Da Nang with Gunfighter 2 on his wing. They both landed safely even on a dark, stormy night with a rain soaked runway. Peterson grew that night as a pilot, a warrior and as a human being. For better or for worse, like so many young men in Vietnam, he would never view the world the same. Had he killed men that night or only monkeys? He would never know. He did his duty, and that was what he and countless others came to Vietnam to do.

2

A Milk Run

The alert shack was quiet at the Phu Cat Air Base, Republic of South Vietnam. The four F-4D crews were resting after a hard set of two missions. The crews sat alert for 24-hour shifts, eating and sleeping in the facility during this time. Actually, the eating was not really eating. It was involving oneself with MCIs or C rations. They were said to contain all the calories that a person needed to stay alive, but there was no claim as to quality or taste. Usually, a person could eat one, maybe two boxes of the rations before they were through. The C ration contents would just sit in the stomach and swell up, completely filling the abdominal cavity. One got the feeling that just one more meal of these things and the body might explode.

The F-4 crewmembers were restricted by regulation to flying only three combat missions during their 24 hours in the alert shack. This may sound easy, but in fact was a very difficult thing. Crews had to be ready to launch with only a three-minute warning. The instant the phone rang, the crews would start their run to the planes. It made no difference what a crewmember was doing: sleeping, eating, or playing cards. The clock started when the phone rang. The crews had to get to the planes, start them, taxi to the runway, and take off within the three-minute limit.

What made these missions extremely difficult was that the pilots had to brief for the flight on the go. The pilots never knew where they were going, what type mission or what the risk was from enemy fire. Some missions were routine and were affectionately called a "milk run." At other times the missions were extremely dangerous. Often however, many of the alert missions were troops in contact (TIC). This meant that the good guys were in trouble. It could be that American or South Vietnamese troops were caught in the open and under attack; an isolated army or marine firebase could be under attack or any number of other life and death situations. A call for airpower in the middle of the night or early morning before the sun came up was plain bad news.

In this particular alert compound there were three sections: an open area with several tables and chairs and a side kitchen where pilots could make coffee or hot tea. The third section was a separate room with six or seven double deck bunks. This room was kept completely dark at all times, which allowed aircrew members to go in and try to get a little sleep. However, sleep was hard to come by in the bunkroom. With crewmembers coming or going, the room was flooded with light, disturbing all within. However, the biggest obstacle to sleep was the pilot's constant awareness of the ring of the phone. Any noise at all caused the pilot to move from a light sleep to wide-awake with his adrenaline flowing. It was a rare thing for a pilot to get any meaningful rest during the 24-hour alert.

The F-4Ds carried a large assortment of weapons and were armed depending on each individual mission. They almost always carried two missiles, the AIM-7 or AIM-9. The AIM-9 missile was a heat seeker. When launched, it would fly toward the heat generated by the enemy aircraft. It was a great missile and it could be relied on for a high percentage of kills. For alert missions the usual load of weapons included several 500-pound bombs (either in high drag or slick configuration), cluster bomb units (CBUs), napalm and the 20 mm Gatling gun. The Gatling gun could fire six thousand 20 mm rounds per minute. The enemy hated the Gatling gun. It destroyed anything it hit and the pilots could put the rounds right on target. This night, each of the F-4s was loaded with six high drag 500-pound bombs, two canisters of napalm, and the 20 mm gun.

The F-4D's crew was composed of two crewmembers: a pilot in the front seat, the frontseater, who was the aircraft commander, and a backseat pilot, or navigator, who was the plane's weapons officer.

The backseater was affectionately referred to as the Guy in the Back (GIB). His job, as weapons officer, was to primarily operate the inertial navigation system (INS), bombing computer, and the radar system. All of these systems would, or could, be used in air-to-air combat situations or air to ground bombing modes. The radar on the F-4 was especially good. It could pick up any traffic, friendly or not, over a hundred miles away and could lock on to that traffic at 50 miles and track its flight path. The F-4's AIM 7 radar guided missile could then be fired to destroy the target if it was determined to be hostile.

Captain Ron F. Kilmer was an F-4D aircraft commander. He was a good pilot, a good man and well respected. He was all business and he "got it." He had a built in crap detector that allowed him to see every assignment or mission for what it was. He got the important stuff done and was able to shake off the rest. This was important to those who flew with him because he did not put others' lives at risk without reason. If the mission was important, he got it done! If it was a crap mission that was dreamed up by some feather merchant or military dipstick in Saigon, then he went through the drill, but put no lives at risk unnecessarily. He had a lot of combat experience with 192 combat missions and ten months in country. Time spent in Vietnam was called in country time.

The combat flights of the F-4 were almost always composed of two aircraft, a flight lead and a wingman. An unusual mission might require a flight of four.

Captain Kilmer was the flight Lead for this alert period. His wingman was Captain John Curtis with his GIB, Lieutenant Larry Brown. Captain Curtis was a new guy in country, he had been in Vietnam for only a month.

It was during ones' first few months in country that the highest risk of loss was encountered. Flying on the target range for practice in the States was not the same as flying real combat missions. On the practice target range the pilots flew slower to get a better score hitting the target. In country, the faster you went the less chance you had of being hit by enemy fire. It was affectionately referred to as "hauling ass." On the range, pilots made multiple passes on the target. Practice makes perfect, so to speak.

In country, multiple passes got you killed. Statistics of downed aircraft during the war showed that the more passes made on the target, the higher the risk of being shot down. So a saying was coined from this research that stated, "One pass and haul ass!"

However, this axiom did not apply to aircraft sitting alert. With so many of their missions aiding troops in contact with the enemy, everything that could be done to help, was done. Pushing the limits for the pilots, the aircraft, and the flight conditions was always expected. When the troops needed help, they got it even if it meant putting the aircraft and crews at risk. Everyone knew, accepted and embraced this concept. To help, or save, a brother in arms was the highest calling. All willingly signed on to this unwritten code of warrior conduct.

Lieutenant Brown, in contrast to Curtis, was not a new guy. He was on the eleventh month of his year tour and had completed 191 combat missions. He knew the game and how it was played. He knew all that mattered to him was: do I go home soon or not? It was the practice in Vietnam to pair an experienced GIB with a new aircraft commander. The experienced GIB would, with all he had learned in combat, help the new aircraft commander get through the first few months alive. The rest of the tour would be the responsibility of the newly trained aircraft commander to keep himself alive. Some learned and made it home, others didn't and several paid a huge price.

It was early in the morning, about 0200 (zero-two-hundred hours). Kilmer's GIB, Lieutenant Ben Stone was back in the dark room trying to get some sleep. Lieutenant Stone was young, right out of pilot training, but smart. He was a fast learner and had no illusions about what this war was all about. He knew that the bottom line, politics or no, was the hard cold fact, do you go home at the end of your year tour. This fact eluded some, and in too many cases, it cost them their lives. His belief was, get the job done, but make it home when the tour is completed.

But now at 0200, all was quiet in the alert compound. Captain Kilmer was relaxing in his bamboo chair, Lieutenant Stone was resting in the dark room. Captain Curtis and Lieutenant Brown were involved in a game of poker. Poker was popular on the base and five-card stud was the most common game. Little money ever changed hands but lots of stories both about home and about former combat missions were shared. Of course the faults of military life were the topic of many a conversation and always fair game.

"Ring. Ring." All hearts began to beat faster. Kilmer grabbed the phone, "Alert shack, Cobra 1 here Sir." With a momentary pause Kilmer yelled out, "It's a go."

The crews began their sprint to the aircraft.

"Damn, it's raining like hell," yelled Captain Curtis as he ran into a wall of water.

The crews had about 25 yards to run, as they were hit by rain coming down in sheets during this monsoon night. When they reached the concrete revetments where the F-4s were parked, all were dripping wet. Up the ladder and into the cockpits the crewmembers crawled, while the crew chiefs helped them get their parachute harness attached to their Martin-Baker ejection seats. Both aircraft commanders went to the

Starting Engines Checklist.

Kilmer recited over the intercom:
"External air - Connect to right starter
Engine master switches - ON
Engine - Crank
10% rpm, ignition button - DEPRESS WHILE ADVANCING THROTTLE
Ignition - RELEASE AT LIGHTOFF
At 45% rpm, ground card air - OFF
EGT - WITHIN LIMITS
Fuel flow - WITHIN LIMITS
Idle rpm - 65% + or -1%
Oil pressure - 12 PSI MIN
Hydraulic pressure - WITHIN LIMITS
Generators - GEN ON."

The Checklist was continued until both engines were running with all instruments normal.

"Phu Cat Tower, Cobra Flight taxi, scramble," Kilmer called over the UHF radio.

"Cobra Flight cleared to taxi runway three-three," responded the tower.

"Roger, Cobra Flight," followed Kilmer.

Cobra 1, the Lead aircraft containing Kilmer and Stone, pulled from the revetment with Cobra 2, Curtis and Brown, right behind. Two minutes had passed and they still had a lot to do before takeoff.

The **Before Takeoff Checklist** was read out loud by Kilmer in Cobra 1:

"Stab Aug - ENGAGE
Canopies - CLOSED & LOCKED
Lower ejection guards - CLEAR
Fuel panel - SET & CHECKED
Flaps - 1/2
Anti - skid - ON
Warning lights - Checked
Pitot heat / anti - ice - AS DESIRED
Shoulder harness - AS DESIRED
Variable ramp - CHECK FULLY RETRACTED."

As Cobra Flight reached the end of the runway, the arming crew began to pull the safety pins from the armaments. Within seconds the arming crew leader held up all the arming pins with their red flags. This was to ensure the pilots that all their assortment of ordnance was "hot."

Good, Stone thought as he looked at the pins and red flags, *we are ready to launch.*

"Phu Cat Tower, Cobra 1 and Cobra 2 are ready to go," radioed Kilmer.

Immediately the tower came back, "Cobra 1 and Cobra 2 cleared for immediate takeoff, runway three-three."

Without pause, Kilmer began advancing the throttles on the two J-79 engines. The fully loaded F-4 began to move slowly. Then the afterburners ignited and down the runway Cobra 1 accelerated until it reached rotation speed. Within seconds they were airborne. Cobra 2 trailed only 30 seconds behind.

"Not too bad," Stone remarked to Kilmer over the intercom, "we were airborne in 2 minutes and 52 seconds."

Cobra 2 joined on Cobra 1's right wing. In bad weather it was common for aircraft to fly in close formation. That meant that they flew formation only three feet away from each other. This was tough to do and it took a lot of energy no matter what the weather or in-flight visibility might be. However, it kept them together and this was important for their mutual safety.

Ten minutes later Kilmer made a call to the forward air controller (FAC). His job was to control the air strike on the target. The FAC's call sign was Covey 1.

"Covey 1, Cobra 1 and 2 with you, a flight of two F-4s overhead at Angels One-Six-Zero, what do you have for us this morning?"

"Cobra Flight, Covey 1 with you, we have troops in contact at a firebase. It's not looking good for the good guys. The bad guys are attacking on three sides and are coming over the wire on the west side of the firebase. The friendlies are asking that you concentrate your fire on the west base perimeter. They know the distance is too close for you guys to insure their safety, but feel that they really have no choice. If the enemy makes it into the compound, the outcome for the base will be in doubt. That's the bad news; the worse news is that the weather down here is dog crap. You have fifteen-hundred-foot overcast with hills extending up into the clouds. There is light rain with the visibility about one mile. You will have to work under the overcast with flares for lights so that you can identify the line of fire. I'll do the best I can to keep the lights on, but it's hard to keep several flares working at the same time."

"Great!" was Cobra 1's response. "We're on our way down."

Penetrating an overcast sky, at night, with reduced visibility is one of the most dangerous things for an aircraft. The elevation of the terrain was, at best, uncertain due to the incomplete mapping of Southeast Asia. However, even with good maps, considering the speed of fast movers like the F-4, it was hard to know exact locations within a mile or two.

Down, down went the two aircraft. The F-4s descended through ten thousand feet, nine thousand feet, eight thousand feet, and then seven thousand feet. Nothing.

"Stone, if we don't see something soon," barked Kilmer over the intercom, "we'll have to come up with another plan."

"There, over there. I see light," responded Stone, "check 3 o'clock position, slightly low."

"I have it," yelled Kilmer.

Just then both aircraft broke through the overcast at 5,800 feet MSL, only 1600 feet above the ground.

"Covey 1, Cobra Lead, keep the lights on. We cannot operate in the dark at this altitude with all the rocks around."

"Will do," responded Covey 1. "Do you have the target, west side of the compound one thousand meters at your 11 o'clock position?"

"Got it," answered Kilmer.

"Hit my smoke, cleared for attack from your position," responded Covey 1.

"I'll make the first run, you come in behind me," ordered Cobra 1. "Drop only two at a time. We'll need multiple runs to make sure we get this thing done right."

"Roger that," responded Cobra 2.

Cobra 1 began his first run.

"I can see the bad guys climbing over the wire," remarked Stone, "they are half way through the perimeter."

"Got 'em," responded Kilmer, "we'll stop them right there."

Thump. The sound of two napalm canisters coming off the F-4 was heard in the cockpit. Within seconds Covey 1 reported the results.

"Ordinance on target, Cobra 2 you're cleared on target now."

"Roger," responded Cobra 2.

Both F-4s made it around the pattern, dodging hilltops, and staying out of the clouds, to make another run on the target. This time 500-pound, Snake Eye, high-drag bombs were used. These weapons had fins that opened up when released from the aircraft and allowed the bombs to slow down and give the F-4s time to escape the fragmentation (frag) pattern. Escaping frag patterns enabled them to avoid being hit by their own bomb blast. The high drag nature of these bombs also allowed them to be placed accurately on target at very low altitudes, sometimes as low as 100 feet above the target.

"Well great. What the hell is going on," yelled Kilmer. "The lights have gone out."

What happened was that all the flares had burned out.

"Sorry about that. I'll have lights up in a sec," replied Covey 1.

Within seconds flares ignited. A bright burst of light was everywhere.

"There goes our night vision," yelled Stone.

Kilmer responded, "Yeah, help me watch for the rocks as best you can. I can hardly see anything."

Minutes passed that seemed like hours, but both F-4 crews managed to dodge the hilltops and stay below the cloud deck as their night vision slowly returned.

The two F-4s continued to make bombing and strafing runs on the target area. Each pass on the target brought increased risk from enemy ground fire. Thump, thump, thump sounds were heard and felt on Lead's aircraft.

"Sir, we are taking hits from that hill just to our right on final. I felt impacts just behind my canopy. Do you see any problems with the bird?" inquired Stone.

"No, she's doing well. All the gauges show normal. We're just about out of bombs but we have the ability for one more pass to put that gun out of operation," responded Kilmer.

"Sounds good Sir, let's do it and get the hell out of here, I think we have stopped the bad guys' progress going over the wire."

"You guys are taking fire from the hill just west of you on approach to the target," reported Covey 1. "If you want to take them out, you are cleared in."

"Roger," answered Kilmer, "we have enough ordinance for one more pass. We will quiet that gun."

Cobra 1 made a final run around the pattern and turned on final. Kilmer lined up on the gun's approximate position. It was just too dark to see the gun's exact location. However, with a 500-pound bomb, close was good enough.

"The automatic weapon fire is coming hot and heavy your way," called out Covey 1. "Give them something to remember you by."

Kilmer passed within yards of the machine gun location and about 200 feet above it. He released a 500-pound high-drag bomb and quickly pulled up and away from the target in a five G maneuver while igniting the F-4's afterburners.

There was a burst of light and rolling fire and flames from the target's location.

"You got the gun," reported Covey 1. "That group won't shoot at any more aircraft. Good job."

Both F-4s expended all their ordnance and informed Covey 1 they were off the target and on their way home.

Covey 1 responded, "Thanks guys, you've saved some butts tonight. Good job. Take the rest of the night off," he said with a laugh. "Covey 1 out."

The climb to altitude and safety was welcome for both crews. The flight back to base was uneventful. There was even a clearing sky for their recovery and landing. After the two crews put their F-4s to bed they went to debrief the mission in the intelligence shack.

"How did it go?" asked the Intel officer.

"Just another milk run," responded Captain Kilmer as he turned his head and winked at his fellow crewmembers.

3

Run to the Coast

What a pleasant morning in the Republic of Vietnam. The sun had climbed above the horizon in a clear sky increasing the temperature to 73 degrees Fahrenheit. At 0520, all the aircrew members who had not flown combat missions the night before, awakened and started planning for the day. The typical day started with crewmembers getting up, showering, shaving, putting on their flight suits and boots and heading out to the chow hall to get the usual breakfast.

Breakfast options consisted of cold cereal, hash browns, toast, powered eggs, bacon, and of course the ever-present SOS or creamed beef on toast. Creamed beef on toast was affectionately given the name SOS, because of its unusually greasy nature and salty as hell taste. With little imagination one could tell why it was given the SOS name. The naming for this entree option went back to World War II when the GIs of that era first bestowed the title.

Captain Ron Kilmer got an early start to the day getting up at 0400. He finished breakfast and pulled his maps and flight logs together and was ready to go to the squadron to prepare for the mission scheduled later that morning.

Lieutenant Ben Stone entered the chow hall and hollered to Kilmer, "Ready for our mission Sir? Do you have any idea what it is?"

"Not a clue Ben, I'm on my way to check it out. Grab some grub and hurry down to the squadron and let's check."

"I'll be down in less than fifteen minutes Sir," Stone replied, "just have to have some powered eggs, fake meat, extra grease, and some non-fresh bread." He grinned at Kilmer.

"Great, see you in 15," Kilmer responded, laughing about Stone's comment.

Stone went through the chow line and headed for an empty seat at a half full table. As he sat down, one of the GIBs, Lieutenant Larry Williams, sitting at the next table, spoke to him.

"Hi Stone! Ready to fly?" asked Williams.

Lieutenant Williams was an experienced backseater. He had been in country for almost eight months. He was smart, a hard worker and respected by those who knew him. He was a good pilot and very often paired with new aircraft commanders to help them get up to speed on how to stay alive as newbies. He could get a little pushy when dealing with others, but he was usually on the right side of an issue. If someone would take him on in an argument, it didn't end well for the challenger because Williams knew his stuff.

"I understand we're going on a mission in country," remarked Williams.

In country missions were those where the flight didn't leave the borders of South Vietnam. Out-of-country missions were those that took place in North Vietnam or secretly in Laos or Cambodia. The in country missions were usually shorter in duration and didn't have some of the risks associated with flying in Laos or Cambodia and certainly not those associated with flying in the North.

Stone looked at the food on his plate with disgust, "I haven't heard a word. In country huh? That'll make it easier for the search and rescue crews to pick you up when you go down! Don't worry, Kilmer and I'll stay with you overhead and protect your butt until they arrive."

It was very common for the crewmembers to tease one another about the outcome of a mission and joke about the other crew getting shot down.

"Don't worry Stone, we'll stay with you and Kilmer. Well, until we get a little short on fuel, then you're on your own. Oh! By the way, can I have your stereo if you don't make it back?" continued Williams with a big grin.

"Sure," replied Stone, "anything for you. Who's your frontseater?"

Williams snarled back, "You'd have to bring that up at breakfast. I got the short straw - Captain Benson."

Stone dropped his fork, "Not Benson, that arrogant weasel. That's just great, now I know it'll be a perfect day."

Captain Sam Benson wasn't really a bad guy. He was relatively new to the squadron, being in country for only about two months. However, he was arrogant, haughty, and only fairly smart. He wasn't nearly as smart as he thought. He didn't learn anything from others and was stubborn about changing some of his bad flying habits. Even those who out ranked him, and who had a lot more flying experience than Benson, had trouble teaching him anything. He always seemed to resist learning. It was a dangerous attitude to have in a combat zone. No one can come into a combat situation possessing all the needed flying skills necessary to survive. That was what made a man like Benson so dangerous and why GIBs didn't want to fly with him. However, on this mission Williams had been teamed with Benson and he needed to make the most of it. Both Stone and Williams were thankful that the flight Lead would be Captain Kilmer. They knew he wouldn't put up with any of Benson's crap. Benson wouldn't intimidate Kilmer and Kilmer had ways of making damn sure that Benson would be kept on a short leash.

As soon as breakfast was ingested all crewmembers came together in the squadron briefing room. Kilmer, as usual, had a good idea what the mission was and gave a short overview of it before he instructed all crewmembers to head next door to the intelligence briefing. Before each combat mission crewmembers would attend an intelligence briefing where officers would give up-to-date intelligence about the mission's target and the area around it. They discussed all known target facts. Information such as: location of the target, its appearance, surrounding terrain and particularly important, how well defended, were always discussed. If other crews had attacked the target recently, then what to expect concerning enemy fire certainly became part of the discussion. Target reports would contain information on small arms and automatic weapons fire, 37 mm and 57 mm anti-aircraft fire, and even surface to air missiles (SAMs).

On today's mission, an attack on a suspected weapons cache, the Intel officer warned of at least small arms fire coming from the target area. As soon as the Intel officer completed his briefing, the two crews continued to the second phase of their briefing, weather in the target area. The weather officer gave a briefing on what to expect. He provided forecast weather for home plate, the departing base, weather en route to the target area, weather in the target area and for return to home plate. The weather forecasts included several emergency airfields around the target area, just in case one of the aircraft received battle damage and needed to land quickly.

After completion of the Intel and weather briefings, the two crews went into a room for a briefing for the flight itself. The Lead aircraft commander gave this briefing. In this case it was Captain Kilmer. Kilmer quickly but very thoroughly went over every aspect of the mission. This included aircraft takeoff, rejoin and the navigation route to the target area. Instructions, given by Kilmer, stated that he would lead the attack on the target and that Benson, following his lead, needed to execute the exact same attack plan. This was standard operating procedure (SOP) but Kilmer said it out loud for all to hear so that crewmembers would know what he wanted done. Kilmer knew of Benson's reputation. Benson, likely to do his own thing, could get someone in trouble. His history reflected the fact of a reluctance to follow Lead's leadership. At least with Kilmer's briefing, everyone would know the expectations.

With the briefings completed, it was time to head to the aircraft and accomplish the preflight on both the aircraft and its weapons. First, the crewmembers went into the staging area where they put on their G-suits, survival vests, inflatable life preservers, and checked their survival radios in the vests for proper operation.

The G-suits helped protect the crewmembers from excessive gravitational forces placed on them during aircraft maneuvers. Compressed air was forced into the G-suit's bladders located on the crewmember's abdomen, thighs and calf muscles. Under heavy G loads the bladders would inflate with compressed air and help keep the blood in the upper part of the body. This prevented the crewmember from blacking out or losing consciousness.

The crews then went to the weapons locker and picked up their Smith & Wesson 38 caliber revolvers. With this accomplished, the four crewmembers proceeded to the crew van and climbed inside. The squadron scheduling officer drove them to their aircraft.

All crewmembers knew their responsibilities and the aircraft and weapons systems underwent a quick but accurate check. Kilmer briefed a start engine time of five minutes after the hour with a takeoff time of ten minutes after the hour. With both aircraft parked side by side in the revetment rows, each crew could see the others' progress.

When the watch on Kilmer's wrist showed one minute after the hour, Kilmer yelled at Benson, "Let's do it."

Both crews climbed into the cockpits and started their engines. Soon the INS was aligned and all pre-taxi checks completed.

Stone informed Kilmer, "The INS is up Sir."

The INS was slow to get aligned and was usually the last item ready before taxi.

"Thanks Ben." Kilmer then initiated the mandatory call to the tower for taxi instructions.

"Phu Cat Tower, Cobra 1 and Cobra 2 ready to taxi."

The tower came back with, "Cobra 1 and 2 taxi to runway one-five."

"Wilco, Cobra 1. Cobra 2 are you up?" continued Kilmer.

"Roger that," responded Cobra 2.

Both F-4Ds taxied to the end of runway one-five where they stopped for the final check of the aircraft, their bombs, and for the removal of all safety pins from the weapons. The weapons crew chief held up two handfuls of pins with their red safety flags showing that the weapons had all been armed.

Kilmer nodded approval and asked, "Stone, is your checklist complete?"

"Good to go Sir."

"Okay, let's go," responded Kilmer as he called the tower.

"Phu Cat Tower, two F4s ready for departure."

"Cobra 1 and Cobra 2 cleared for take off runway one five."

"Cobra 1 on the roll."

Benson radioed 30 seconds later, "Cobra 2 on the roll."

As Cobra 1 was accelerating down the runway, Stone came over the intercom, "Fifty knots Sir."

This was not a mandatory checklist item but a meaningful call made by some of the GIBs. It meant that if anything went wrong from this point on both pilots could eject from the F-4 and the Martin-

Baker ejection seat was guaranteed to give them a full chute before the crewmembers hit the ground. Of course, the guarantee wasn't really worth much, but the Department of Defense (DOD) had conducted a lot of research and made needed changes to the seat to make this a reality. Earlier versions had boasted that it was a zero-zero system. This meant that a crew member could sit in the seat and fire the ejection sequence on the ground with zero altitude and zero airspeed and get a full chute before ground impact. However, it turned out with some unfortunate ejections on the ground, under zero-zero conditions, that they weren't successful. With some modifications to the seat, the ejection parameters had now been changed to the 50 knots and zero altitude condition.

It was a welcome thought knowing that after 50 knots of acceleration, any hazardous aircraft emergency could be handled with crewmember ejection. During takeoff and the climb to a thousand feet or so, if anything went wrong with the aircraft with tons of bombs on board, a couple of seconds saved in the ejection from the aircraft could mean the difference between life and death. The short time of the takeoff roll provided little time for thought and analyzing, knowing that ejection was now an option was a comforting thought.

The two F-4s joined into formation and proceeded to the target coordinates. As they approached the target area Kilmer switched the radio to the FAC's radio frequency.

The FAC's call sign was Covey 1.

Kilmer made the call, "Covey 1, Cobra 1 and Cobra 2, two fast movers with you at fifteen thousand feet."

"Good morning Cobra Flight," responded Covey 1. "I have a suspected troop concentration with some possible automatic weapons fire. A fight of F-100s just left the area and one aircraft observed automatic weapons fire on their last pass. So, keep your eyes open, the bad guys would just love to take down an F-4."

"Our heads are up and scanning the area. Thanks for the update," remarked Kilmer. "Can you give us some smoke and update on any friendlies in the area?"

"No friendlies and I am releasing my smoke now," reported Covey 1. "Hit my smoke and make your run to the southeast. Staying out of your way southwest of the target."

"Roger that," Kilmer answered. "Cobra 1 is turning final on the target and is hot. Cobra 2 you're cleared in as soon as I report off the target."

"Wilco," replied Cobra 2.

Responding with Wilco, meant that Cobra 2 understood the order and would comply.

Cobra 1 was on the target within seconds. Kilmer could see the enemy on the ground. Some were running for cover while others just stood in the open firing their AK-47s at the approaching F-4. They had little chance of hitting the descending aircraft but the possibility always existed. Two canisters of napalm were released from the F-4. Within a second or two the target area burst into an inferno. The ground exploded in a blaze of fire and smoke covering an area at least 100 yards long and 25 yards wide.

"Damn, how do they take that kind of punishment and keep on fighting?" asked Stone as the big F-4 began its defensive climbing turn away from the target.

"We're off the target," radioed Kilmer.

"Cobra 2 on final," came a call from Benson.

The FAC interrupted Benson's call. "I have an active 50 cal sight just west of the original target area and it's shooting like hell at you guys. Switch to the 50 cal sight and take them out. Do you have them in sight, west of my smoke twenty to fifty meters?"

"Cobra 2 has the new target, we're switching to it now," yelled Benson.

Williams could feel the corrective turns that Benson was making on final approach trying to get lined up on the new target. These turns seemed excessive and the angles of bank too large. This just didn't seem right to Williams but he didn't say anything.

"Damn, Damn," came the words from Benson as he continued to turn the aircraft back and forth across the final approach path to the target.

"What's wrong Sir?" asked Williams.

"I can't get the reticle exactly on the damn gun's location. We're too close. I'll just have to make another pass," responded Benson.

The F-4 stopped turning and flew straight and level over the target.

Wow, this sure seems strange, thought Williams.

"We'll come back and get the gun on our next pass," radioed Benson.

Then the unthinkable happened. Thud, thud, thud, the big F-4 shook, and the right wing dipped over 30 degrees.

"What the hell was that," cried Williams.

"I don't know," replied Benson, "it felt like something hit the aircraft."

Something had hit the F-4. The active 50 cal site sprayed the F-4 with several rounds of high-explosive 50 cal ammo. One thing a new guy should learn and learn quickly was that you never turned your back on an active gun site without leaving their ears ringing. That meant don't ever make a dry run over an active target. Always drop something so that the enemy kept their heads down when you flew over. If the enemy saw anything come off the rails in their direction, they would not chance certain death just to shoot a couple more rounds. On the other hand, if they didn't see anything coming their way, they shot hard and fast as the aircraft went by.

That was exactly what happened and now the big F-4 had been wounded. No one knew to what degree the F-4 had been injured but it received a beating.

"Cobra 1, Cobra 2, we have taken a hit."

"How bad have you been hit?"

"I don't know," there was a pause then Benson continued, "we have a Fire Light on number one engine."

"Listen carefully," commanded Kilmer, "turn due east now and climb as fast as you can. Try and make the coastline just in case you have to eject. Have the GIB run through the Engine Fire checklist with you. I'll declare an emergency and get the search and rescue guys coming your way."

"Roger Lead, thanks."

Kilmer continued to take charge, "Search and Rescue, Cobra 1 on Guard. Come up please, we have an F-4, Cobra 2, with battle damage and a Fire Light on one of his engines. He is declaring an emergency! We're on the one-six-five degree radial at thirty seven miles off Da Nang, heading zero-niner-zero degrees, reaching for feet-wet."

The term feet-wet let others know you were no longer over land but over the water. Being over the ocean upon ejection increased the chances of being picked up by friendlies.

Little time went by before air rescue came back with a call to Cobra 2.

"Cobra 2, Rescue 1 on Guard, how do you read me?" radioed the rescue Jolly Green helicopter.

"Loud and clear," responded Cobra 2.

Rescue 1 continued, "Change to my frequency 274.6."

"Roger."

Cobra Flight and Rescue 1 all changed to the frequency.

"Cobra 2, Rescue 1 with you, we're on our way. How long till you reach the coast, and how is the aircraft? Do you think you can make it to the coastline?"

"I don't know," answered Benson, "I can see the coastline up ahead, but the aircraft isn't flying well."

Williams started calling out the ENGINE FIRE checklist over the intercom:

"Bad engine - IDLE

Light out - CHECK DETECTOR SYSTEM

If detector system is O.K. - LAND AS SOON AS PRACTICABLE

Light / Fire confirmed - SHUTDOWN ENGINE

If fire persists – EJECT."

Benson responded verbally to the checklist. "Engine at idle, the detector system is good, fire is confirmed, I'm shutting down the number one engine. Do you concur Williams?"

"Damn right I do," answered Williams. "I can see fire coming through the engine panels on number one engine."

"Shutting down number one," called out Benson.

Things didn't get any better. The F-4 was sluggish, slowing down and beginning to shake. Then the unthinkable happened, the Fire Light on engine number two came on.

"Crap, crap, crap," yelled Williams, "we have flames coming from the number two engine."

"You see flames Williams, I now have a Fire Light on number two engine?"

"I sure as hell do."

The cockpit fell silent; both pilots knew that they were in big trouble.

Then a strong voice came over the radio, "Cobra 2, Lead here. You have a lot of fire coming from the number two engine. You're going to have to eject, but we're going to get you to the coast first. Everything is going to be all right. Push the nose of the aircraft over and start giving up altitude for airspeed. We have to keep you flying. We'll stay with you all the way. The Air Rescue people are only a short distance out."

The F-4 seemed like it would never reach the coastline. However, very slowly the burning F-4 did reach the coastline and flew over the water's edge and out over the ocean.

Kilmer came back on the radio, "Okay Cobra 2, you're over the water. You're in good shape. Trim the aircraft up and punch out now."

Benson responded, "The right engine just quit. We're burning and losing airspeed quickly."

Williams yelled in the intercom, "Captain, we need to eject. I'm turning the ejection valve back here so that when I eject, you'll come with me."

This valve was a modification made to the F-4D so that if the frontseater became incapacitated for any reason, the backseater could eject them both.

Kilmer screamed over the radio, "Cobra 2, your aircraft is starting to break up, pull the nose of your aircraft up slightly above the horizon and eject. You're only about two thousand feet above the water. Do it now!"

Benson did what he was told, pulling the nose of the F-4 slightly higher to get a positive climb rate for the ejection. He established about a 500 feet per minute climb but the airspeed was decaying rapidly. It went from 250 knots down to 230 then 200 knots.

Benson called to Williams, "I'm giving the order to eject."

That order was to call out Eject, Eject, Eject, three times. As quickly as Benson said eject the second time, Williams had reached his lower ejection handle and had given it a powerful pull. For about a half a second nothing seemed to happen, and then the sequencing began. A charge went off in the ejection seat that retracted straps that pulled the pilots into position for ejection. Another charge went off that blew the backseater's canopy off, then the larger dynamite charge went off blowing the backseater's ejection seat, with him in it, out of the aircraft. Once the seat had traveled about 3 feet a rocket pack attached under the seat ignited and propelled the seat about 200 feet above the aircraft.

In less than a second these same events occurred with the frontseater and his ejection seat. Both men had been successfully separated from their burning, crippled ship. However, the pilots were not yet safe. They needed to get their parachutes opened and free themselves from their ejection seats. This was designed to be an automatic response from the Martin-Baker seat. In this case, that was just what happened. Two separate charges went off in each of the seats and both pilots' parachutes were pulled out of their cases. When both chutes opened, the resulting force separated both men from their seats.

The two men began their slow descent to the ocean surface. Both were in different states of shock, but were alive and working hard to stay that way. Aircrew training stressed that if they ejected over water, on descent as soon as their boots touched the water, they were to release the parachute from their harness, allowing the chute to float free of them. The danger, if this wasn't completed in a timely way, involved the possibility that the parachute might come down on top of the crewmember, entangling him in the parachute lines. The crewmember risked drowning because he couldn't swim free of the lines.

Williams remembered his training and just as he entered the water he released his chute. Benson wasn't so fortunate. He entered the water with his parachute attached and it covered him as it settled to the water. He was immediately covered with a sinking parachute and encircled with scores of tangled parachute cords. In his dazed state he started to struggle against the encircling lines. This only entangled him more and began to increase the odds that he would drown.

Williams observed what was happening to Benson and began to swim toward him. When he was only a few feet away he yelled at Benson to take out his parachute survival knife, open the blade and stick it straight up into the air and cut a hole in the chute so that Benson could stick his head up in the air to breathe. Benson responded to the instructions. He reached down in the water to the small pouch on his right leg that held his parachute knife. Taking the knife out he pushed the button to extend the blade. Out came the blade and up went Benson's arm cutting through the canopy of the parachute. Benson then forced his head through the hole. His head came up into the clear air, and then precious oxygen filled his lungs.

Oh, how good that felt, he thought.

"Captain, pull the tabs on your life preserver. You need to stay above the water."

Benson didn't need to hear this plea twice. He yanked on the left tab of his life preserver and then on the right tab. Swoosh, both sides of the preserver inflated.

Williams with his preserver already inflated, now helped Benson free himself from his sinking chute.

The burning crippled airship slowly descended through the air. It hit the water with unusual smoothness and didn't explode. It seemed to display a quality of grace and seemed satisfied that both of its crewmembers were safely down.

Benson and Williams, in the water for only about five minutes, heard the sound of the rescue Jolly Green helicopter coming for them. Quickly it was overhead. A rescue crewmember jumped out of the Jolly Green and into the water.

"Hello Sirs," he said, "we're here to take you home. You're our responsibility now and you're safe."

Both Benson and Williams were safely taken into the rescue helicopter and appeared unhurt from their ordeal. The rescue chopper took them directly back to Phu Cat where the whole squadron turned out to welcome them. They got off the crew van that picked them up on the flight line and walked into the squadron still dripping wet.

"Hey!" came a loud cry from one of the pilots. "How was it?"

Benson, wringing water out from the sleeve of his flight suit, looked at Williams and responded, "Just another day at the beach."

4

The Failed Run

Fighter pilots are a rare and distinct group of human beings. They are usually thought of as self assured, of relatively high intelligence, somewhat loners, and just a little bit on the arrogant side. As in all generalizations, there is only some truth in these beliefs. First, fighter pilots tend to have, on average, a higher intelligence than the general population. They are all college graduates, many with majors that are highly technical and require some advanced mathematics. They have to be self-assured to be able to pilot a highly sophisticated, modern, supersonic fighter-bomber. It takes self-confidence and excellent flying skills to fly in all weather conditions to accomplish difficult missions where there are lives that hang in the balance. Being self-assured is a major prerequisite for being a fighter pilot.

Fighter pilots on the other hand are not loners. They're just a tight group of professional individuals who have learned to stick together to accomplish their difficult missions. This small select group also understands and gives support to each other as life and death decisions are faced and made. They understand the ever-present possibility of something going wrong, resulting in not only the deaths or injuries of the crew but of innocents on the ground.

As far as the label of arrogance, there could certainly be some truth to this allegation. But why not! The fighter pilot is selected from the very top of a large group of individuals. They cannot have any physical deficiencies that might interfere with their flying requirements. There cannot be history of asthma, heart conditions, diabetes, mental illness, history of drug use or criminal convictions. Most importantly, their vision must be perfect. With all of these restrictions and requirements for a near perfect physical body and a higher than average intelligence, it is natural for pilots to have a high self-concept and perhaps to be a little on the arrogant side.

Flying has a way of taking arrogance and moderating it and keeping it in check. That is because of the nature of human flight. It's not natural for humans to fly and so every moment in the air is fraught with danger. If one becomes too arrogant in the flight experience and pushes the limits of personal skill or the performance of the aircraft, independent physical laws will exert themselves resulting in loss of the aircraft, loss of the pilots, or both.

Colonel Thomas M. Spiker was such an arrogant pilot. He had been very fortunate throughout his career not to have hurt or killed anyone. He was reckless in his flying. He was always pushing the limits of flight operational assignments. He had been a Group Commander back in the "world." As Group Commander he could fly any day he wanted and with whomever he wished. He raised alarm and brought fear to those who were assigned to fly with him during their training. He always pushed the limits of safety while teaching and practicing all the many aerial flight maneuvers and the assorted bombing and strafing assignments on the target range.

As a habit, he entered the range and began his practice bombing and strafing runs by pressing his attack on the target. This meant he would dive too low to the ground or fly too close to the target putting both the aircraft and crew at risk. He was good at flying the airplane, but he was always pressing his luck.

There is a saying among pilots, "There are old pilots and there are bold pilots, but there are no old, bold pilots." Pilots know that flying is inherently dangerous and to survive many years of aerial experience one needs to fly within the limits of safety.

Many times the range control officer warned Spiker about his risky flying. Spiker was told that if he continued to break the safety rules he would be asked to leave the range. He laughed at the warning, made one more low pass on the target with his aircraft in a dangerously low altitude, and in a high G turn headed for home base.

Colonel Spiker had been in Vietnam for three weeks. His reputation from his last assignment had preceded him to the Da Nang Air Base. It was clear from his flying behaviors, after flying on a few missions in country, that his reckless attitude had come with him.

Pilots and navigators talked non-stop about him and his flying. No one wanted to fly with him, either as a wingman or as a crewmember. However, in the military, rank has its privileges, and the colonel could pick what flights he wanted to fly and even select crewmembers with whom to fly. This was beginning to cause some morale problems in the wing and the three flying squadrons that composed it. However the squadron commanders were all lieutenant colonels and hadn't come up with any kind of workable solution to this difficult issue. They needed a reason, an incident, to be able to remove the colonel from flying status. They knew that this would be difficult and full of risk for their military careers. They all agreed that when Spiker did come to fly with their squadron, they would assign the most experienced, toughest GIBs to fly with him. In this way they thought safety would be enhanced by the experienced GIB watching and checking everything that the colonel did.

Well, it didn't take long for the colonel to show up in one of the squadrons. He wanted a daytime attack mission and wanted to fly as soon as possible. The squadron was abuzz with discussion and anticipation. Who was going to fly with the colonel? The squadron commander didn't take part in these discussions. He had already decided who the backseater would be, Lieutenant Ben Stone. The squadron commander believed that if anyone could keep the colonel from killing someone it would be Stone.

Stone was experienced, perceptive, smart and to the point. In short, he wouldn't take any crap from anyone. He had talked to the squadron commander earlier about another pilot who had put lives at unnecessary risk by not following standard operating procedures regarding flight operations. Stone, on this occasion, after being given permission to enter the commander's office, saluted in a respectful way, and in a clear strong voice reported, "This pilot is unsafe, he is going to get somebody killed. He needs to be fixed and until this is done I won't fly with him... Sir!"

The squadron commander just smiled as Stone was making his report. Stone reminded the colonel so much of himself when he was younger.

It was very rare for Stone to show this type of behavior because he was a real military man. He believed in the chain of command and lived by the military's code. However, Stone didn't suffer fools well and he knew to go to the source of authority when something needed to get done and get done quickly. Stone understood that sometimes military rules and regulations were restrictive and some were just plain dumb. However, many of them made sense and should be followed for safety concerns.

The choice had been made; Stone would be the colonel's back seat pilot for this mission. The colonel and Stone would be Lead and Captain Lee Young and Lieutenant Bill Johnson would be number two in the flight. Both Young and Johnson were experienced crewmembers. Young was a great pilot who was an Academy graduate. He had been in Vietnam for about six months and was well respected by his peers. Johnson was an older navigator/weapons officer who had years of radar time in the F-101 aircraft. He had only four years left in the Air Force before he was going to retire. That was something he was looking forward to with some excitement.

Colonel Spiker took both crews through the Intel and weather briefings for the assigned mission. He then went through the flight briefing for the target and the SOPs for the mission. Everything seemed right, but everyone just had a strange feeling about this mission. They didn't trust the colonel and were continually thinking: *What the hell is this guy going to do today that will get us all killed?*

Everything was normal/normal as the two crews went through the required aircraft checklists, engine startup and taxi to the runway for takeoff. The weapons were armed and clearance for takeoff was given by the tower. The two F-4s began their takeoff rolls with thirty seconds of separation between the two aircraft. They rejoined in close formation and headed for the target area.

As they approached the target area Spiker made a call to the FAC whose call sign was Covey 1.

"Covey 1, Gunfighters 1 and 2, two F-4s, over your station. We are each carrying 750-pound slick bombs. What do you have for us today?"

"Gunfighter Flight, Covey 1, I have some suspected underground bunkers with confirmed enemy troops in the area. I'll lay down some smoke and give you directions from there."

"Roger." responded Spiker. "Looking for your smoke."

The slow moving FAC aircraft maneuvered into position to fire a smoke rocket to mark the target. The FAC pilots were brave men who risked their lives daily marking targets for the fast moving fighter-bombers. Many of the FAC aircraft were single engine, slow moving propeller aircraft that had little or no defenses from attack. Their only defense was that the enemy would not normally shoot at them for fear that the FAC would call in an air strike on their position. Usually the enemy would hide from them. However, once the FAC saw them, and marked their position with a rocket, there was no reason for the bad guys not to shoot at them. In fact, there was every reason to shoot the FAC down so it couldn't continually mark their movements.

"Gunfighter 1, Covey 1, do you see my smoke? The target is twenty meters east of my smoke. Once you see my smoke, you are cleared in on the target."

"We have your smoke and the target," replied Spiker.

Colonel Spiker rolled the heavy F-4 over on its side and pushed the nose over into a 55 to 60 degree nose down attitude. This was the normal attack attitude with slick iron bombs. The aircraft would begin the attack at about ten to twelve thousand feet with a 60-degree steep dive angle. The frontseater would maneuver the aircraft to place the target reticle on the target with a correction for any wind drift. As this occurred the backseater called off the altitudes of the diving aircraft by thousands of feet. The intercom call would be*: Ten thousand feet, nine thousand feet, eight thousand, seven thousand, six thousand, ready, pickle.* The ready was given a thousand feet above the pickle altitude. At the pickle altitude the frontseater was to press the bomb release button and begin pulling off the target with a five to six G pull out. One G is the force of gravity exerted on a person or any object on the earth. In a high performance fighter-bomber the speed of the aircraft during a turn or pulling out of a dive could result in a G or load factor being placed on the aircraft and crew that was many times the normal force of gravity. It was not uncommon for the F-4 to pull six or seven Gs in flight while bombing or in air-to-air combat.

If the frontseater did not pickle at the prearranged altitude the backseater would call out a thousand feet below the pickle altitude and warn the frontseater to begin the dive recovery. Before takeoff the two crewmembers discussed what the expectation would be should the frontseater not pickle and pull at the agreed altitude. Most agreed that if the frontseater became fixated on the target for some reason, the GIB would pull on the stick and begin the dive recovery 1,000 feet below the pickle attitude. For some crews this was not discussed because it became an ego issue for the frontseater. However, it was important to discuss and know the expectations, because the massive F-4 had so much speed and inertia in a 60-degree dive angle that it took several thousand feet to recover from the dive. A descent of a couple of thousand feet below the pickle altitude could mean that the F-4 wouldn't have enough altitude to recover and would impact the ground. This was known to happen and crews were aware that a couple of seconds of indecision could spell death for both crewmembers.

Suddenly, Spiker did something very strange on this attack on the target. He pulled out of the dive smoothly and leveled the aircraft at about 100 feet above the ground. Stone was just about to ask the colonel what he was going to do when the FAC asked the same question.

"Gunfighter 1, what are your intentions? The target is now at your 12 o'clock position."

"I am in hot and on to the target," responded Spiker.

Stone's thoughts were racing through his head. He couldn't figure what Spiker was going to do given their bomb load. He had never seen anything like this before. Almost without thinking he called over the intercom.

"Sir, do you remember we only have slick bombs on board?"

Stone didn't know for sure what Spiker had in mind but he did know that if Spiker released the slick bombs at this altitude, the bombs would trail along the flight path of their aircraft and hit the ground and explode with the F-4 in the bomb's fragmentation pattern. In short, if Spiker released the slick bombs at their current altitude it could blow them out of the sky.

Spiker responded to Stone, "Keep the intercom quiet lieutenant, I've got this covered."

Stone came back, "Do not drop the bombs, you will blow us out of the air!"

Just then the unthinkable happened. Spiker pressed the pickle button and two 750-pound bombs were released from under the wings of the F-4.

"What the hell did you just do?" yelled Stone over the intercom.

There was no answer from Spiker, but there was a very quick response from the bombs. They hit the ground within a second and a half. There was a huge explosion that shook the F-4 violently. It rolled to a forty-degree bank angle to the right and then back to the left. Stone had turned his head to the right just as the bombs exploded. Immediately he observed large chunks of metal blasting through the wings. Some of the larger pieces of the bomb fragments were four to six inches long and two to three inches wide.

Stone thought: *Damn, he almost blew the wings off!*

The F-4 continued to respond to the damage. The aircraft's Master Caution light came on announcing that something was wrong with the aircraft's systems. Along with this general warning came a Fire Light illumination for both engines. The FAC was saying something over the radio but it couldn't be understood.

Stone came on strong, "Sir, what are our warning indications?"

Spiker responded, "We have Engine Fire lights on both engines."

Stone barked, "We need to climb to altitude now and declare an emergency. We also need to go through the Engine Fire checklist."

Spiker responded with a statement that was beyond belief, "We're okay, we just got hit with a little 50 cal stuff. No problems. The Fire Lights are just a malfunction of the alert system. We'll turn for home but everything is fine."

"Covey 1," radioed Spiker, "Gunfighter 1 has been hit with 50 cal ground fire and we're off the target for home."

"Gunfighter 1, Covey 1, understands you are off the target. I did not observe any ground fire, but I sure observed the effects of the 750-pounders. I thought you were goners! Good luck on your return to the base."

"Lieutenant, we don't need to declare an emergency. The Fire Lights are only a malfunction of our warning systems," Spiker finally responded to Stone.

Stone would have none of it. “The Fire Lights are real. I can see fire coming up between the metal panels on the right engine nacelle. I’m declaring an emergency, you climb this damn thing now!”

Spiker responded with a climbing turn toward home base.

Stone made the call over Guard channel, “Mayday! Mayday! Mayday! Cobra 1 climbing through eight thousand feet, on the two-zero-zero degree radial from Da Nang for thirty-seven miles. We have battle damage and Fire Lights on both engines. We have a confirmed fire on the number two engine. We need to get on the ground now.”

Within seconds, Air Traffic Control (ATC) came back over the radio.

“Roger, Gunfighter 1, we have you on radar and are sending a rescue helicopter to your location. Climb to ten thousand feet, and stay in touch with me. Change to my frequency 325.5.”

“325.5,” Stone radioed back.

“Stone,” asked Spiker, “those 50 cal can really do some damage can’t they?”

“Yeah, if they ever hit you with one,” responded Stone with a sarcastic tone.

“Well, that’s what hit us,” Spiker yelled over the intercom. “You need to come to grips with it.”

Stone didn’t respond to Spiker’s challenge. He knew what had happened and this egotistic mad man was not going to change his mind or cover it up. He looked outside again at the short reddish blue flames jumping up between the engine panels. Then he noticed fuel was flowing out of the large uneven holes in the right wing.

“Damn it,” he said to himself.

Turning his head to the left he looked at the top of the left wing. He saw the same thing, fuel was flowing unevenly from the battle damaged holes in the wings.

“Colonel,” Stone called to Spiker, “we’re venting fuel from both wings. It’s coming from the holes caused by the explosion. We need to shut the number two engine down to stop the fire. The escaping fuel could cause us to blow up in flight. I don’t see flames on number one engine yet.”

Spiker reluctantly agreed, going to the Engine Fire checklist. He read through the checklist quickly and then announced,

"Right engine, SHUTDOWN."

The aircraft, with its almost full load of bombs was now very much underpowered. It could no longer climb. In fact, Spiker had to put the crippled aircraft into a shallow descent in order to maintain flying speed.

Spiker talked to Stone over the intercom, "We're going to have to get rid of this load if we're going to make it back to base."

Stone thought, *Well the man is starting to get the big picture after all.*

"Yes Sir, I think you're right. We need to jettison our load. Do you want me to call for a location and permission to do so?" requested Stone.

Before Spiker could respond Stone was on the radio calling for a radial and DME to jettison their bomb load. The military had many pre-determined locations where bombs could be jettisoned safely. A bomb load jettisoned in this manner almost never exploded because of spin-up safety fuses on the bombs. The fuses on the bombs had to spin up from air resistance after normal release to be armed to explode on impact with the ground. By jettisoning the bombs the fuses could not spin-up and arm and thus wouldn't explode on impact.

The crippled aircraft was given a small break. The jettison location was only a few miles from their location. Spiker and Stone were able to make it there quickly and Spiker punched off their remaining bomb load. The crippled F-4 responded with a new burst of energy and airspeed. However, the good news didn't last long.

"Stone," announced Spiker, "we have low fuel and partial hydraulic failure lights. The aircraft is flying heavy and not responding well to command inputs."

Stone responded to Spiker's announcement, "Well that is just great news, Sir. Yeah. Great news!"

As Stone finished his response to Spiker he turned and looked at the number one engine. Fire! Stone could hardly believe his eyes.

"Sir, we have fire, number 1 engine. We have got to get this thing on the ground and on the ground now."

Spiker agreed and called Da Nang, which could be seen in the distance.

"Da Nang Tower, Gunfighter 1 is emergency, twenty miles out. We are single engine with a fire burning in the good engine. We will need foam on the runway and will use the hook to take the cable."

The tower responded, "Roger, you are cleared to land on runway three-five right. Cleared for the cable and the runway will be foamed."

The F-4 was designed originally as a navy aircraft. As such, it had a large tail hook on the aft section of the plane that could grab a steel cable on touchdown. By grabbing the cable, the landing could be completed in a few hundred feet instead of the normal several thousand feet. The aircraft decelerated from about 130 knots upon taking the cable, to a full stop in about a second and a half. This could enhance the safety of a landing aircraft especially one that had been damaged or lost certain aircraft systems. With foam on the runway, and with the fire trucks spraying the foam on the aircraft, it reduced the risk of the aircraft exploding when its fuel came in contact with the fire.

The crippled, burning F-4 turned and made a long, straight in final approach.

"The gear, flaps and hook are down," announced Spiker to Stone.

"Roger, don't forget to lock your shoulder harness, Sir," responded Stone. "If you forget, your face will be smashed against the instrument panel."

Both pilots reached down and locked their shoulder harnesses. Then they reeled themselves backwards to lock the upper section of their bodies flat against their seats.

The F-4 flew across the runway threshold and hit the runway about 70 feet in front of the steel arresting cable. Within seconds the tail hook grabbed the cable and the aircraft began decelerating immediately. The decelerating of the F-4 was accompanied by a loud screeching noise outside the aircraft. The noise came from the steel cable that was attached to a thick, strong, flat ribbon material. This flat ribbon ran through specially modified B-52 brakes that had been redesigned for this braking procedure. As the tape was pulled through the brakes, the lining of the brakes grabbed onto the tape. This provided tons of resistance that very quickly slowed the aircraft and brought it to a stop.

Immediately, both canopies opened and the pilots began exiting the smoldering remains of a once powerful, fully functioning aircraft. The fire trucks arrived and began spraying foam on the entire surface of the plane and directly on and into its engines. It didn't take but a moment or two and the broken F-4 cooled and waited for a tow to take it to the maintenance hangar.

Spiker and Stone didn't say a word to each other as they went into the Intel shack for debriefing of the mission. Spiker insisted that the aircraft was damaged by ground fire. Stone didn't say a word but left the Intel shack, jumped in a crew van and drove to the squadron building. As he arrived at the squadron a dozen pilots and navigators greeted him. All of them wanted to know what happened on the mission.

Stone only replied, "He blew us up."

Stone proceeded to the squadron commander's office, knocked once, opened the door and walked into the room. The commander knew why Stone had come to see him and invited him to come in and to have a seat. Stone told the story of what had happened. The commander could hardly believe what he was told. He knew Stone well and knew that if Stone said it, then it was the truth.

Somehow, word of both accounts of the mission quickly spread throughout the squadron. The damaged F-4 was placed in isolation with a yellow tape barrier placed all around it to try and prevent individuals from coming close to inspect it. This was a feeble effort at best to try and hide the truth of the mission. The squadron commander ordered two crew vans filled with volunteers, both pilots and navigators, to go down to the flight line to inspect the damaged F-4.

When they arrived at the flight line no one attempted to stop the group from inspecting the plane. It was clear looking at the battle damage that it had not been inflicted by ground fire. Huge holes in the fuselage, tail section and in the wings showed without a doubt that its own bombs had blown up the once proud bird.

Within days the F-4 was disassembled, crated up and shipped back to the States. The colonel was reassigned to another base. No one knew what base he had gone to, or at least no one ever spoke of it.

It took Stone a day or two to put this flight behind him. Very soon he was flying again and even joked about this almost fatal mission.

"Don't let 'em go too low, or you might blow," he would jest with other crewmembers.

They all knew what happened that day and how the tough, strong, powerful F-4 brought both crewmembers back alive.

5

Hitting the Ground

Major Richard White was not liked by many of the flight crewmembers at Da Nang. He was arrogant, overly proud, a loner, and not a particularly good pilot. He didn't try to establish positive relationships with anyone. He didn't really seem to care about others nor about the war effort. He wanted to fly missions and fly them his way.

It wasn't uncommon for him to put himself and other crewmembers in harm's way unnecessarily. For example, on flights in Laos he would disregard proper mission safety protocol by descending his F-4 to a very low altitude, 100 to 150 feet above the trees. He would slow the aircraft down to final approach airspeed, about 150 knots. He would do this to try and get the enemy to fire on his low and slow aircraft. He hoped to see the enemy's firing location, then turn the F-4 around, go back and attack their position. This was called trolling and was very dangerous for the aircraft and its crew. It was not a recommended practice and the backseaters or GIBs who had this happen to them refused to fly with Major White again.

Major White was also known to press the targets by descending below the proper altitude to release the bombs. This altitude is called the pickle altitude. Under some conditions this was an accepted way to acquire the target, if both the backseater and the aircraft commander had communicated about the situation in advance and an escape plan had been developed. Such a plan would designate a minimum descent altitude when the backseater must begin the dive recovery should the frontseater fail to do so. Frontseaters have been known to become fixated on a target and simply drive the aircraft into the ground.

Major White wouldn't discuss these kinds of safety issues with his backseaters. In fact, Major White's custom was to communicate very little with the backseater. He expected him to just do his job, keep quiet, and let the frontseater fly the aircraft. Other pilots seemed to intimidate White or threaten his ego so he just didn't like to be around them. Whatever the case, it seemed to work better if a navigator backseater, rather than a pilot, was assigned to fly with White. He didn't seem to be threatened by a navigator because what could they tell him about flying? However the use of only navigators as GIBs in the F-4 with White put both crewmembers and the aircraft at increased risk. Navigators, particularly new ones, wouldn't know that many of the things that White did with the aircraft during missions weren't SOPs and were in fact dangerous and plain stupid.

Those who out ranked White knew of his dangerous flying tendencies but seemed unable or unwilling to take him off flying status and place him at a desk job. They continued to assign him a navigator backseater or at least a new in county pilot, and hoped that it would all work out.

With the use of a rotating schedule within the squadron, it didn't take long for White's name to appear on the schedule. The combat mission assigned this day was an out of country target in Laos. It was a suspected enemy truck parking area along the Ho Chi Minh Trail. Out of country missions were those that were flown out of South Vietnam. These could be missions in Laos, North Vietnam or Cambodia. Missions flown out of country were considered especially hazardous or dangerous. There were many reasons these missions were considered dangerous. They included the fact that there was usually more enemy ground fire on these missions. The North Vietnamese Army (NVA) would set up permanent gun locations out of country to protect targets of opportunity, such as truck stops, troop concentrations, and stored supplies and guns that would normally move down the Trail.

These missions took place in isolated and remote locations that made access difficult for rescue personnel should there be a problem and aircrews were downed. There were always numerous enemy soldiers in these remote locations and any friendly help needed in an emergency would be sparse or non-existent.

It was also known that in these isolated, remote locations a crewmember who ejected and was captured by the enemy, was usually killed on the spot. The enemy soldiers didn't have the desire or will to spend months taking prisoners back up the Ho Chi Minh Trail to North Vietnam and to prison. It was easier for them to kill the crewmembers immediately and be done with it.

The other members of the flight crew this day were Captain Kilmer and Lieutenant Stone in the Lead aircraft and Major White and Lieutenant Bill Black in the wingman position. Lieutenant Black was a navigator weapons officer and had been in country only about two months. He was a quiet, good looking young man who would hang out with pilots and other navigators but usually didn't say very much. He was shy in his interaction with others. He was liked by all around him, probably because he left the impression that he was vulnerable and in need of help to survive this war. He left the impression that*: He was the younger brother that you had left at home.*

The crews arrived for the mission briefing the required two hours before takeoff. Kilmer, as Lead aircraft commander, was responsible for the flight and for the preflight briefing. Both crews went into the target briefing room and began studying the target. The target was situated in a mountainous area that had steep karst valley walls and rugged tree covered hills. The Ho Chi Minh Trail was cut through the mountainous valleys and through streams and rivers that ran through the area. The Ho Chi Minh Trail was called a trail but it was more like an interstate highway in some of its locations. The Trail was made up of complex patterns of truck routes, foot and bike paths and river crossings. The NVA troops worked on the Trail for years to make it a highway system that would allow them to bring supplies and equipment down from North Vietnam through Laos and Cambodia to South Vietnam.

After the crews studied the target area, Kilmer took the crewmembers to the Intel briefing room where the Intel officer presented a briefing that warned enemy ground fire was almost a certainty. There had been enemy fire in the target area four out of the last five days. One F-4 had received battle damage in the target area two days earlier and had to make an emergency landing in Thailand. The Intel briefing also included the fact that if there was an emergency on the mission, and the crew was forced to eject, there would be absolutely no friendly troops in the area. In the case of battle damage, the Intel officer suggested flying as far as possible away from the target area before ejecting. This warning had been given before to aircrew members and it never resulted in feelings of hope or security.

After the Intel briefing was completed, the weather officer provided the briefing. The forecast in the target area predicted good weather. No rain was forecast and the visibility was to be better than five miles. There was a chance of scattered to broken clouds above 15,000 feet, but that would present no real problem for the F-4s or to the mission.

After the weather briefing the crews went to the equipment shack to retrieve their flight gear. Their G-suits, parachute harnesses, and survival vests were put on. Their 38 caliber Smith and Wesson revolvers were placed in their shoulder holsters. Emergency radios were checked to make sure that they were operating properly. Extra 38 cartridges, emergency batteries and emergency flares were also stored in the survival vest. Many pilots and navigators took extra cartridges for their revolvers purely for psychological reasons. It made them feel better to have a few extra rounds of ammo with them. Few of them saw themselves getting into a gun battle with the bad guys. They knew that more than likely this would be an unproductive choice that would result in a bad ending.

Once the crews were fully dressed for flight, they left the equipment shack, went to the parking lot, and climbed into the crew van for transport to the aircraft. The crew van driver then dropped each of the crews at their aircraft revetments. Kilmer and Stone began to pre-flight their aircraft and weapons. White and Black also began the pre-flight of their F-4. No problems were found on either of the two birds, nor their weapons. Both crews then climbed into the cockpits and began the sequence to start their engines. The engines were started, checklists completed and the two F-4s rolled out of their concrete revetments. As Lead aircraft, Kilmer and Stone pulled out while White and Black pulled into second place.

"Da Nang Tower," called Kilmer over the radio, "Gunfighters 1 and 2 taxi, two F-4s."

"Gunfighter 1 and 2 cleared to taxi, runway one-seven left," responded the tower.

"Cleared to taxi, runway one-seven left," responded Kilmer.

Both aircraft taxied to the arming area of runway one-seven. The arming crews began arming the bombs. One of the arming crewmembers found a problem with one of the attachment lugs holding a 500-lb bomb onto a rail attached to White's wing.

"Sir, we have an attachment lug problem on the left wing," called the arming crew chief. "One bomb is only attached at one end but we will get it corrected immediately."

"Roger," responded White, "we need to get this show on the road."

About five minutes went by and the hung bomb problem had not been corrected. White became very irritated and called the arming chief over the intercom.

"What's the status of the hung bomb? We need to get on with the mission. We are burning JP-4 and daylight."

"We'll have it done in one," responded the chief.

"Well get it done or yank the bomb off the plane now, we need to get these birds in the air," yelled White.

"Yes Sir," responded the chief.

Another five minutes went by and White was getting more and more irritated.

He was just about to yell at the crew chief again to take the hung bomb off of the plane when the crew chief came on the intercom.

"Sir, we have the problem corrected, you are ready to go."

"Well, it's about damn time," responded White.

"Gunfighter 1, Gunfighter 2, we are ready to go," called White to Kilmer.

Kilmer didn't answer White directly but let him know that he understood his transmission by calling the tower for takeoff.

"Da Nang Tower, Gunfighter 1 and 2 ready for departure, runway one-seven left," announced Kilmer.

"Gunfighter 1 and 2, you are cleared for takeoff, runway one-seven left. Have a good mission," responded the tower.

"Roger, understand cleared for takeoff, you have a good morning."

Kilmer released the brakes on the fully loaded F-4, pulled onto the runway, and positioned both throttles to full military power position. The heavy F-4 slowly began to roll down the runway. Then Kilmer moved both throttles to the outboard position and pushed them forward igniting both afterburners on the powerful J-79 engines. Immediately the afterburners ignited and both engines began to deliver on their advertised 17,000 lbs. of thrust. This provides the F-4 a total of 34,000 lbs. of thrust. A clean F-4, one that is not carrying any ordnance or fuel, weighs in at 29,632 lbs. This provides a clean F-4 a thrust to weight ratio of about 1:1: one pound of thrust to one pound of weight. This means that an F-4 in such a configuration could theoretically fly straight up through the atmosphere. However with fuel, the thrust to weight ratio of the F-4 isn't quite 1:1. So aerodynamically, sustained flight straight up through the atmosphere isn't possible in the F-4. However with this power to weight ratio, the F-4 held the world's zoom climb record in the 1960's, climbing to an altitude of over 96,000 feet. It also held the world's aircraft speed record by flying 1600 miles per hour. The F-4 is capable of achieving a speed of over Mach 2, or over twice the speed of sound. Very few fighter-bombers of the era were able to accomplish this feat.

The F-4 had an abundance of power. This was a characteristic that would serve it well in carrying and delivering ordnance in Southeast Asia. It also assisted them in dogfights with Russian built MIG fighters over North Vietnam. It's well known by F-4 pilots, that in a dogfight with a MIG, unloading the F-4 by pushing the nose over toward the ground to establish a negative G condition and igniting the afterburners, the F-4's airspeed instantly increased by 100 knots. This gave the F-4 a distinct advantage over the MIG. All fighter pilots understand that airspeed is life and the greater the airspeed the greater the chance of surviving in a combat environment.

Kilmer's F-4 continued to accelerate and reached rotation speed. Kilmer pulled back on the stick and established a ten-degree nose high aircraft attitude. The aircraft lifted off the ground with a huge roaring sound that was characteristic of the F-4. Kilmer retracted the landing gear and the flaps as the F-4 began its climb to altitude while accelerating in airspeed.

White began his takeoff roll 30 seconds after Kilmer. After lift off White's F-4 began to accelerate to an airspeed that would allow him to close the distance from Lead. As was the practice for formation flying, Lead pulled back his throttles and reduced his power by 2% to allow the number two aircraft to have extra power and speed to join on the Lead aircraft. The extra power provided to White allowed him to quickly join on Kilmer's right wing.

The flight then headed for Laos to join up with the FAC that would control the attack on the ground target. Many things go through the minds of the crewmembers while they are flying to the target. It usually doesn't take a lot of time to get to a target, whether it's in county or out of country. The F-4 was so fast that it could reach a normal target in 20-25 minutes. During these 20 minutes or so the thoughts of a crewmember could cover many topics: what might happen over the target, what could happen if the aircraft should sustain battle damage, what ejection would be like.

Ejection from a relatively safe, quiet cockpit into a violent 500-knot wind stream while riding an uncontrollable rocket seat brings thoughts of fear and uncertainty, especially if this should happen over the target area. Probably the most overwhelming thought that goes through the mind of crewmembers is: *Please God, don't let me screw up.* Crewmembers were very concerned about making a mistake that might cost the life of a friendly on the ground or one of the flight crewmembers in the air.

On this particular day, friendlies on the ground was not an issue, but making a mistake on in-flight duties might have very serious consequences. Thoughts of loved ones and of home are topics that didn't go through the minds of crewmembers during a mission. There were just too many duties and responsibilities that needed to be attended to and thinking about loved ones was a clear invitation for disaster.

Stone had dialed in the Tactical Air Navigation System (TACAN) channel frequency for the closest station to the target. The station was Channel 72 and the target was on the three-five-zero-degree radial for 47 DME. The Distance Measurement Equipment (DME), measured the distance the aircraft was from a TACAN station. It was one of two ways the F-4 crew had to determine their location.

The other way was the Inertial Navigation System or INS. The INS was a self-contained navigation unit that was able to use accelerometers to find the center of the earth and to measure any movement of the aircraft either accelerating or decelerating as it flew through the sky. When the pilot gave the INS the takeoff location in longitude and latitude, and the destination location in longitude and latitude, the INS was able to solve the mathematical operations necessary to navigate to the desired destination. It had an operation error of approximately one-half mile per hour of operation. That was very good especially in the era in which it was developed and utilized. On an aircraft mission of about one and one half hours long it was rare if the INS had an error of more than a mile or two. It was able to give the F-4 crewmembers directed steering, with distance information, to any location on the earth up to 9,999 miles away. The enemy couldn't jam the INS with false electronic signals from the ground.

Coming upon the target area, Kilmer gave the FAC a call on the radio. "Misty 1, Gunfighter 1 and 2 with you. We are approximately five miles from your location at Angels One-Five-Zero. We have 500-lb Mark 82 slick bombs on board today."

"Gunfighter 1, Misty 1. I have a visual on you two miles south of my location. The target is active. We've had ground fire all morning. It seems to be mostly small arms fire but I wouldn't rule out some 37 mm coming on line. I'm firing my smoke now. When you see my smoke, give me a tally ho."

Within seconds Gunfighter 1 radioed the FAC. "Misty 1, Gunfighter 1, I have your smoke."

"Roger that," responded Misty 1. "Hit my smoke. Make your run into the target from east to west."

"Wilco," called Kilmer, "Gunfighter 1 is onto the target, Gunfighter 2 you come in behind me. Heads up for ground fire."

"Roger, Gunfighter 2," radioed White.

Gunfighter 1 rolled in on the target. They started their attack at 12,000 feet above ground level (AGL). The heavy F-4 rolled over on its side while the nose of the aircraft dipped to a 60-degree angle below the horizon. Down the huge bird went rushing toward the ground, accelerating through 500 knots of airspeed.

Inside the cockpit, a 60-degree nose low attitude looks and feels like the aircraft is 90 degrees to the ground. It gives the experience of a roller coaster that is going straight down. The ground rushes up toward the aircraft, slowly at first, then speeding faster and faster toward the aircraft until it fills the entire view in the windscreen. The sky is gone from view with only the earth closing quickly. Seconds to use for recovery are vital.

Stone began to call off the altitudes to Kilmer: "Ten thousand feet, eight thousand, seven thousand, six thousand, ready pickle." The thump sound of two Mark-82 bombs leaving the F-4 was heard.

"Pull, pull," Stone yelled over the intercom.

Kilmer didn't need to hear Stone yelling, "Pull." He was pulling on the flight controls with all his strength. The big F-4 rotated in space and seemed to switch ends as the inertia of the aircraft carried it downward while the blasting J-79s were now pushing it skyward. Slowly the F-4 stopped its descent and began to gain altitude, missing the karst ridges by only a few hundred feet.

"Damn," exclaimed Kilmer. "That was a real eye opener, a little too low. Did you happen to see any ground fire Stone?"

Stone replied, "I didn't see a damn thing except us just barely missing that ridge line on pull out. Maybe we need to release a little higher on the next round. What do you think?"

"I think you might be on to something," Kilmer responded with a laugh. "I believe the terrain around here is higher than is printed on the charts."

Gunfighter 1 continued their flight pattern to line up on the target for a second run. Then out of the blue Misty 1 called on the radio in an excited, strange voice.

"My God, did you see that fireball? I have never seen anything like it," called Misty 1.

"I see it," responded Kilmer. "Did Gunfighter 2's bombs hit a weapon storage area? It looks like that's what happened. That was a horrible explosion."

"Gunfighter 2, Misty 1, can you read me? Gunfighter 2, Misty 1, can you read my transmission?"

There was no response to Misty 1's radio call to Gunfighter 2.

"Gunfighter 2, Misty 1, can you read me?"

Again there was silence and an awful sense that something was horribly wrong.

"Gunfighter 2, Gunfighter 1, do you read me? Do you read my transmission?" called Kilmer over the radio.

"Gunfighter 1, Misty 1. I am flying low over the target area and I believe Gunfighter 2 has hit the ground. I see what looks like aircraft wreckage all over the hillside with fires everywhere. I believe Gunfighter 2 is down."

There was a silence over the radio for about 30 seconds as Gunfighter 1 flew over the impact sight of Gunfighter 2's aircraft. The 30 seconds seemed like 30 minutes.

Finally Gunfighter 1 came up on the radio.

"Roger, Misty 1, I copy your transmission. Did you observe any chutes or do you hear any beepers?"

"That is a negative," responded Misty 1. "I'll alert air rescue to the situation, and stay on the scene until they arrive. I'll also make some lower level passes over the area to check for any chutes on the ground or beepers. How is your fuel situation?"

"We are good on fuel and can stay on site as long as you need us."

"Roger, understand," radioed Misty 1.

Both Misty 1 and Gunfighter 1 stayed at the accident site until the rescue helicopter arrived on scene. There was no observed evidence that either of the pilots had ejected from the downed F-4. No beepers could be heard.

"Gunfighter 1, what is your fuel status?" radioed Misty 1.

"We're getting close to emergency fuel, we better head for home," responded Kilmer.

"Roger that, you're cleared to exit the area. Have a safe one home."

"Wilco," responded Kilmer, "I will inform Intel of the situation when I get back to base. We are off your station. Thanks for anything you can do to help on the ground."

"Roger," radioed Misty 1, "I'm really sorry about your wingman."

Kilmer and Stone didn't say a word on the flight back to Da Nang. They were in shock over the event that so quickly took two of their fellow aviators. When they landed they went into the Intel shack to inform the Intel officers what happened.

Word already reached the base about the tragedy. The wing and squadron commanders were in the Intel shack to hear first hand the story of the loss of one of their aircraft and two of their aircrew members. Kilmer and Stone told what they had seen and heard but neither could really explain what had happened. Had Gunfighter 2 been hit by enemy fire, was there a malfunction with the aircraft or did the aircraft commander press the target too low and not have the altitude to recover from the steep dive angle? No one knew and no one ever found the answer to what really happened that day. However what happened had a profound effect on the surviving aircrews at the squadron. It pointed out all too clearly how one mistake, one aircraft malfunction, or one hit by enemy fire could have quick and deadly results.

It became very clear to the pilots and navigators in the squadron that life was very precious and fragile and that seconds or even fractions of a second could mean the difference between life and death. The consequences of seconds lost this day meant that Captain White and Lieutenant Black would never go home again.

6

Escorting B-52s and North Vietnam

"Bang. Bang," came a knock on Lieutenant Stone's BOQ door. "Bang. Bang," the knock came again.

"Hey Stone, get your butt up, it's getting late," yelled Lieutenant Bill Weatherby. "You get to go to Laos today you lucky dog. You don't want to miss that," Weatherby continued, while he laughed.

It was a nervous laugh because he was going on the same mission. He knew of its dangers, but as always, never showed his concern. Crewmembers remarked only jokingly about the dangers and hazards of flying the combat missions assigned. Assigned missions were never officially questioned or refused because of their dangerous conditions. They were bravely accepted and accomplished.

Lieutenant Weatherby went down to the squadron building early to check on his scheduled flying mission for that morning. It was a special mission. It would take them into a dangerous part of Laos for an Arc Light mission. An Arc Light mission usually involved a group of three B-52 bombers escorted by protective fighters. Each bomber was loaded with 500-pound hard bombs and each B-52 could carry over 100 of these Mark 82s. With three B-52s on an Arc Light mission, just under 400 bombs could be delivered at one time in a very small area. It was a devastating attack, covering an area about two miles long and about a half mile wide. The NVA hated the B-52 attacks. Captured enemy soldiers told of the results of the Arc Lights. They revealed that while sitting around a fire to have a meal, without warning, the whole world around them exploded. Any enemy soldiers who were in the vicinity, even close to the area covered by the bombings, were terrified by the horrific blast of the bombs, the convulsive shaking of the earth, and the deafening sound of the hundreds of bombs tearing their way through the jungle. For those unfortunate enough to be caught in the kill zone, approximately two miles long by half-mile wide, their war and their lives were over.

Stone rolled out of bed, reached over and opened the door to his BOQ room and grabbed a towel and a bar of soap.

"Hi Bill," said Stone, "I'll run down and take a quick shower and be right with you. Did you say Laos? That's just great! What kind of mission have we been assigned, do you know?"

"Yep, Northeastern Laos. We're going to fly cap for the B-52s that are conducting an Arc Light mission," replied Lieutenant Weatherby. "A lot of bombs are going to the bad guys today."

Stone showered, shaved, and dressed. He slid into his flight suit, zipped up its long zipper and put on his flying boots.

"Let's get to the chow hall and fill up our tanks," remarked Stone.

"You got it," Bill remarked, "I have a crew van out front."

Both Stone and Weatherby climbed into the van and drove to the chow hall to eat breakfast. Before a mission most crewmembers didn't feel like eating, but they knew it was wise to at least eat something. Most forced themselves to eat a small meal. It might be hours before they had an opportunity to eat again because the crew duty day could be 16 hours long and access to food very limited.

The breakfast meal served was a normal one. It included powered eggs, greasy bacon, SOS, toasted white bread, hash brown potatoes, powered milk, dried cereal, reconstituted orange juice, and coffee. The menu usually never changed for either good or bad. It was just what it was.

Stone and Weatherby finished in short time and climbed into the crew van and drove to the squadron building. They walked inside and went directly to the target planning room to get the information on the mission. The veteran Lead aircraft commander, Captain Ron Kilmer and his wingman, aircraft commander Captain Douglas Robertson joined them. There was not a type of mission that Kilmer hadn't flown in Vietnam. He had been in country for almost nine months and had a ton of experience in the mission requirements of the F-4D. Captain Robertson on the other hand had only been in the Vietnam Theater for two months. He still had a lot to learn about staying alive in a combat environment. The good thing was that he recognized this fact and did not miss an opportunity to learn from combat veterans like Kilmer. He asked questions and really studied each mission and its target. By the time he left the squadron planning room, he had the planning for the whole mission in his head and written down. He developed a plan of action from engine start up to engine shut down. It was because of his desire to learn the requirements of each mission and to get it done right that he earned the respect of even the most senior pilots in the squadron.

It quickly became very clear what the mission would involve. It directed that two F-4s take off armed with air-to-air missiles, and rendezvous with tankers and refuel. They would join-up with three B-52s, or Buffs, who were carrying the bombs to be delivered to weapons storage and troop concentration areas in northeastern Laos. The job of the F-4s was to fly Sky Cap for the B-52s and protect them against a possible threat from North Vietnamese MIG aircraft that might come up and attack the Buffs. Northeastern Laos was very close to the border of North Vietnam and it would be a short flight for the MIGs to take off from Hanoi and fly to intercept the Buffs. The B-52s would usually fly high, at about 30,000 feet; however, they had to fly straight and level to deliver their bombs onto their target. This made them a perfect target for the MIGs who could attack using an assortment of weapons.

Sending the F-4s along to protect the Buffs was a great strategy. The F-4 was a perfect aircraft to be used to protect the B-52s. It was designed as an air-to-air fighter interceptor by the Navy to protect the fleet, and it was an excellent platform for this role. The F-4 was Mach 2 capable and could carry two exceptional types of air-to-air missiles. The primary missile weapon was the AIM-7 or Sparrow missile. It was a radar guided missile that could fly at several times the speed of sound toward its target. The powerful radar on the F-4 that guided the missile could reach out and "paint" targets at well over 50 miles out. It could lock-on and track targets at a 25-35 mile range. The Sparrow could then be fired, and with a high degree of certainty, destroy the target within these distances. The closer the target got, the deadlier the Sparrow became.

The second excellent missile that was carried by the F-4 was the heat-seeking missile known as the AIM-9 or Sidewinder. A heat-seeking missile looked for an infrared (IR) heat source, like the tail pipe of the jet engine on the enemy aircraft, lock onto that heat source for guidance, and fly to it. As soon as the Sidewinder's computer indicated that the missile was as close as it could get to the target, it would explode the warhead. The warhead had hundreds of steel rods that would expand out from the explosion and destroy the enemy aircraft.

The F-4 had a unique way of launching the Sidewinder. The pilot could select a setting on his fire-control panel called the bore-sight mode. This would line up and then cage the infrared tracking head of the Sidewinder with the pilot's reticle on his target display. This would allow the attacking pilot to fly and position the F-4 in a 6 o'clock position of the enemy aircraft and place his target reticle on the tailpipe of the enemy. The Sidewinder tracking head would detect this strong IR source and give out a characteristic growling sound that announced the target had been acquired and was being tracked. The attacking F-4 pilot had only to pull the trigger on his control stick and the Sidewinder launched off the carrying rails, tracked to and destroyed the target aircraft.

The Sidewinder had a much shorter range than the AIM-7 Sparrow missile. However, after several modifications, when the target came within range, the missile was reliable and deadly.

Pilots liked both missiles even though each went through their early growing pains. The early AIM-7 would not arm itself rapidly enough flying off the F-4s. They weren't good for dog fighting in close quarters, within 1,500 to 2,000 feet. In F-4 encounters with MIGs in the early part of the Vietnam War, Air Force pilots struggled to get into proper firing position on the MIGs, launch the Sparrow only to have it not arm and just fly passed the fleeing MIG. This was very frustrating for the pilots. By the late '60s this problem had been corrected and the Sparrow could be launched and armed in a shorter distance. However, the Sparrow's strongest characteristic was its ability to track, attack and destroy targets at long distances. It was extremely deadly at distances from five to fifteen miles. Unfortunately, this advantage was defeated by the military's rules of engagement that required that aerial targets be identified visually before they were attacked. This took away much of the Sparrow's advantage.

The four F-4 crewmembers completed their required mission planning, Intel and weather briefings and suited up for the mission. They climbed into crewmember vans and were driven to their F-4 aircraft revetments. As they drove up to their respective aircraft they noticed the F-4s looked uncharacteristically strange. This strange appearance was due to their somewhat slim and sleek appearance. There was not a huge bomb load on-board for this flight, only the Sparrow missiles loaded under the F-4's huge body and the Sidewinders loaded on the outer wing stations. With only the small light missiles loaded on the F-4 the craft would be extremely fast and responsive. It was a real joy to fly the F-4 in this configuration. This was what the aircraft had been designed to do, and did it better than any aircraft in the Air Force or Navy inventory at the time.

Both crews completed the pre-flight of their aircraft and onboard missiles. The crewmembers climbed aboard their aircraft and quickly started the engines. They completed all pre-taxi checklists.

"Phu Cat Tower, Cobra 1 and Cobra 2, two F-4s taxi," radioed Kilmer.

"Cobra 1 and Cobra 2," responded the tower, "good morning, you are cleared to taxi to runway one-five. The wind is one-seven-zero degrees at seven knots."

"Cleared taxi to runway one-five," responded Kilmer, "good morning to you sir.

"Cobra 2, are you up on freq?"

"Cobra 2 up," radioed Robertson.

Both F-4s taxied to the runway arming area where the arming crews readied the Sparrow and Sidewinder missiles for operational readiness. Both crews got thumbs up from the crew chief that the missiles had been armed for possible launch.

"Doug, you ready?" radioed Kilmer to Robertson.

"Cobra 2 ready to go."

"Phu Cat Tower, Cobra 1 and 2 are ready for takeoff," radioed Kilmer.

"Cobra Flight, cleared for takeoff. Caution, there have been reports of small arms fire off the departure end of the runway. Have a good mission."

"Cleared for takeoff," radioed Kilmer.

Both F-4s taxied into position on the 10,000-foot runway and began going through their pre-takeoff checks. As the powerful J-79 engines were advanced to full Military (Mil) power, the F-4s attempted to leap forward but were held back by the aircraft's powerful brakes. In response to the powerful thrust from the engines, and being locked in place by its brakes, the F-4's fuselages lowered and pitched forward, giving the appearance of large powerful animals ready to leap onto their prey.

With all checklists completed Kilmer quickly looked over his right shoulder at Robertson. Robertson indicated he was ready for takeoff and gave him a thumbs-up. Kilmer released the brakes and smoothly brought the throttles from full Mil power into the afterburner position. This action gave the crewmembers a response like none that can be experienced outside a fighter-bomber. The light F-4 began to rapidly accelerate down the runway like a German sports car. The afterburners ignited to give a surge forward that was simply exhilarating. The F-4 accelerated faster and faster until it reached rotation speed and the nose of the aircraft rose 12 degrees toward the sky. Within seconds the sleek bird took to the air, began its climb for altitude, and reached a speed of 300 knots before clearing the field boundary. Flying a clean or lightly loaded F-4 is a fighter pilot's dream. It was just an amazing flight experience.

Kilmer pulled the nose of the F-4 up to increase its climb performance. He wanted as much altitude as possible passing the spot where ground fire had been reported. He also wanted to slow the aircraft some so that Robertson would have an easier time in the rejoin. Robertson quickly joined on Kilmer's right wing only feet away from the Lead.

"Stone, do you have a heading for me to the Cherry Tanker Track?" requested Kilmer.

"Yes Sir, I do," responded Stone, "for Cherry Track pick up a heading of three-zero-zero-degrees. That will take us to the southern end of the track."

The aerial tankers of the Air Force constantly flew prearranged racetrack patterns that ran in northeastern and southwestern directions.

Several of those tracks were in use at any one time to provide needed additional fuel for mission requirements. Fighter-bombers on prearranged missions or fighters who were running low on fuel could intercept these Air Force tankers and refuel their aircraft. Fuel is life to a fighter aircraft and the history of these aerial tankers in the air war in Southeast Asia was one of saving the lives of our aircrew members with their fuel assistance.

A great deal of the fuel burned on a mission is burned during taxi, takeoff, climb to altitude, and navigating to the target location. If a fighter is refueled at altitude, close to the target or escort, then the flying time of the mission can be extended by at least an hour.

"Stone," radioed Kilmer, "see if you can pick up the tanker on your radar scope and then give me a heading for intercept."

"Will do Sir," responded Stone. "I am looking out now on the two-hundred mile range. I don't have him yet, but will give you a call when I pick him up."

Stone continued to scan with the radar to pick up the Air Force tanker on Cherry Track. No targets appeared on the radar for seven to eight minutes, then, a small blip appeared at the top of the scope. The blip became more pronounced, as it quickly started moving down the scope. Stone adjusted the radar antenna up and down to try and determine if the tanker was above or below them in altitude. The tanker was scheduled to be 2000 feet above their altitude. It was confirmed by Stone that the target was in fact above them in altitude and approximately 150 miles out.

"Sir," called Stone over the intercom, "I have the tanker on radar. He is approximately one hundred fifty miles from our current position and 1500 to 2000 feet above us. A good heading to intercept him would be three-one-zero-degrees."

"Thanks Ben," replied Kilmer. "In a few minutes I'll try to bring them up on the radio."

"Cobra 2, switch to the tanker's frequency on 232.2," radioed Kilmer.

"232.2," repeated Robertson.

"Cobra 2 up with you on 232.2."

"Roger," responded Kilmer. He waited a couple of minutes and then made the radio call to the tanker.

"Cherry 1, Cobra 1 and 2 with you at Angels Two-Two-Zero, ninety miles out. We are two Fox 4s who would like to top off our tanks."

"Cobra 1 and 2," answered Cherry 1. "I have a pair of F-100s taking fuel presently, but they should be on their way before you rendezvous with us. Continue to join on us and give a call when three to five miles out."

"Wilco," replied Kilmer. "Will give you a call in a few."

It didn't take long to close the 90-mile distance between the F-4s and the tanker. The closure speed between the tanker and the F-4s was about 800 knots. With that kind of closure speed the tanker would be in visual contact in less than ten minutes. The time seemed to go extremely fast and soon Stone called over the intercom to Kilmer.

"Sir, I have a visual on the tankers at 11 o'clock, slightly high, about three miles."

"I have them."

"Cherry 1, Cobra 1, we have a visual. We are about three miles out."

"Cobra 1 and 2, you are cleared to join on us," radioed the tanker, "Cobra 1 you connect first, followed by Cobra 2."

"We copy," responded Kilmer. Kilmer joined on the tanker and slid the F-4 into position and opened the F-4's refueling door.

"Cherry 1, Cobra 1 is in position and ready to connect."

"Roger," the boom operator responded, "you are in great position, I am sticking you now."

The tanker's refueling boom connected with the F-4's refueling receptacle, just ahead of the aircraft's open refueling door. The thirsty F-4 took on all the fuel it could hold.

"Cobra 1, you're topped off and cleared to disconnect. Cobra 2, when Lead is clear, you can move into position," commanded the boom operator.

Cobra 1 disconnected from the refueling boom and moved to the left wing on the tanker. Cobra 2 slid from the right wing of the tanker and moved into position to take on fuel. As he flew into position Cobra 2 opened his refueling door.

"Cobra 2," radioed the boom operator, "you're in perfect position, hold right there. I'm going to connect with you now."

"Roger," responded Robertson, "fill it all the way to the top."

"Will do Sir," replied the boom operator, "this is what we do, we pass gas."

"Well, I must say you do it quite well," replied Robertson, "I only wish you gave Green Stamps."

In less than ten minutes both the F-4s had refueled and were ready to depart the tanker.

"That's all I can do for you today," radioed the boom operator. "You're cleared off."

"Thanks for your help today," radioed Kilmer, "see you later on in the war."

Both F-4s slid back away from the tanker and Robertson rejoined on Kilmer's right wing. Kilmer then made a smooth but steep right turn toward the northeast and began to climb to 30,000 feet.

"Stone," called Kilmer on the intercom, "now we need to find those damn Buffs. Put the rendezvous coordinates in the INS and give me a heading. I'll try and contact them on the join frequency."

"It's done Sir," replied Stone, "turn to zero-five-zero degrees, that will get us in the neighborhood."

"Cobra 2, Cobra 1," radioed Kilmer, "switch to the Buff's frequency now."

"Roger," responded Robertson, "changing over now."

Both aircraft changed to the prearranged intercept frequency for the B-52 bombers.

"Cobra 2," radioed Kilmer, "are you up on freq?"

"Cobra 2 with you," answered Robertson.

"Arc Light Lead, Cobra 1 and 2, two F-4s on your frequency," radioed Kilmer. "How do you read me?"

"Good morning Cobra Flight, Arc Light 1 reads you loud and clear, how me?" responded the B-52 Lead aircraft.

"Arc Light 1, I read you loud and clear," radioed Kilmer. "We are approximately five zero miles southwest from the rendezvous point at Angels Three-Zero-Zero."

"Standby one," radioed Arc Light 1, "let me see if we have you on the scope."

Within 20 seconds Arc Light 1 came back on the air.

"Cobra Flight, Arc Light 1, we have you on our scopes. We show your position forty-three miles out at our 7 o'clock position. You are cleared to join with us. Please stay above us. We're about twenty-five minutes from the target."

"We confirm with our radar," responded Kilmer, "we'll join high and be looking for any unwanted visitors. You will be covered."

"Thanks," responded Arc Light 1, "it's nice to have a little brother cover our backs."

"We'll be with you in a few," responded Kilmer.

Soon visual contact was made with the three B-52s. The two F-4s joined on them in loose formation and in a slightly high position. The F-4 crewmembers knew that soon hundreds of 500-pound bombs would be falling from the Buffs and they didn't want to be underneath them when the bombs were dropped. That could ruin their whole day.

The five-ship formation of three B-52s and two F-4s proceeded in formation flight toward the assigned target in northeastern Laos. Suddenly a call came up on Guard frequency from an AWACS aircraft that was on station in the Gulf of Tonkin.

"Two bandits, taxiing at Bull's-eye," announced the AWACS.

The AWACS or Airborne Warning and Control System aircraft were modified with large radar domes attached to the top of the aircraft. They were used to help direct allied flight operations in North Vietnam and to provide early warning of North Vietnamese MIG fighter activity for American strike aircraft.

"Two MIGs airborne at Bull's-eye, climbing on a heading of two-four-zero degrees," warned the AWACS.

Bulls-eye was the code name for Hanoi and with the heading of two-four-zero degrees the MIGs were heading straight toward the B-52 formation.

"Cobra 2, Cobra 1," radioed Kilmer, "they're coming our way. Let's go meet them."

"Roger, Cobra 1," answered Robertson.

"Arc Light 1, Cobra 1," radioed Kilmer, "we're going to intercept the threat. You guys all right on your own?"

"We're fine, give 'em hell!"

Cobra Flight broke from the Buffs and picked up a heading toward the approaching MIG threat.

"Pick them up as quickly as you can on the radar Ben," requested

Kilmer over the intercom. "I'd like you to vector us around to their 6 or 7 o'clock position so I can put a Sidewinder up their ass."

"I am all over it Sir," responded Stone.

"Cobra 2, Cobra 1," radioed Kilmer, "we're going to try and maneuver to their 6 o'clock for a visual ID and a Sidewinder shot. I'll target the wingman first and then go for Lead. If I screw up the shot and they break formation, I'll make a call, until then keep my six clear."

"Will do," responded Robertson.

"Sir," radioed Stone, "I have them on the scope fifty miles out. There are two targets and they are a few thousand feet below us. Suggest a heading of one-five-zero to one-six-zero degrees to start our intercept angle attack."

"Turning to one-five-zero," responded Kilmer, "I have the switches ready for either a Sidewinder or Sparrow shot. Do you have a radar lock on the bastards?"

"No Sir," answered Stone, "I'm not getting a damn lock-on. Working on it. Turn left one-four-zero-degrees to continue intercept."

"Roger. How many miles out?"

"Targets, forty miles, I have a lock-on Lead," responded Stone, "just a little closer and they will be ours. Thirty-five miles."

"Ben, I have the switches set-up for a Sparrow shot. Are we good?"

"No, hell no," answered Stone. "We've broken lock on our target."

"Stone, can you get another lock! What are they doing?"

"Negative," answered Stone, "they seem to be diving toward the ground. I can't pick them up in the radar ground clutter."

The AWACS broadcast again on Guard. "Bandits have reversed their course and are returning to Bull's-eye. They are down on the deck and speeding like a bat out of hell. Airspace currently clear of threat."

"Cobra 2, safety your switches," radioed Kilmer, "let's get back to the Buffs."

"Roger, switches safe," radioed Robertson, "I'm coming back on your wing."

The two F-4s reversed their flight path and flew out of North Vietnam and rendezvoused again with the B-52s.

"They chickened out, did they?" radioed Arc Light 1.

"Yeah, I guess so," responded Kilmer, "if they had pressed the attack another minute or two, all hell would have broken loose. We would have nailed them."

"Well, it's good to have you back with us. Thanks for the help. Bombs away in about three minutes," cautioned Arc Light 1.

The three minutes went quickly and the call came over the radio from Arc Light 1, "Bombs away."

Cobra Flight watched as hundreds of bombs departed the Buffs and descended toward the jungle floor. Then explosions below burst forth everywhere! It was like the whole jungle erupted into fire and flames. The exploding bombs moved north rapidly as they impacted the ground and established their destructive pathway. Bright flashes of light and billowing clouds of smoke revealed the bombs striking the ground. Within less than a minute a section of jungle two miles long was in flames from the impacting bombs and multiple secondary explosions from stockpiled weapons.

"Wow," remarked Kilmer, "I think the Buffs hit a home run on this one."

"Yeah," answered Stone, "a lot of people down there just had their day ruined. It's good to be up here and not down there."

Cobra Flight stayed with the Buffs until they had cleared Laotian and Vietnamese airspace and were safely on their way back to their off shore base.

"Arc Light 1," called Kilmer, "good job today. Have a safe flight home. If it's okay with you we will be heading back to the barn."

"Roger," responded Arc Light 1. "Thanks for your help today. We make a damn good team. You have a safe flight home as well."

The two F-4s left the B-52s and both flights turned to go back to their respective bases. All crewmembers were happy to return to base alive and well and with each of their different missions completed as advertised. However, that night, each of the F-4 and B-52 crewmembers discussed and reflected on what happened and what could have happened this day.

7

Loss of a Friend

The day was hot and humid in the Republic of Vietnam. It had been raining on and off for days. This was not rain that was normal in the States, but rain that came down in sheets, like pouring water out of a large bucket or tub. However, for now the rain had stopped and the sun was pouring through the scattered clouds to heat up the earth, and the effect was staggering. The heat was so intense and the humidity so high that it made it difficult for one to breathe. The water vapor in the air was so thick that it seemed like it could be cut with a knife. Just trying to get enough oxygen was an effort and bringing air into the body was like breathing through a straw.

Captain James Lawson was enjoying a day of crew rest and relaxing out of the heat and humidity in his air-conditioned BOQ. He had flown several missions in the last few days and the pilot scheduler had decided that Jim had earned a day of rest. Actually Jim had another nickname crewmembers used when talking to him. That name was Captain America, after the popular comic book hero of the time. Jim loved to be called Captain America and he played the part very well. He had a tough appearance, was outgoing, loud, and opinionated. He was also friendly, funny and usually had a drink in his hand.

He could be found at the Officers Club every evening and during days when he wasn't flying. He'd be playing cards and telling exciting stories of his combat flying experiences. He would also be entertaining with his favorite jokes at the Club, all while in the company of his flying and drinking buddies. He was on his second voluntary tour in Vietnam. He had well over 300 combat missions and he was always ready to tell the stories about each and every one of them. Captain America was good at story telling. He captured the attention of anyone within earshot. One got the feeling that Jim had done all the things that he said he had done. His stories were not only exciting, but believable.

All who knew him liked Captain America. He was considered a friend by most and even loved by those who had the chance to spend a little time with him. Everyone was his friend and he would buy drinks for all who would stay and listen to his tales of the day. Equally important was the fact that people also respected Jim. He did his job very well and was always ready to help new guys coming in country. He was an excellent pilot and he had lived through so many dangerous missions that he'd earned the respect of all within the squadron and the wing.

Jim had a lot of friends but some of his friends were special. He had a strange, very strong bond with four or five men who had been through some of the same combat flight experiences. Whenever possible, considering the flying schedule, they were together at the Officers Club, drinking and playing cards or at the BOQ drinking and just hanging out together and laughing at all the oddities of the war. It seemed as though all the laughing and drinking was an attempt to hide something that none of them wanted to talk about. You could catch a glimpse of it every now and again in either their comments or in things that were not said. It was hard to put a finger on it, but it was equally hard to miss. Whatever it was it had a power and a sense of cold darkness about it, but then it would be gone in a laugh or another shot of alcohol.

One of Captain America's special friends was Captain Larry Cline. Larry was always in the inner circle with Jim, laughing, drinking and enjoying the true life of a fighter pilot. Larry was an F-4D aircraft commander and was also on his second voluntary tour in Vietnam. He had 262 combat missions and a goal of completing over 300 missions before he went back to the world, as the States were called in Vietnam. Today, Larry and his flight had been assigned a mission that involved attacking a suspected truck park and ammunition storage area in central Laos. These were always dangerous missions.

The bad guys owned most of Laos. If an aircraft got in trouble and the pilots had to eject over Laos they knew that there would be little or no help on the ground. The response time for rescue operations in Laos was always very long. A crewmember knew he could have several hours to wait on the ground for rescue, and depending on the weather and time of day, it could even be days. If a crewmember was injured during ejection he knew that he would have to supply all of his medical needs until help arrived. It was very common for an aircrew member to experience a broken arm or a broken leg or another major injury during the ejection itself. If the F-4 was badly damaged from ground fire and became uncontrollable before ejection was initiated, then the high airspeed and high G loads could cause even more serious injuries. Ejection airspeeds over 500 knots created a violent and disorientating wind blast that could injure the crewmember severely. The ejection seat with the pilot attached could tumble uncontrollably until a small stabilizing chute was eventually deployed from the seat. All of these violent events increased the possibility of injury upon ejection. All injuries had to be taken care of by the crewmember himself until help could arrive. Many times pilots suffered shock during ejection and became unable to care for their medical needs.

This was where the survival training of crewmembers took over, allowing them to try and think clearly enough to call for help on the emergency radio. They may also have to splint a broken limb, put a tourniquet on to stop a bleeding artery, or take care of some other life-threatening situation. All of these threats, including the risk of increased enemy ground fire, made missions into Laos very dangerous.

Captain Cline had been assigned this Laotian mission and he accepted it, as always, without any discussion or comment. This wasn't strange or an exception. All assigned combat missions were handled the same. Pilots never complained or challenged any assigned mission. Aircrew members accepted each mission as their duty to complete. Each was considered a part of a larger war effort that one-day would bring victory in Southeast Asia.

Captain Cline's other flight members included Cline's GIB, Lieutenant Sam Williamson. Williamson was a young navigator who had been in country only a couple of months. He had sat through the regular target planning, intelligence and weather briefings earlier in the day. All the conditions seemed to be normal for the mission. The weather was forecast to be fair in the target area. No ground fire had been reported over the last couple of days. Intelligence reports indicated enemy truck parks and possibly a weapons storage area as the primary targets.

The flight's engine start, taxi and takeoff all went without problems. The flight to the target area was also normal. There were no indications that trouble was ahead for the flight.

Captain Cline's flight reached the target area. Cline contacted the FAC and requested information on the target's exact location and its threat level. This information was radioed to the flight. Captain Cline, as Lead aircraft, made the first run on the target. It was at this point that things began to go terribly wrong.

Back at the base information started to come in that there had been trouble during the mission. At first, very few facts filtered back to the base, and the entire wing became concerned about what may have happened.

Captain American received word that something had happened during the mission with his very good friend Captain Cline. He immediately climbed into his flight suit, slipped on his flying boots and pulled up the zippers that held them on. He ran out of the BOQ building and jumped in a crew van that he had driven home from the squadron the night before. As he started the van several pilots and navigators from the squadron also ran from their rooms and jumped into the van. They quickly drove the one-half mile from the living area to the squadron building and ran into the main large squadron assembly room.

Limited reports were beginning to trickle in about what had happened on the mission. The wing headquarters communication unit was talking to 7th Air Force about the current status of the rescue operation. These reports were relayed in real time to the squadron assembly room on the public speaker system. It was then that the report came into the squadron from 7th Air Force, "Jolly Green Rescue 1 has picked up two crewmembers."

"Yea!" A roar of cheer came up from all the pilots and navigators in the room. Captain America was ecstatic. He decided that he would get to the Club as fast as he could and purchase a fifth of champagne to take to his friend. He would present it to Captain Cline as soon as he landed in the rescue helicopter. Off he went to the Club to purchase the champagne. Within eight to nine minutes he made it to the Club, purchased the bottle, and drove to the flight line to meet the arriving rescue helicopter. He could hardly wait to see his friend again and celebrate his safe rescue from being shot down.

Within minutes, Captain America heard the approach of the huge Jolly Green Rescue helicopter. It soon reached the base and made a half circle around the field to line up for a landing on the base taxiway. The Jolly Greens were Sikorsky HH-3E helicopters. They were widely used in Vietnam for Combat Search and Rescue missions and at times used the radio call sign "Pedro." They were loud and really ugly to look at, but their work and the dedication of their crews were well respected. The rescue chopper soon touched down and reduced the RPM of its engines. The crew chief stepped out of the chopper immediately followed by the rescued GIB, Lieutenant Sam Williamson. Lieutenant Williamson was a weapons officer who had originally trained as a navigator. Williamson quickly walked over to Captain America to tell him not to go to the chopper. However, the noise from the jet engines was still too great for any conversation to take place even though the pilot was in the process of shutting down both engines.

Williamson was unable to stop a rejoicing and ecstatic Captain America from running to the open door of the Jolly Green. As he reached the door and looked inside Captain America could not believe his eyes. Both crewmembers had been picked up, but what the report from the rescue helicopter had not detailed, was that Captain Cline's parachute had not opened after ejection from the aircraft and that his friend was dead.

It was determined later that Captain Cline had ejected from the aircraft successfully, but did so out of the success envelope of the ejection seat. He ejected at an airspeed of between 500 and 600 knots with the F-4 very near the ground in an out of control condition, only 100 to 150 feet elevation above the trees. Under these conditions Captain Cline never had a chance to escape from his crippled F-4. Captain Cline's body had hit the trees at such a speed that he suffered multiple fatal injuries. He had been killed almost instantly after ejection.

Captain America looked at the broken, lifeless body of his lost friend lying on the floor of the helicopter. His body was half covered in a blood soaked parachute. He dropped the bottle of champagne to the ground where it broke. He then turned around and fell to his knees, placed his head in his hands and began to weep uncontrollably for his lost friend.

The shock and the realization of the death of his friend, and the way in which he had died, was almost too much to deal with for Captain America. He had seen death close at hand as he had lost friends in combat, but this was different. Maybe it was the suddenness of it. Maybe it was the change from an expectation of joy and deliverance to a reality of death and brokenness. It was an unbelievably hard blow for him. It also had a huge impact on all of the squadron members who knew and respected Captain Cline. It took them months to begin to recover from Cline's loss and the manner in which it was reported. For some, they would never be the same.

Captain America changed that day. It was difficult to really know how much he had changed, and to what depth, but he had changed. He never took life or friendship as candidly, flippantly or perhaps even as thoughtlessly as before the accident. He never laughed as loud or as long. Captain America had seen a vivid reality of war with the death of a warrior friend. This experience rotated his kaleidoscopic view of life forever and he would never be the same again.

Concrete Revetments: Workers of the 820th Civil Engineering Squadron completing aircraft shelters at Da Nang AB, South Vietnam, 1969. (Photo Courtesy of National Museum of U.S. Air Force)

F-4 Wild Weasel on Tarmac. (Photo Courtesy of National Museum of U.S. Air Force)

F-4 Phantom flying over North Vietnam. (Photo Courtesy of National Museum of U.S. Air Force)

Side view of McDonnell Douglas F-4 Phantom II. (Photo Courtesy of National Museum of U.S. Air Force)

2 F-4s on KC-135 Tanker taking fuel. (Photo Courtesy of National Museum of U.S. Air Force)

Forward Air Controller (FAC) flying O-1. (Photo Courtesy of National Museum of U.S. Air Force)

Forward Air Controller (FAC) in 0-2 aircraft. (Photo Courtesy of National Museum of U.S. Air Force)

Forward Air Controller (FAC) in OV-10 aircraft. (Photo Courtesy of National Museum of U.S. Air Force)

HH-3 Jolly Green Rescue Helicopter (Photo Courtesy of National Museum of U.S. Air Force)

B-52 Bomber: type used in "Sky Spot" bombing operations, South Vietnam, North Vietnam and Laos. (Photo Courtesy of National Museum of U.S. Air Force)

McDonnell Douglas RF-4C cockpit. (Photo Courtesy of National Museum of U.S. Air Force)

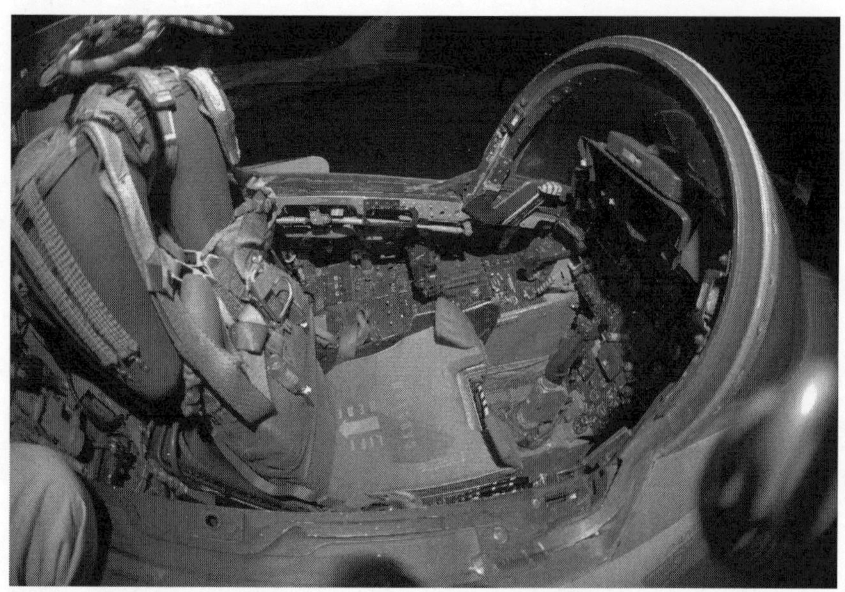

Front seat cockpit of F-4 and Martin-Baker Ejection Seat. (Photo Courtesy of National Museum of U.S. Air Force)

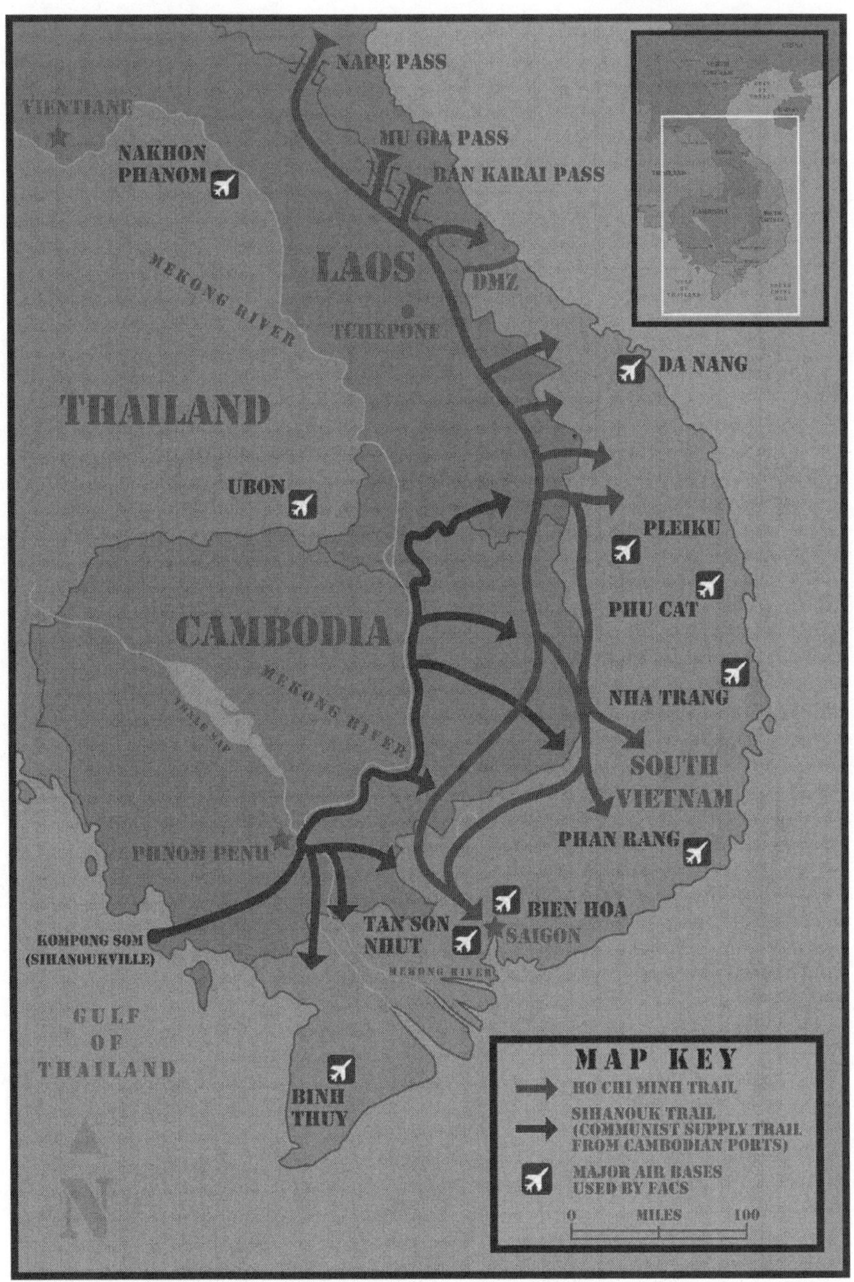

Map of South Vietnam, Laos with the Ho Chi Minh Trail. Note location of U.S. Air Bases. (Photo Courtesy of National Museum of U.S. Air Force)

Mark-82 500 lb. "Slick" bomb. (Photo Courtesy of National Museum of U.S. Air Force)

MLU 750lb. Land Mine Bomb. (Photo Courtesy of National Museum of U.S. Air Force)

8

Deadly Mission

The warm, humid day was typical at the Phu Cat Air Base, Republic of Vietnam. In 1969 Phu Cat was a relatively new base, it was built to support the American and South Vietnamese war effort. It was completed in 1967 and began as a primary staging base for F-100 fighter-bombers. However, the F-100s were not destined to stay long at Phu Cat. They were replaced in less than two years with F-4C and F-4D Phantom II fighter-bombers that were transferred down from Da Nang Air Base, the northern most air base in South Vietnam. The pilots at Phu Cat, who flew the F-100s and F-4s had very good housing quarters by wartime standards. They lived in Bachelor's Officers Quarters with each aircrew member assigned a separate room of a two room suite. Each pair of rooms had a short hallway in between the rooms to provide some privacy. Each room had a refrigerator and all the rooms were air-conditioned. Aircrew members were required by regulation to have air-conditioned housing at Phu Cat. Each BOQ building had several sets of these paired rooms, thus housing a number of aircrews per building. The rooms were not large, but made a great gathering place in the evenings for the pilots and navigators of the F-4s. Between 1900 and 2000 most of the flights of the day had been completed. There were some night missions taking place, but there were usually fewer of them scheduled than day missions. Six to eight crewmembers would get together in a BOQ room, select their favorite beverage and discuss all that had happened on their missions that day. Stories were told about enemy fire, targets attacked, helping troops in contact, and various other issues or problems of military life. These discussions would very often continue until the early morning hours of the next day. Even though to a casual observer it might appear that these were no more than B.S. sessions, these meetings were of vital importance. They gave the crewmembers a chance to let off steam and to give those in authority hell for all of the political mistakes, military blunders and just plain stupid mistakes that seemed too often to be part of the war effort. It also gave the crewmembers a chance to learn from the mistakes of others. Mistakes and errors are made in war with disaster always near. By listening to others talk about their errors and what they would do differently to correct them, crewmembers could learn and live to be smarter and safer warriors.

Today, despite a beautiful start to the morning, for those who would be flying there would be many challenges and dangers.

Captain Kilmer and Lieutenant Stone were scheduled to fly as Lead. Flying with them in the number two aircraft were Captain James Williams, the front seat pilot, and Lieutenant Jerry Thomas, a navigator in the backseat. The takeoff time for the mission was scheduled for 1000. Both of the crews met at the briefing shack at 0800 hours for the pre-flight briefing. They met in the planning room to get the day's target information and plan the navigation route to the target and the return route to the base. The mission was to be an in country mission to destroy a suspected arms cache and truck staging area in the western part of Vietnam.

After the target photos were examined and planning was completed, the crews went into the Intel briefing room. The Intel officer gave a very thorough target briefing. He particularly stressed that recently there had been intense hostile small arms and automatic weapons fire in the target area. Two days before this mission, two F-100s had attack missions in the area and received hostile fire with one of the F-100s being hit and having to make an emergency landing at Da Nang. The crewmembers looked at each other and showed respectful concern over the Intel officer's information. After the Intel briefing, the two crews were given the weather briefing in and around the target area. The weather in the area was forecast to be good to excellent. There was no ceiling and the prognosis for visibility was to be greater than ten miles.

After target planning and the briefings, the two crews went to the equipment room to put on their flight gear. There were several items that the flight crewmembers had to wear. All crewmembers had to put on their G-suit, survival vest, parachute harness and helmet. The survival vest contained various items including the extremely important emergency radio. The crewmembers always carried a Smith & Wesson 38 caliber revolver and extra batteries for the emergency radio. Many pilots included other items such as a pen flare gun with extra flares, extra cartridges for the 38 revolvers, one or two knives, and an extra emergency radio beacon transmitter.

As soon as the crews had their equipment on, they proceeded out of the squadron building and climbed into the crew van for transportation to their planes. The squadron scheduling officer, who had the responsibility to take crews to their planes, drove the crews to their concrete revetments. Kilmer and Stone jumped out of the van and began the preflight procedures for their aircraft and its weapons. Williams and Thomas proceeded to their F-4 to start their preflight. Today both F-4s were carrying eighteen, 500-pound high drag bombs. Stone began the check of the bombs while Kilmer started the preflight on the aircraft.

As soon the crews checked both the aircraft and the bombs, they climbed into their cockpits to get the aircraft systems up and running and the engines started. The Lead F-4 was quickly ready and Kilmer gave the signal for the external air cart to send high-pressure air to the J-79 engines to begin the starting procedure. Both engines were started and Kilmer pushed the throttles up to pull out of the revetment. As Kilmer and Stone taxied by Williams and Thomas, Williams gave a thumbs up signal indicating that he and Thomas were ready to pull in behind Kilmer and Stone to taxi out to the runway.

"Phu Cat Tower, Cobra 1 and 2 taxi, two F-4s," called Kilmer over the radio.

"Cobra 1 and Cobra 2, taxi runway three-three," responded the tower.

"Cobra 1 and 2, Roger, runway three-three."

Both F-4s taxied to runway three-three and turned into the arming area. The arming crews began pulling the pins from the Mark-82 high drag bombs. Within minutes the arming of the bombs was complete and the weapons chief held up the safety pins with their red streamers for the aircraft commanders to see, indicating that the weapons were armed. Both crews completed their aircraft checklists readying their aircraft for takeoff.

"Phu Cat Tower, Cobra 1 and 2 ready for takeoff runway three-three," radioed Kilmer.

"Cobra 1 and 2 cleared for immediate takeoff runway three-three," responded the tower.

When the tower cleared an aircraft for immediate takeoff, the aircraft was to depart without delay. Usually in-bound aircraft were only minutes away from landing and the departing aircraft needed to get onto the runway and depart as soon as possible.

The two F-4s taxied onto the runway and began their pre-takeoff checks. Kilmer brought up the left engine throttle to Mil power and checked for normal instrument indications. With the instruments indicating normal, he rapidly brought the left engine to idle and the right engine to Mil power, checked for normal instrument readings and then retarded the throttle. Kilmer positioned the flaps to takeoff position and then gave Ben a call.

"Ben, are you ready for takeoff?"

"Yes Sir, let's get this show on the road," responded Stone.

Kilmer looked over at Cobra 2 who gave him the thumbs up again, indicating they had completed their pre-takeoff checklist and were ready for departure. Cobra 1 advanced his throttles and began his takeoff roll.

The heavy machine began to roll, slowly at first, then quickly began to pick up speed as the afterburners ignited. When the afterburners ignited on the F-4 there was a noticeable push against the pilot's seat, indicating that maximum power was coming from the J-79 engines. It was always a good feeling to experience the maximum power coming from the engines. Faster and faster Lead accelerated down the runway. Kilmer had the control stick pulled back against his stomach. This was the normal takeoff procedure for the F-4 and would allow the nose of the aircraft to come off the ground as soon as the plane was ready to fly regardless of what load it was carrying. The nose wheel came off the runway and the nose of the plane began to pitch up. Kilmer released back-pressure on the stick to establish a 10 to 12 degree nose high attitude for takeoff. The heavy F-4 came off the ground reluctantly, but soon established a positive climb and headed for the en route altitude.

After 30 seconds, Cobra 2 began the takeoff roll, and within minutes had joined onto Cobra 1's right wing. With the rejoin completed, the flight navigated toward the target area. The assigned target was less than 20 minutes away, and the flight was soon close enough to call the forward air controller to receive instructions for attacking the target.

Kilmer called the FAC, "Covey 1, Cobra 1 and 2, twenty miles out with Mark-82 high drag bombs. I hope you have something good for us today."

"Roger Cobra Flight, Covey 1 with you, I have a hot one for you. Give me a call when you're overhead. Then I'll mark the target for you with smoke. We are experiencing ground fire in the area, so be careful on your approach to and departure from the target. The bad guys are trying to defend something down there that must be important to them. They're shooting like hell at anything that moves."

"Wilco," responded Kilmer.

It seemed that the distance to the target area was covered in seconds. The F-4s were overhead and gave the required call to the FAC.

"Covey 1, Cobra 1 and 2 overhead," called Kilmer.

"Roger," responded back Covey 1. "I am rolling in now to mark the target. Let me know when you spot my smoke."

"Damn," yelled Covey 1, "they are hosing me big time. My aircraft has been hit. Standby one!"

There was a pause that seemed to last a very long time. Then Covey 1 came back on the air.

"Cobra 1 and 2, I'm still flying but they shot the hell out of my bird. Be careful on your final approach. Make your run from north to south. Do you see my smoke? What is left of me is well out of your way."

"Got your smoke," responded Kilmer.

"Put your bombs one hundred meters to the south of my smoke. Cleared onto the target," commanded Covey 1.

Cobra 1 rolled onto the target. Down, down they went to 100 feet above the ground. The ground and the trees were streaking by the cockpit as the F-4 accelerated to a groundspeed of over 500 knots. At that speed it was possible to see forward clearly, but it was very difficult to focus on objects on the ground to the side of the aircraft. Objects on the left and right of the aircraft were very blurry.

"Captain, we are taking fire from our 2 o'clock position. I can see the tracers coming by us. Let's get onto the target quickly and get the hell out," Stone called over the intercom.

"We'll be off in a second," responded Kilmer.

With a thump sound, two 500-pound high-drag, Snake Eye bombs came off the aircraft. The Snake Eye high drag bombs had fins that were closed while on the aircraft, but on release, opened up and retarded the bomb's flight to earth. This gave the F-4 time to fly away from the bomb release point and be out of the bomb's fragmentation pattern when it exploded.

Kilmer pulled off the target with a five G load on the aircraft and in a 60-degree bank angle. With the pull off escape maneuver Kilmer ignited the afterburners to get additional speed for altitude and lateral separation from the target. The powerful F-4 climbed and accelerated with an awful, deafening noise.

Covey 1 called, "Cobra 1, your bombs were on target. Good job. Cobra 2 you are cleared in on the target. Hit the fire started from Lead's bombs."

"Roger," responded Williams. "I'm turning final onto the target."

Cobra 2 approached the target that was responding with a hail of automatic weapons fire.

"Damn Sir, are you watching 2 on final? They're shooting the hell out of him," called Stone over the intercom.

"Yeah, they're really hosing him, but he's off the target now and looks okay. Here we go again. Hang on to your ass."

Kilmer and Stone were back on final for another pass on the target.

"Cobra 1, Covey 1, keep dropping your ordnance on the same location. Ammo keeps cooking off down there. They must have a lot of crap stored and you guys are blowing the hell out of it. Keep it coming."

"Roger," answered Kilmer, "we're on final and in hot."

Cobra 1 was on final, accelerating quickly to achieve the maximum speed possible. The afterburners were ignited and the bird, in a shallow dive, was screaming toward the target. To confuse the enemy gunners, Kilmer made an early turn on the final approach to the target. This resulted in a shorter final and a different run-in heading. Kilmer's attack angle was 30 degrees off the original heading and the final was a half-mile shorter. This may have helped, however, they were still receiving fire from enemy positions.

"Fantastic Sir," remarked Stone, " good job getting us onto the target."

Kilmer was on the target, dropped two more Snake Eyes and pulled on the control stick with every bit of strength he had. The F-4 pitched up as it reached for altitude and safety. The FAC came back with a report.

"Good strike Lead! Things on the ground are burning and exploding like hell. Man, we sure caught them cold today. Cobra 2 you're cleared in on the target. Concentrate your bombs a little south of the fires, about one hundred fifty meters."

"Roger, we're onto the target," responded Cobra 2.

Williams and Thomas turned final and proceeded in on the target. The powerful F-4 descended until it was only 75 feet above the ground. Cobra 2 continued to accelerate to a groundspeed of 550 knots. They approached the target and Williams punched off two 500-pound high drag bombs. He then started to pull off the target.

Suddenly something very strange happened. The F-4 stopped climbing and started to settle into a shallow descent. Thomas couldn't understand what was happening.

"Captain, what's going on?"

There was no reply. The F-4 continued to settle toward the trees.

"Captain, Captain," called Thomas. "What the hell is going on?"

Thomas grabbed for the control stick to pull the aircraft up away from the trees. However, events happened so quickly that Thomas wasn't in time to stop the F-4's descent. In just seconds the F-4 began to make contact with the treetops. The aircraft began to impact tree limbs and ingest leaves and branches into the engines. The F-4 shook and shuddered as it impacted and ingested the foreign matter.

"Williams, Williams, can you hear me?" called out Thomas as he pulled on the control stick.

The F-4 was in trouble. Smoke began to fill the cockpit and short flames began jumping through the floorboards. Thomas continued to grab onto the controls and tried pulling the F-4 up and out of the trees. It was too late. The controls didn't respond.

Covey 1 called out from his position, "Cobra 2, you are on fire and are breaking up. You need to eject. I repeat! You need to eject and eject now!"

Thomas called one more time to Williams, but with no response. He knew instinctively that he had seconds to live if he did not get out of the aircraft. With rapid and deliberate effort he reached down to the lower ejection handle and pulled it with all his strength.

Thomas didn't remember what happened after that. His ejection seat fired as advertised and Williams was exited out of the disintegrating F-4. His chute fully opened but because of the speed of the F-4, it began to come apart and shred. However, it stayed together long enough to allow Thomas' unconscious body to descend through the trees and to the ground. The F-4 continued to break apart as it moved through the trees and then suddenly disintegrated with a bright flash of light and a huge series of violent explosions.

The radio came alive from Cobra 1, "Covey 1, what happened to Cobra 2? Did you see anything? What was that explosion? Was it Cobra 2?"

Covey 1 replied, "It was Cobra 2. It appears they either hit the ground or were hit and destroyed by enemy fire."

Cobra 1 responded, "Did you see them go in or did you see any chutes?"

Covey 1 came back, "I did see the aircraft descending into the trees and I did observe one chute. I think at least one of the crewmembers made it out. I'm calling in air rescue now."

"Thanks, Covey 1. I'll stay overhead as long as possible to provide assistance, until I am emergency fuel," responded Kilmer.

Cobra 1 stayed overhead and made repeated attacks on the target to suppress enemy fire and assist the Jolly Greens as they came in and looked for survivors. The crash site was about one mile south of the target location. When Cobra 1 reached emergency fuel they had to depart the crash site and head for home plate.

The Jolly Greens worked their way south of the target area and after some time found Thomas still in his parachute harness and attached to his parachute. The chute had done its job. Thomas was alive. He was badly injured with a broken leg, a broken arm and multiple internal injuries, but even with his injuries he did live to fly and fight another day.

The next day a rescue team went to the site of the downed F-4 and began looking for Williams and for an explanation of what had gone wrong. It wasn't long before they discovered William's body and the explanation for the crash. The small arms fire had found its mark. Captain Williams sustained two hits from enemy ground fire. One bullet hit him in the neck and another had hit him in the heart. Either of the wounds would have been instantly fatal. It was surmised that as soon as Williams had released the two bombs he had been hit by the ground fire and was killed. This explained the release of pressure on the aircraft's controls and the decent into the trees of the F-4.

For several days and nights after this mission, stories were told and retold in the BOQ rooms of Phu Cat. Questions were asked and discussions held on what could have been done differently and why the mission turned out the way it did.

Captain Kilmer and Lieutenants Stone and Thomas had different memories of that beautiful but deadly day in the Republic of Vietnam. They all had similar memories and respect for a fallen warrior. This fallen warrior would one day, in the not too distant future, have his name engraved forever on a long black wall in Washington D.C.

9

Hell at 500 Knots

It was a typical day at Da Nang Air Base in the Republic of Vietnam. Busy! It was always busy. Trucks and people were constantly moving war supplies all over the base. Da Nang was home to the Army, Navy and Marines who operated on the west side of the base and the Air Force who operated on the east side. Two parallel runways running North and South divided the base.

Powerful diesel generators were always running providing needed electrical power to all sections of the base. Those generators were noisy and dirty and filled the air with exhaust from the burning diesel fuel. The smell from these generators gave Da Nang a very characteristic odor along with tiresome sounds. It was the smell and sound of war at a very busy level.

The two parallel runways were active 24 hours a day. If Navy, Marine and Air Force fighter-bombers weren't taking off for strike missions, then numerous other aircraft: C-130s, C-141s, O-1s, O-2s and Air America planes were taking off or landing. It was one of the busiest airports in the world. At times during the war, a single day would involve over 2,500 takeoffs and landings at Da Nang. However, it wasn't one of the safest airports. Many times Viet Cong would fire on aircraft as they were taking off or landing. Aircraft on approach for landing would make steep approaches on final to help avoid ground fire. On takeoff, F-4s and other fighters would make maximum power takeoffs and stay in afterburner to climb quickly to altitude, thereby avoiding possible ground fire.

In the late '60s, on the Air Force side of the base, aircrew members lived in two story modular buildings. They were like mobile home trailers stacked on top of each other. They were very plain in design and construction. They were gray in color and seemed out of place at Da Nang. The aircrew members lived four to a room and slept in steel bunk style beds. The rooms weren't large, and with four men in them, it left very little room to move around. Just about all they were used for was sleeping. However, even sleeping in these rooms was difficult because these crew quarters were very close to the flight line, and the construction of the buildings was so flimsy, that every time a jet would take off they would shake and rattle. If crewmembers were asleep the noise from the jet, along with the shake and rattle of the building, would wake them up. There was only one advantage of these buildings and that was that they were air-conditioned. At Da Nang in 1969, this was a requirement for Air Force officer aircrew members. When the humidity and temperature were very high, it was a welcome relief for aircrew members to climb into their bunks and rest in a cool setting, even if the room was vibrating from the noise of each takeoff from departing jets.

However, crew quarters were far from the minds of Captain Ron Kilmer, an F-4D aircraft commander, and his pilot backseater Lieutenant Ben Stone, as they were eating breakfast in the chow hall and talking about their mission for this day. Both Kilmer and Stone were experienced war veterans. Both had been in Vietnam for over six months and had over 200 combat missions between them.

"Do you know what our mission is today Ron?" asked Stone.

"No Ben, I don't," replied Kilmer. "I haven't been down to the squadron today. I got kind of a late start. I was going to get up at 0500 to get a good run in, but just couldn't get away from the rack monster until 0530. Since I was so late, I could only get in a three-mile run and then get to chow. We'll know soon enough where we're going."

"I heard a rumor that we may be going up North," continued Stone. "I really don't like going up there, so much damn anti-aircraft stuff. The radar controlled guns and the SAMS give us a run for our money. But what the hell."

"Yeah, not a fun delivery, but we'll see. I have to survive these powered eggs and all this grease on my hash browns before I can worry about the flight," remarked Kilmer.

Both men laughed. It was common for the men to joke about the food. The chow was usually not all that good, but given the restraints of the war, it was much better than it could have been.

Kilmer and Stone finished breakfast and left the chow hall. They both jumped into a crew van and headed down to the squadron building. Kilmer drove the van and they both continued to talk about what the possible mission would be for the day. They soon arrived at the squadron building. They parked and went inside to start the mission briefings and to check the weather in the target area.

Once inside the squadron building they went to the target planning room. The other crewmembers were already there, studying the target and its location. The two crewmembers in the number two F-4, were Captain Joe Thomas, the aircraft commander, and Captain Bill Johnson, his GIB. Captain Thomas was an experienced aircraft commander. He had been in country for seven months and had flown 125 combat missions. He was a good pilot and had a good handle on the big picture of the war. He knew that whatever the politics or strategies of the war, it all boiled down to "do I go home at the end of this deal or do I die over here?" He was determined to do his duty, get the job done right, and go home to his wife and children when his year was up.

Captain Johnson was much like Thomas but had even more flying experience. His early training in the Air Force was that of a navigator. After serving a short time as a navigator, he received advanced training to become a weapons officer flying in the F-101 Voodoo. He had 20 years of weapons officer duty and several thousand hours of flying time in the F-101. Bill was always calm, relaxed and never seemed to worry about a mission. He was trustful of the aircraft and his aircraft commander's abilities. He was a grandfather figure to the younger pilots and navigators who were mostly in their mid-twenties, as Bill was an aged 48 years old. His advanced age, for the younger aircrew members, along with the fact that Bill was always smoking a pipe, gave him his distinct grandfather persona.

"Hi Bill, Joe," said Kilmer as he and Stone entered the room. "Where are we going today?"

"I hope you guys have paid up your life insurance. We are going to Laos and Ban Phanhop to deliver 500-pound magnetic bombs," replied Johnson.

"Oh! That's just wonderful news," remarked Stone sarcastically. "That just makes my friggin' week."

The Ban Phanhop Valley was an important section of the major roadways coming out of North Vietnam. These roads ran through Laos and then down into South Vietnam. This highway system became known as the Ho Chi Minh Trail. It was the main transportation route to move men, equipment and supplies from the North down South to sustain the war effort. Mountainous terrain limited how supply traffic could leave North Vietnam and move through a few natural passes toward the South. Ban Phanhop Valley was an important section of the Ho Chi Minh Trail as few roads came out of the karst mountains and proceeded South. There was probably no one single area of either North or South Vietnam that had been bombed as much as these highways and roads, particularly those in the Ban Phanhop area. There was bomb crater on top of bomb crater on the valley floor, and all of the trees had been blown apart and looked like large chewed up toothpicks coming out of the ground. There were always small fires in the area with smoke rising and forming several layers of haze above the ground.

There were steep limestone karst cliffs, partially covered by trees, on either side of the valley. Water had dissolved the limestone that made up the mountains and ridges and formed natural holes and caves in the rocks. Within this natural cover the North Vietnamese would set up anti-aircraft installations to protect their road system. Rumor had it that within the caves the NVA had guns on tracks and rollers that could move out of the protection of the cave into firing positions to shoot at allied planes that came to this location. The area looked like Dante's Hell. Pilots who flew missions in this area were always shaken by its eerie appearance and the frightful firepower coming from the enemy weapons along the ridges. No place in Laos was better defended than this location. Once this hell on earth was experienced, it would never be forgotten. Pilots didn't like to fly into the area because they knew, that on that day, their lives would certainly be on the line.

With the addition of the 500-pound magnetic bombs the pilots knew that their mission was going to be a difficult one. With regular slick

500-pound hard bombs the pilots could deliver them in a high altitude, high angle delivery method. This allowed the pilots to begin their attack at high altitude, well above most enemy guns, and drop the bombs 3,000 to 4,000 feet above the target and then escape the maximum kill zone of enemy fire. With the magnetic bombs this advantage had to be given away. The magnetic bombs had to be delivered in a very special envelope for them to work effectively. They had to be dropped at an airspeed of 500 knots and exactly 500 feet above the ground. The 500 knots airspeed was good for escape but not the 500 feet elevation. This placed the fighter-bombers and their crews right in the kill zone of enemy fire. If the fighter was hit at such a low altitude and in such a highly defended enemy area, the chance of flying to safety or surviving an ejection was highly doubtful.

The theory behind the use of these 500-pound magnetic bombs was that they would be dropped along important roadways and road intersections. They would be dropped from the fighter and hit the ground, penetrate the earth without exploding, and be hidden from sight. Whenever enemy trucks would try to drive through the area the metal construction of the trucks would disturb the magnetic field within the bomb. When the truck got close enough the bomb would explode destroying it. This sounded like a great plan and in theory it was, but to the aircrew members who were called on to deliver these weapons it raised great concern about surviving the experience.

The four crewmembers looked at the target information together. This included Intel reports about truck traffic on the roads and enemy fire in the area. There were recent reconnaissance photos of the target area from the North Vietnam border area southwest through the passes for several miles.

"Damn," Thomas remarked, "have you ever seen anything like this in your whole life?"

"I don't believe I ever have," responded Kilmer. "It looks like you would be hard pressed to find a spot that has not had a ton of bombs dropped on it. We want to be real careful today guys. This is a bad place and we have our work cut out for us. Remember, we'll be shot at today more than anyone else in the war. It would make a North Vietnamese soldier's career to bring one of us down. Stay sharp!"

The four crewmembers took more than the usual time studying the target information. They made special plans for the attack because of their unusual bomb load, reviewed emergency procedures, and discussed escape plans should one of the F-4s get hit. That plan was for the wounded bird to turn immediately toward Thailand and head for one of the Air Force bases there. The other F-4 would try and join them and escort them safely there. The two crews discussed what the plan would be if one set of crews had to eject. The major point that was made was – don't eject in the area. All agreed there would be little or no chance for survival if ejecting in this location. The plan that was agreed upon, if the crews needed to eject and if the aircraft was controllable, was that the wounded bird would fly as far and as fast as it could from the target area, and then the crews would eject. The surviving F-4 would stay on the scene until help arrived or until it was emergency fuel. Emergency fuel was the minimum amount of fuel needed to safely get an aircraft to the nearest friendly airfield.

The plan of attack was a simple one; Lead would attack the target first and in one pass over the target drop all of his bombs at the required 500 feet AGL and at 500 knots. Number two aircraft would be seconds behind Lead and drop all of their bombs in one pass within the required elevation and airspeed restriction. Making multiple passes in a target area like Ban Phanhop, while dropping landmines made no sense. Usually in a flight of two fighters, the Lead aircraft would surprise the enemy gunners and get a free first pass without enemy fire. Once the enemy was stirred up by the first attack, the gunners knew the F-4s were in the area and opened up with all their firepower on the second aircraft. Making multiple passes in an area like Ban Phanhop was asking for real trouble.

With the target studied and the plan of attack completed the crewmembers went into the briefing room for an intelligence and weather briefing. The intelligence officer started his briefing with a comment.

"Gentlemen," he said, "I usually have some bad news and some good news about a target. But today I have only bad news and more bad news. Over the last few days we have had extreme enemy ground fire in the area with one aircraft lost and several aircraft damaged by enemy fire. Please monitor Guard carefully today for an emergency beacon from our downed crewmembers and report any contact. Also pass on its location to Air Rescue. Be careful today and come back safe. I don't want to be briefing other crews tomorrow about you." The Intel officer then left the room.

Kilmer looked at Ben and then the other crewmembers. Kilmer didn't say a word but was visibly shaken by the Intel officer's comments. No crewmembers had ever seen Kilmer shaken. He was always cool, calm and professional in his approach to his flying missions. As suddenly as it came, Kilmer's shaken look was gone. He quickly responded to the situation and regained his normal stance and reassured his men.

"All right men," Kilmer commented softly but sternly, " let's get this weather briefing done and get the hell out of here and get this mission in the books. We can get it done safely and done right. We'll all sleep in our own bunks tonight." That was all that needed to be said to settle the two crews down.

The weatherman gave the weather forecast for the target area. The forecast was for good weather with no chance of rain. The visibility would be greater than five miles. The return weather back to the base also looked good. Whatever happened this day, weather would not be part of the problem.

The four crewmembers headed for the equipment room. They started putting on their equipment needed for the flight. The standard equipment included: parachute harness, G-suit, helmet, survival vest, orange colored flip-blade parachute knife, Smith and Wesson 38 caliber revolver, emergency radio and at least one extra battery for the radio. Many crewmembers carried some extra survival gear. Extra items carried included a large K-Bar type knife, extra ammo for the 38 revolver, pencil flare gun with extra flare cartridges, sugar candy, extra radio batteries, and a second small emergency radio. This small emergency radio transmitter was the type contained in the parachute itself.

Crewmembers knew that if they went down out of country their only hope for rescue was the radio. The downed pilot or navigator would have to be able to make contact with the rescue forces and give them his location and authenticate who he was to have a chance to be picked up. It wasn't uncommon for the enemy to use emergency radios to try and bring rescue personnel into an area to trap and try to shoot them down. The enemy would turn on an emergency radio or beacon and wait for the alarm to be picked up by friendly forces. When the rescue forces arrived the enemy would then open fire and kill as many rescuers as possible. It was for this reason that for a rescue to begin, the person on the ground had to give information to authenticate his identity. The downed crewmember would have to give personal information such as his mother's maiden name, wife's first name, type of car back home, place of birth, before the rescue could begin. Without a radio to do this, it just wasn't going to happen.

"Hey Ben, do you think you have enough extra equipment today?" asked Kilmer.

"I don't know Sir," responded Stone, "I'd like to carry another radio or two but I just don't have the room for it."

Stone was known for taking extra radios and batteries with him on missions. It was not unusual for him to take as many as three radios along with as many extra batteries. He believed one couldn't have too many radios on a mission.

The four crewmembers finished getting on all their gear and headed for the crew van. They all climbed into the van along with the squadron-scheduling officer, whose job was to drive them to their aircraft locations. The F-4s were almost always parked in concrete and steel covered revetments.

As each crew arrived at their F-4, they climbed out of the van and started the preflight of their aircraft and its armament. The aircraft commander would usually preflight the aircraft while the backseater would preflight the armament. Each of these jobs was extremely important. The bombs themselves had many items to check: bomb fuse timers had to be set correctly, safety wires and pins installed properly, bombs securely fastened to aircraft and proper bomb type installed.

The preflight of the aircraft was equally important. It was the last chance before flight to find anything that was malfunctioning, installed improperly, or broken on the aircraft before flight. It would be a little late to discover something wrong after they were airborne with several tons of bombs on board.

All checks and inspections were completed and both crews climbed into their F-4s. The crews started their engines and went through their Pre-Taxi checklist. All the checks went well and no problems were found on either of the birds.

"Da Nang Ground," radioed Kilmer, "Gunfighter 1 and Gunfighter 2, a flight of two F-4s, ready to taxi."

"Good morning Gunfighter Flight," responded Ground Control, "taxi runway one-seven left."

"Runway one-seven left," responded Kilmer. "Gunfighter 2, are you up?"

"Roger, Gunfighter 1," radioed Thomas.

The two F-4s pulled out of their revetments and began to taxi to the runway armament area. The revetments were steel constructed hangars that were covered with about a foot of concrete. These structures protected the aircraft against rocket attacks the VC often fired onto military bases.

Each of the aircraft was armed with eighteen, Mark-82 500-pound landmine bombs. It was a sight to see. It was hard to believe that two fighter-bomber aircraft could carry that load of bombs. The two F-4s jointly, could carry 36,500-pounds of bombs or over 18 tons of explosives. That was more explosive weight than four B-17 heavy bombers could carry on a mission during World War II.

The two F-4s taxied into the armament area adjacent to runway one-seven left. The arming crew quickly did a double check of all the bombs to make sure all safety pins had been removed. Safety pins were used to keep the ordnance unarmed while the aircraft was on the ground. The armament crew chief came in front of both aircraft and held up the arming pins, with their attached red flags, giving a visual check to the aircraft commanders that their bombs were indeed armed and ready for delivery.

"Are you ready to go Ben?" Kilmer asked.

"Yes Sir, I'm ready," responded Stone.

"All right, let's get this show on the road."

Kilmer looked over his shoulder at Captain Thomas and gave him thumbs up signal. Thomas responded with thumbs up. This indicated that both aircraft commanders were ready for takeoff.

"Gunfighter 2, go to the tower," radioed Kilmer.

"Roger, Gunfighter 2," responded Thomas.

Kilmer changed to Da Nang Tower's radio frequency.

"Gunfighter 1," radioed Kilmer.

"Gunfighter 2," responded Thomas.

"Da Nang Tower, Gunfighter Flight ready for takeoff runway one-seven left."

"Gunfighter 1 and 2, you are cleared for immediate takeoff runway one-seven left. Caution, small arms fire has been reported three quarters of a mile off the end of the runway. Suggest you climb as quickly as possible and make an immediate right turn after takeoff, then proceed on course," responded the tower.

"Roger, Da Nang Tower, understand cleared for takeoff runway one-seven left, max climb and right turn immediately after takeoff," answered Kilmer.

"Gunfighter 2, do you copy?" radioed Kilmer.

"Copy," responded Thomas.

Both heavy F-4s taxied onto the runway and began to go through their takeoff checklist. This required that each of the J-79 jet engines be brought up to Mil power, engine instruments checked and the throttles quickly brought back to idle power to check for smooth operation. The noise created by these powerful engines running at Mil power was deafening. The F-4s themselves shook and tried to surge forward as the power was advanced but the huge powerful brakes of the fighters kept them in place.

Finally all the checks were completed and Kilmer once again looked back at his wingman and gave the thumbs up signal. Thomas returned the ready sign. The two mighty F-4s were ready to takeoff. Kilmer slowly, but steadily brought both throttles up to Mil power and the aircraft began to roll. He pushed the throttles outboard and upward to light both afterburners of the roaring engines. The F-4 Lead began its roll down the two miles of concrete that made up runway one-seven left. The burners ignited and gave an immediate push to the backs of each of the pilots in Gunfighter 1. Kilmer pulled the control stick as far back as it would go. This rotated the huge stabilator that controlled the pitch of the aircraft. This control input allowed the aircraft to rotate into flying position as soon as enough speed was obtained to create the lift needed for takeoff and flight. The F-4 quickly accelerated to rotation speed and Kilmer released the control stick pressure to obtain a ten degrees nose-up pitch attitude. This gave maximum takeoff and climb attitude for the aircraft. The F-4 was a little slow to respond in climb and pitch control because of the great weight of the bombs.

However, Kilmer kept the F-4 in afterburner and the additional power from the burners allowed the aircraft to climb at several thousand feet per minute. As soon as safely airborne Kilmer made a right turn on course to stay away from the anticipated ground fire off the end of the runway. Gunfighter 2 repeated the same maneuver and quickly joined Gunfighter 1 on his right wing in proper formation position. To stay in proper formation position, the wingtip light was placed in the middle of the large American star on the F-4's fuselage. By keeping the wingtip light from moving forward or back within the star, the wingman would stay in proper position.

The two F-4s climbed to altitude, leveled off and the crews went through the proper climb and level-off checklists. They also checked for proper positioning of their fuel tank switches. This was important in the F-4D model because if the switches weren't properly positioned, the J-79 engines could flame out from fuel starvation.

The familiar, somewhat comfortable countryside of South Vietnam swiftly passed underneath the F-4s and the uncomfortable landscape of Laos replaced it. It wasn't that the landscape of Laos wasn't beautiful. In fact it was very beautiful with rolling mountains, triple canopy jungles and dazzling waterfalls. However, all knew it was a treacherous beauty. Underneath the jungle canopy of trees were NVA regulars who traveled the Ho Chi Minh Trail and kept the roadways protected and repaired while carrying war supplies and equipment to the south. There were special locations where there were concentrations of NVA regulars that manned anti-aircraft sites to protect the moving truck traffic and supply locations. Each of these sites was more than willing to take on an attacking fighter-bomber in the hopes of shooting it down.

The pair of F-4s arrived high over the target area. Looking down on the area was a frightful sight. Severe bomb damaged roads were winding down from the mountainous areas of North Vietnam, proceeding through northeastern Laos and then down toward South Vietnam. The area was completely devastated by continuous bombings that had hit the truck routes. Small fires were burning all around the valley floor that ran through the tall karst ridges.

"Misty 1," called Kilmer over the radio. "Gunfighter 1 and Gunfighter 2 with you. We're a flight of two Fox-4s with thirty-six Mark 82 magnetic bombs."

Misty 1 was the fast moving FAC that was the target controller for this mission. The Misty FACs flew the F-100 Super Saber. The F-100 was the first supersonic fighter developed by the Air Force and had done an outstanding job in Vietnam. It was showing its age during the Vietnam War but it performed its role as a fighter-bomber very well during the early part of the war. Because of its speed, the F-100 was also used as a fast moving forward air controller, or FastFACs, in out of country bombing missions. It had established a fair survivability record as a fast moving FAC in a very difficult combat environment. The men who flew the Misty FACs were brave and courageous and had an outstanding record of service.

"Gunfighter Flight, Misty 1. Good to see you guys today. The valley floor is open to you. Presently there are no other flights in the area. I'm on final approach now to fire a smoke rocket to mark where I'd like you to drop your Mark 82s. The smoke is away. Do you have my mark?"

"Roger," Kilmer responded. "Gunfighter 1 has your smoke. Are we cleared onto the target?"

"It's all yours," answered Misty 1. "Cleared onto the target. We're having a lot of response from ground fire today so be careful. We're also seeing a lot of fire coming from the caves along the karst ridges. Keep an eye out for that."

"Gunfighter 2, Gunfighter 1 is on base turning final for the target," radioed Kilmer. "You come in behind me as quickly as you can. They're already opening fire on me."

"Copy Gunfighter 1," radioed Thomas.

"Here we go Ben. Watch for ground fire as we get on final," Kilmer radioed over the intercom to Stone.

"Will do Sir," Stone responded.

The Lead F-4 turned final toward the target and the accelerating F-4 descended toward the 500-foot altitude as it raced to establish 500 knots. Kilmer set the necessary switches to allow the Mark 82s to be dropped on command. It took only seconds to travel down final toward the target. The F-4 was below the tops of the cliffs as it sped across the valley floor. Stone's head moved like it was on a swivel looking to the left and then to the right checking for enemy fire. He could see nothing coming their way. Thump! The bombs could be felt coming off the aircraft. Kilmer began pulling the speeding jet up toward the sky and lit the afterburners to get the hell out of there.

"Damn it," yelled Kilmer. "I screwed up the switches on bomb release and we only released half of the damn bombs. We're going to have to make another pass. I'm not going to take these bombs home."

"Got it Sir," replied Stone, "if you don't mind, let's just do this one more time."

"Roger," answered Kilmer, "one more time around will do it for me."

Kilmer pulled the F-4 up above the karst ridges on a downwind leg and set the switches up correctly to drop all the remaining bombs. Just then a radio call came.

"Gunfighter 1," radioed Thomas. "We received a hit from ground fire as we pulled off the target. I'm not sure how badly we've been hurt. We delivered the ordnance, but took several hits after bomb release. We're flying okay but we're heading for Thailand and an emergency landing."

"Copy your status," answered Kilmer, "we're going to complete one more pass and we'll catch up with you and escort you to Thailand."

The damage to Gunfighter 2 was severe. When they were first hit Johnson thought the aircraft was going to come apart. The explosion and vibration from the anti-aircraft fire had caused the F-4 to roll and yaw excessively. Johnson had reached for his lower ejection handle and pulled it to begin the ejection sequence. Nothing happened. Johnson looked out the canopy at the harsh terrain and at the hellish sights around him. The thought raced through his head: *If I eject here I'm a dead man*. For a few seconds he didn't know what to do. He had the ejection handle in his hand with a slack cable that ran to the ejection seat igniter. Why the seat hadn't fired was a mystery to him. He only knew that if he completed the ejection now he was a goner. He carefully placed the ejection handle back into its retaining bracket and prayed that the seat wouldn't fire. He then informed Thomas of what he had attempted.

"Sir," radioed Johnson over the intercom to Thomas. "I thought we were going in back there and I tried to eject. I guess I didn't pull the cable hard enough to start the ejection sequence. The seat might fire at anytime. So if you hear a loud noise and a lot of rushing air it's just me going for a smoke."

"Damn it Johnson," answered Thomas. "Can't you wait till tonight to smoke that damn pipe? If we make it to Thailand, I'll try and make a smooth landing so we don't eject you on touchdown. This mission just keeps getting better and better."

Gunfighter 1 was turning final to drop the remainder of its bombs. Kilmer and Stone couldn't keep their thoughts off of their buddies in Gunfighter 2. They could hardly wait to get the bombs away and hurry to assist them. As Kilmer and Stone came up on the target all hell broke lose. Enemy fire came from every direction. It was coming from the karst ridges on the left and on the right. It was like a ribbon of death that ran across their flight path from left to right and right to left. Enemy fire was also coming from the valley floor. Both pilots could hardly believe their eyes. They had been fired on before but nothing like this. At 500 feet above the ground it was really up close and personal. Thump. Kilmer released the bombs and was just about to pull the accelerating F-4 up into a maximum climb when it happened. A large explosion occurred at the rear of the aircraft.

The F-4 immediately pitched up in attitude to about 60 degrees nose high in response to the explosion. The F-4 had taken a powerful hit! The violent pitch up in attitude put a seven G load on the aircraft. Next the out of control F-4 pitched down in the opposite direction with a force of negative three Gs. Then it pitched up again with a seven G load and a 60 degrees nose up attitude. The F-4 repeated a violent pitch down attitude. Over and over this savage porpoising motion occurred. Both pilots felt helpless as they tried to get the F-4 under control. Their bodies were violently thrown around in the cockpit. Neither of the pilots had trained for anything like these vicious uncontrollable pitching oscillations. The exploding shell at the rear of the stabilator had caused the aircraft to be uncontrollable in pitch. Both pilots grabbed the control stick and firmly held it in a neutral position. They'd been trained to do this if the pilot himself had caused a situation known as a Pilot Induced Oscillation (PIO). The PIO condition was caused by the pilot giving inputs to control the pitch of the aircraft that were out of sync with the correct control inputs. The pilot would give an up or down command opposite to the input needed to regain control of the aircraft. The only way to correct this was to freeze the controls and let the aircraft settle down into a proper and controllable attitude.

Their training was helping them save themselves and the aircraft. They both hung onto the control stick and froze it in position while the F-4 pitched uncontrollably through 110 degrees of movement. Both pilots continued to be wildly thrown about in the cockpit held in place only by their seat belts and shoulder harnesses. As the F-4 was pitching out of control down the valley floor the anti-aircraft batteries were trying to finish it off before it flew out of the valley. The steep karst cliffs at the western end of the valley were rapidly coming toward the injured F-4. All Kilmer and Stone saw out of the corner of their eyes was the dark brown ridgeline running toward them. If the pitching didn't stop and the F-4 begin to climb PDQ, it would fly into the approaching wall of rock. This happened so fast that the pilots couldn't communicate with each other. The shock of the circumstance left both pilots speechless. They fought to try and get the F-4 under control before it impacted the karst ridge ahead.

Suddenly, the F-4's pitching motion began to dampen out. At first, less violent motions, and then less steep pitch changes. The F-4 was flying again. Both pilots began to pull back on the control stick. Dark brown surrounded the canopy allowing their eyes to see only the passing terrain. At that moment it flashed through the minds of both that they were going to hit the karst ridge and that would be the end.

Suddenly, just as rapidly as all of this had begun, the fierce, powerful F-4 reached for the heavens and burst over the top of the ridgeline into the bright blue of the sky. It took a moment for both men to say a word. Then Kilmer called to Stone.

"Damn Stone, are you okay?" radioed Kilmer.

"Uh, yes Sir, I'm okay," answered Stone. "I had my doubts there for a moment or two. They sure kicked the hell out of us. I've never ridden an aircraft through anything like that. Are you okay Sir? Do you want me to try and give Gunfighter 2 a call?"

"I'm okay," responded Kilmer. "Yeah, give Gunfighter 2 a call and check on their status. I'm going over the gauges here to check to see what damage we may have."

"Roger," replied Stone. "Gunfighter 2, Gunfighter 1, what's your status?"

There was no reply.

Stone radioed again, "Gunfighter 2, Gunfighter 1, we've been hit and are off the target heading for emergency field. What's your status?"

Again there was no response.

Stone radioed again, "Gunfighter 2 or Misty 1 how do you read Gunfighter 1?"

There was no reply.

"Sir," called Stone, "we appear to have lost our radios. Damn if I know what's wrong with them, but I'll start troubleshooting. How's the aircraft?"

"It's doing okay. Yes, check to see if you can get the radios back. I'm heading to the closest field until I get a better picture of how the bird is doing. It sure took a beating back there."

Stone started going over the radios to see if he could get them back online. The frequencies were right and the volume controls were good. Then he noticed that the push button switches that should be down to select the radios were out of position, they were positioned in the neutral setting. Stone immediately pushed the switches down into their proper positions. The negative G forces experienced in the out of control situation had evidently moved them to the neutral position.

"Gunfighter 2, Gunfighter 1, how do you read me?" radioed Stone.

"We read you loud and clear. What happened to you? We were afraid you had been hit," radioed Thomas.

"We were hit," answered Kilmer as he took over the radios. "We're okay, only lost the radios for a period of time. We're headed toward home or nearest field. How are you?"

"We're almost at Udorn. We're okay, but will make an emergency landing and might take the barrier," radioed Thomas. "We'll give the squadron a call and give a report as soon as we get this bird on the ground."

"Great," Kilmer reported on the radio. "Good to hear you're okay. Yeah, give us a call on the landline when you're safely on the ground. We're going to head back to Da Nang. I think we're okay. Maybe a little bent, but the bird is flying well. We'll work on getting you back to Da Nang ASAP."

Gunfighter 2 made an emergency landing at Udorn Air Base in

Thailand. While landing Johnson prayed that the seat wouldn't fire and eject him on touchdown. Thomas made an exceptionally smooth landing and the seat didn't fire. After parking the F-4, Johnson was very slow in climbing out of his ejection seat and was very careful not to make any unnecessary movements. He reported to maintenance that an ejection attempt had been made, however, with no effect. After inspecting the seat it was found that Johnson hadn't pulled on the ejection handle with enough force to start the ejection sequence. The life support specialist estimated he had come close, but was shy by about a pound of pressure. Johnson was glad that he had been a pound weak that day.

Kilmer and Stone landed safely at Da Nang. The inspection of their aircraft revealed that there was battle damage on the lower left side of the stabilator. It was determined that a 57mm anti-aircraft shell had probably exploded underneath the stabilator and the force of the explosion had caused the F-4 to go out of control.

Kilmer and Stone went into the intelligence debriefing session with a good story to tell. The mission had been accomplished and both F-4s and their crews had returned safely. However for months, both crews had disturbed sleep with memories and nightmares of their journey to hell and their flight back to safety.

10

Hill Tops

The weather was good today in the Republic of Vietnam. The rains that had been pounding most of the country had stopped and the sky was mostly clear. However, clouds were still present over the tops of some of the higher hills and mountains around Phu Cat. Weather forecasters and pilots call this condition mountain obscuration. It usually wasn't a problem during takeoff for the F-4 who had the power to climb quickly to altitude and avoid these clouds with their "hard centers." Pilots refer humorously to cloud-covered mountaintops as *Cumulo-Granitus* clouds after the names of different cloud types and granite rock.

A mountain obscuration condition can raise serious safety concerns for some aircraft; especially lighter piston engine aircraft that have limited power and climb capability. These aircraft have difficulty getting around or through mountainous regions with clouds hiding their tops. With the rains gone and only isolated cloud conditions, pilots of fast mover aircraft like the F-4 had little concern for the weather.

Lieutenant Ben Stone had been in country for eleven months and completed almost 200 combat missions in the F-4. He was a seasoned pilot and had flown with at least two-dozen frontseaters. Most of these were good pilots for whom Ben had great respect, but today Ben had been selected to fly with a new front seat pilot that had just arrived from his training in the States. This would be the new pilot's third mission. Stone, a pilot backseater, wasn't really happy about this mission assignment. Ben didn't want to fly with a new guy any more. He'd been selected many times to fly with new guys to help them get accustomed to flying in combat and give them some well learned combat safety tips. Ben had been selected to fly with new guys because he was smart, had good flying skills, and had particularly good judgment. He had a way of expressing himself to others and providing useful instruction without getting ego involved in the discussion. Most new pilots were thankful for the opportunity to learn as much as they could and as fast as they could about flying and surviving in a combat environment. However, today was different for Stone, he was a short timer. He only had three weeks left in his yearlong combat tour. He didn't want to take any more chances than he had to, because his tour was about over and he was to rotate home. Flying with a new guy was always unsettling, but today Stone was really concerned about this new pilot. He'd heard from his flying buddies that this guy had an ego the size of Texas and was always telling others at the bar that he was over here to win the war.

The new guy's name was Captain David E. Turner. He was in his early thirties and had been a pilot only a short time. He'd been a navigator for several years with the Strategic Air Command and had flown in KC-135 tankers before going to pilot training 18 months earlier. The F-4 was his first flying assignment out of pilot training. Turner was nice enough to talk to on a surface level; however, move beyond the weather and sports and he revealed a difficult personality. Turner was stubborn about most things. He'd already made up his mind on most issues concerning the war and it would do no good to try and get him to look at other points of view. He believed he always knew best and was very resistant to changing his mind on most subjects.

Stone didn't like the idea of flying with this guy; however, he was a team player and he would make the best of the situation. Stone had been flying most of his missions with Captain Ron Kilmer the last two months. They liked flying together because they were both good pilots and they had the same view of the war. Their view was to get the job done as well as possible and then get the hell home. Neither of them had any illusions about winning the war. They knew the politicians back in the world would screw that up. They both had seen the war up close and personal and knew the flying side of it exceptionally well. They had lost friends and had plenty of close calls themselves. They were willing to help where they could make a difference but weren't willing to take foolish, unnecessary chances. They had over 400 combat missions between them and were looking forward to their last mission party and the freedom flight back to the States.

However, today Stone wouldn't be flying with Kilmer; he would be flying with the new guy, and would have to make the best of it. Stone decided to get a head start on the mission by going out early and completing a pre-flight on the bird. Stone climbed all over the F-4 checking every inch of it. He checked the bomb load. Everything looked good. Stone didn't find any problems with either the aircraft or the munitions. This at least gave him a good feeling about the start of the mission.

Stone walked from the aircraft revetment area to the squadron building. It was only about 150 yards and he thought that the exercise would do him good. He quickly arrived at the squadron and proceeded to the mission planning room. The other flight crewmembers had just arrived to start the flight planning and mission briefings. The Lead aircraft crew consisted of Major John Watson and Captain Tommy Custer. Both Watson and Custer were experienced combat veterans, both had been in Vietnam for six months. Watson had been an F-102 pilot before moving to the F-4 and Custer, a navigator, had been a weapons officer in the F-101 Voodoo for several years. Turner would be the aircraft commander in number two aircraft with Stone as the backseater.

Stone immediately went over to Turner and introduced himself.

"Good morning Sir, we will be teamed up today. Good to have you in the squadron."

"Thanks," replied Turner, "good to be over here. I've heard good things about you Stone. Glad we're flying together today."

"Thank you Sir, it looks like a good day to fly."

The two crews studied the target photos, planned the navigation route to the target and established target attack strategies. From the very beginning Stone didn't like the unusual location of the target. It was an in country suspected weapons storage area. That was not unusual but its location was. The target was situated in a box canyon surrounded on one side by rising terrain and two sides by steep mountain ridges. There was only one way into the target area and only one way out. Because of the high terrain the escape away from the target required a 180-degree turn within the box canyon. The distance across the canyon floor was narrow. It wouldn't allow much room for the F-4s to get to the target, which was on the northwest side of the canyon, make a steep right turn to miss the canyon walls on the north and east, and fly back out the southern entrance of the canyon. Stone knew it would require a high degree of flying skill to drop the bombs with enough speed to make a high G, tight 180-degree turn. The pilot couldn't allow the F-4 to gain too much airspeed, that would result in the turn radius being too wide and result in the F-4 not being able to complete the 180-degree turn and impact the eastern mountain slope. Stone voiced his concern about the location of the target, along with its hazards to the others during the briefing. It appeared, after their discussions, all understood the existing dangers of the target's physical location.

The customary Intel and weather briefings were given to the aircrews. The Intel officer had little to say about the ground threat in the area. There hadn't been any flights in the target area for some time, so no reports had been received concerning enemy ground fire. The most helpful information from the Intel briefing was that if either of the F-4s was damaged by enemy fire the best alternative for escape was a turn to the east. The escape plan was to fly away from the target area, climb over the eastern mountain tops and make for "feet wet" over the ocean. The ocean was only about 20 miles to the east of the target and would make for a good ejection location. The Navy had patrol boats off the coast of Vietnam and stood ready to rescue downed airmen.

With the exception of possible mountain obscuration in the target area, the weather briefing provided little that might suggest problems for the flight. The forecast was for good weather throughout the mission including the return flight to Phu Cat.

After the Intel and weather briefings, the crewmembers proceeded to the mission planning room where Watson covered all aspects of the mission from engine start to engine shut down. He wanted to make sure that Turner understood every possible aspect of the mission before they went out to fly. There was little time for clearing up issues or answering questions in the air. Watson wanted everything to go like clockwork once the engines were started.

After Watson had completed his briefing, there were very few questions. He did an excellent job on the brief and he made sure all major parts of it were clear.

The men left the briefing room and went to suit up for the mission. They climbed into their required equipment, which included their G-suit, parachute harness and survival vest. Everyone had special items that they wanted to carry in case of ejection. Some crewmembers took extra cartridges for their revolver believing that having the revolver would help protect them from enemy soldiers searching for them. Other crewmembers believed the revolver would be of limited or no value to them so only took the required six rounds of ammo. Others believed the pencil flare gun would be invaluable to signal their location to the rescue aircraft. They would take extra flare cartridges. Still others believed that an extra radio with extra batteries provided the best chance of rescue. Each had their own reasons for taking sometimes unique and certainly different items with them on their missions. In all cases each aircrew member had their own view of what they would need to take with them in order to survive and be rescued after ejection.

After getting suited up, the four aircrew members left the squadron building and climbed into the crew van for transport to their aircraft. The squadron scheduling officer drove them to the locations of their aircraft and dropped them off. The two crews then began the pre-flights of their F-4s and their bomb loads.

Turner began the preflight of the aircraft while Stone made a second check of the bomb load. He didn't tell Turner that he had already been out to the aircraft and had given it an initial check. Stone felt good that he had spent some extra time checking out the bird and its load. During a preflight it was rare to find anything significantly wrong with either the aircraft or the bomb load. The crew chiefs of the aircraft and the ordnance load always did an exceptional job of getting the F-4s ready for flight. If there was a minor problem, the crew chief would inform the pilots so they would be aware of it and make any needed adjustments.

Stone finished his check of the bomb load and climbed into the backseat of the F-4 while the crew chief helped him strap into the ejection seat. The crew chief helped attach the parachute connectors to his harness. He removed the safety pins from the ejection seat thus arming it. It was important to safety the ejection seat while on the ground and to make sure it was armed for flight. There had been inadvertent ground ejections with the F-4 with serious consequences.

Turner climbed into the front seat and began the same sequence of hooking up to the aircraft. Stone attached the leg straps from the ejection seat onto his lower legs. The leg straps were important, as they would pull the crewmember's legs from the rudder pedals and into proper position during an ejection event. This prevented the crewmember's legs from hitting the canopy rails during ejection. If this were to happen it would probably break both of the pilot's legs. These restraining leg straps also helped prevent the pilot's legs from flailing in the wind-stream at high ejection speeds. Allowing the pilot's legs to forcibly and uncontrollably flail in the high-speed airstream could inflict serious injuries.

Both pilots performed their Starting Engines checklist and Turner brought both the J-79 engines to life.

"Radios on, set and INS operational," Stone radioed over the intercom.

"Roger," Turner replied.

"Phu Cat Tower, Cobra Flight ready to taxi," radioed Watson.

"Cobra Flight, taxi to runway three-three," replied Phu Cat Tower.

"Taxi runway three-three. Cobra 2, are you on frequency?" radioed Watson.

"Cobra 2, up," answered Turner.

Both F-4s pulled from their concrete revetments as Turner pulled into position about 200 feet behind Lead aircraft. Pilots were careful not to get too close behind each other because the burning JP-4 fuel exhaust could be overwhelming, especially on a hot, humid tropical day. They taxied to the ordnance arming area where both F-4s had the safety pins removed from their bombs. With a signal from the armament crew chief that they were armed and ready, Watson responded with a thumbs up signal.

"Phu Cat Tower," radioed Watson, "Cobra Flight ready for takeoff."

"Cobra 1 and 2 cleared for takeoff runway three-three," responded the tower.

"Cobras, cleared for takeoff," continued Watson, "Cobra 2, did you copy?"

"Copied," responded Turner.

Both F-4s taxied onto the runway and began their Before Takeoff checklist. In less than a minute Watson looked over at Turner and gave a thumbs up signal. Turner replied with thumbs up signaling that both aircraft were ready for departure.

Watson brought both throttles up to full Mil power. The big F-4 started to roll and then in one smooth motion Watson pushed outboard and forward on the throttles to move them into full afterburner position. In less than a second the J-79s responded with a sudden burst of thrust coming from the powerful afterburners. The F-4 quickly began to accelerate. This was a rush for the pilots. For many it was like their old drag strip days when they would race their souped up cars down the quarter mile speedway. However, the F-4 didn't stop accelerating at a quarter mile mark, it just continued accelerating, rotated and took to the sky.

Takeoff was an cautious time for the crewmembers. There was a short period of time during the takeoff sequence, beginning at rotation speed and continuing to a thousand feet above the ground, when loss of an engine or another emergency could mean possible disaster for the crew. All crewmembers were especially alert during this critical time of flight. Ejection was an option but with a load of bombs on board it would be difficult to escape the bomb blast should the bombs explode during the crash. At or above a thousand feet above the ground, chances for survival increased significantly for the crews.

Watson completed his takeoff without difficulty and began a climbing right turn toward the south. Turner soon joined on his right wing in close formation. After the turn to a southerly heading the two F-4s proceeded to the target area. The target was only 70 miles from Phu Cat. The two F-4s covered the distance in quick fashion and Watson radioed to Cobra 2 to change the radio frequency to that of the FAC.

"Cobra 2, Cobra 1, change to FAC frequency now."

"Roger, Cobra 2 changing frequency," replied Turner.

"Cobra 2, how do you read Cobra 1?"

"I read you loud and clear," responded Turner.

"Covey 1, Cobra 1 and 2 with you. We're three minutes from the target area. Today we're carrying Mark 82 high drag bombs," radioed Watson.

"Good morning Cobra Flight," Covey 1 replied. "I have a visual on you at my 9 o'clock position. I'm firing a smoke rocket now to mark the target. Do you see my smoke?" radioed Covey 1.

"I have your smoke and I have you in sight," radioed Watson.

"Place your bombs fifty meters north of my smoke. Make your run from the south to the north up the canyon. Turn right to recover to the south," instructed Covey 1.

"Roger," responded Watson, "Cobra 2, you come in behind me and keep an eye on the mountains to the east. Keep your speed up."

"Roger," responded Cobra 2.

Cobra 1 made his first pass on the target. He attacked the target at a high speed, dropped four of his high drag bombs, ignited his afterburners and began a tight high G climbing turn to the right.

"Cobra 2 onto the target," radioed Turner.

"You're cleared onto the target," responded Covey 1.

Turner turned into the target but instead of accelerating to over 500 knots for the run he pulled the power back. The airspeed began to decay and passed through 400 knots.

"Sir, you want to attack as fast as you can," radioed Stone over the intercom.

As he made the call to Turner he pushed the throttle up to full Mil power.

"I want 400 knots for the run," replied Turner.

He pulled the throttles back to idle to regain the 400-knot speed. Back in the States on the practice range, pilots had been taught to use an airspeed of 400 knots so there would be more time to place the bomb on target. This would give them a better range score; however, this wasn't the range. In Vietnam their F-4s were heavy and there could be ground fire heading their way. Stone knew from experience that speed in combat was not only your friend but also your life. Being slow in a heavy F-4 close to the ground in the target area was stupid. He pushed the throttles up again.

"Leave the damn throttles alone," responded Turner. "I want these bombs right on the target."

Again Turner pulled the throttles to idle power. The big heavy F-4 just seemed to float toward the target and the wall of granite that was to their north.

"Sir," responded Stone, "if you don't give us power we won't be able to make the turn back to the south."

"I can't get the reticle on the target," responded Turner. "I'm not going to drop anything this run. We'll just have to make another pass."

With this announcement Turner started a slow, shallow turn toward the east. He was slowly, very slowly bringing the power up from idle. Alarm bells were going off in Stone's head. His eyes tracked from their current location toward the cloud covered mountain cliffs to the east. It was as if his eyes were marking a dashed red line from their location to a big red X on the canyon wall to the east.

"Damn it Sir," called Stone over the intercom, "can't you see that we're not going to make this turn if you don't get the power in and increase our rate of turn?"

It seemed like the huge F-4 was just hanging in the air waiting for something important to happen. Turner made no response. Stone did, he slammed the throttle to full military power.

"Turner, light the afterburners, start climbing, we're not going to make this damn turn," yelled Stone over the intercom.

It was only seconds but it seemed like minutes before Turner responded. He pulled the nose of the F-4 up. However, he pulled it up too high and didn't add power nor did he light the afterburners. At once the airspeed began to decay. Stone glanced at the airspeed indicator as it passed through 300 knots and headed quickly toward 250 knots.

"Get the nose down some and light the burners, we're getting too slow. We're going to fall out of the sky if we keep this up," yelled Stone over the intercom.

"Light the burners, light the damn burners," he continued.

The throttles in the backseat of the F-4 can only be controlled up to full military power. The afterburners can't be ignited from the backseat. For some reason this was how the bird was designed and Stone was regretting that decision.

Suddenly Stone felt a soft thump as the afterburners ignited. It was too little too late. Afterburners work best when there is a lot of air going through the engines. When the aircraft's speed is slow, with very little air going through the engines, the afterburners are not very effective and don't provide the power experienced at high airspeeds.

The huge, fully loaded, heavy F-4 seemed to stumble toward the wall of granite that was approaching quickly. Clouds covered the tops of the mountains so there was no way of knowing where there might be a pass to fly through. Both men were silent as the F-4 entered the clouds around the mountain cliffs.

Thoughts raced through Stone's mind. *What will it be like to hit a wall of rock at 300 knots? Will I know it's coming or will it happen so fast I won't realize it? Will I know this idiot gets it before I do?* Then the thoughts just stopped.

The aircraft seemed still, motionless, surrounded by the gray clouds that hid the mountaintops. Time seemed to stop as the F-4 and its two crewmembers remained suspended in the gray mass. They were engulfed in a dangerous world with no sight, sound or sense of movement. It was an uncomfortable world that neither pilot had ever experienced before.

Suddenly a brilliant light illuminated the inside of the F-4. It was the blinding light from a brilliant radiating sun. The F-4 had broken through the gray clouds and had topped the mountain ridges. They had escaped this mountainous death trap.

Stone resisted screaming at Turner. He was fuming inside. How could a pilot be so stupid? But what could Stone say to Turner? There were just too many damn dumb things that Turner did during that pass on the target. He almost killed them both.

They got the mission accomplished with a second run on the target. Turner flew a faster final, dropped all of the damn bombs on one pass and made the necessary high G turn with full power to stay away from the cloud covered mountains to the east.

Stone was silent and didn't say a word to Turner during the flight home. He was so angry he couldn't put his words together to say what he wanted. The landing back at Phu Cat was uneventful. The two crews put their F-4s to bed and walked together toward the Intel shack for their debrief. Then Stone found his voice. He began yelling at Turner all the way to the Intel shack. Turner was very defensive and yelled back at Stone. It was unclear to all if he had learned anything that day. However, Stone was clear about his relationship with Turner. He told him he would never fly with him again and that he doubted if Turner would survive his tour of duty. They both agreed that it would be best if they were never assigned to fly together again, and for whatever the reason, they never were. Turner was alive when Stone left Vietnam to return to the world, but Stone never checked to see if Turner survived the war.

11

Jerry's Big Watch

It was just after 1600 at Da Nang Air Base, Republic of Vietnam. Inside the 480th TAC Fighter Squadron, a dozen pilots and navigators were captivated by Captain Jerry Evans and his fun personality and riveting stories. This was usual for Jerry, wherever he went he would always draw a crowd with his story telling, jokes and clever statements. Everyone liked Jerry and liked to hear his entertaining stories. People also liked Jerry because he was so damn good at everything he did. He always got the job done, no matter what it was or how difficult it might be. Afterwards Jerry would tell you how hard the job was and how good he was at getting it done. Somehow you just couldn't get upset with Jerry and his boastful attitude. He always made you smile, even when he was telling everyone how great a pilot he was and how he was going to win this war all by himself if that's the way it had to be.

Jerry had a practice of telling every new member coming into the squadron that he was the best fighter pilot in the Air Force. The most famous line that Jerry asked every new squadron member was, "Do you know how you can tell the best fighter pilots in the Air Force?" Jerry would continue, "You can tell how good a fighter pilot is by the size of his wristwatch. The bigger the watch the better the pilot!"

Jerry continued, "Just look at the size of my watch." Jerry then pulled up the sleeve of his flight suit and showed the biggest wristwatch you could possibly imagine. It had dials on top of dials. For a 1960's vintage watch it was amazing. It could do anything, from solving mathematical problems to timing multiple events.

If, in fact, the size of a pilot's watch made that pilot a good flyer, then Jerry would definitely be one of the best pilots around. Regardless of the size of Jerry's watch, he was a good pilot. He had a lot of flight time in fighters including the F-4D. He was smart, knowledgeable, experienced and self-assured. Perhaps he was a little too self-assured for his own good.

In one of Jerry's story lines, he talked about what he would do if his aircraft was hit by ground fire and severely damaged. He remarked, "If my aircraft gets damaged and I need to eject, no problem. I have a 38 caliber revolver and after I eject and land on the ground, I'll pull out my trusty gun and take the fight to the bad guys. They won't have a chance against me."

Jerry repeated this same story many times in many different places. Fellow squadron members would just smile and remark, "That's just Jerry, the best fighter pilot in the world. The pilot with the biggest watch."

On today's mission, Jerry was scheduled to lead a two ship F-4D formation to strike a suspected enemy troop location in the southern part of South Vietnam. His GIB was Lieutenant James White. Lieutenant White was fresh out of pilot training and F-4 training school. His first assignment was Southeast Asia with a scheduled year tour at Da Nang Air Base. White was young and inexperienced, however he was a good pilot and wanted to be a great fighter pilot. Jerry and White had flown several combat missions together and had built up a trust. White was just a younger, smaller version of Jerry. He looked up to Jerry and wanted to someday be as good a pilot and perhaps have as big a watch as Jerry's.

Captain Ira Thomas and Lieutenant Sam Franklin were the two crewmembers in the second F-4 scheduled for Jerry's mission. Thomas and Franklin were experienced combat pilots. Captain Thomas had been in country for seven months and Franklin had eight months of his tour behind him. Both were respected for their flying abilities and good judgment. Captain Thomas' last assignment was that of an Undergraduate Pilot Training (UPT) instructor in the T-38 aircraft. For the last five years, he had been an instructor in T-38s. Flying with student pilots for this long, he had seen just about all the mistakes a pilot can make in an aircraft. He would tell stories about his time as an instructor with undergraduate pilots who were trying to complete their pilot training. Many of the stories he told were both funny and terrifying at the same time.

Lieutenant Franklin had been assigned to the F-4 straight out of pilot training. He had graduated from pilot training in the top quarter of his class. He requested a fighter for his first assignment out of pilot training and he was very pleased when he received his orders assigned to the F-4. Franklin was good at flying the F-4, but he was exceptional with his knowledge of the aircraft. He knew all about every system that comprised the plane. He was an expert in every detail of its many systems. If anyone ever had a question about the F-4's hydraulic, fuel, electrical, or emergency systems they went to Franklin for the answer. He loved studying about the F-4's systems and how every part came together to make up the aircraft. His degree from the university was in mechanical engineering and his understanding of engineering showed in his knowledge of the aircraft.

On today's mission the crewmembers had completed their briefings with the Intel officer and the weatherman. The briefings had been normal with nothing special to report. The weather was forecast to be good throughout the day and there had been no reports of enemy fire in the target area. However, as usual Jerry took extra time in his flight briefing. He liked to be extremely thorough in every aspect of a mission. He reminded all of the other flight members that every flight had its dangers and not to let down their guard but to do everything right.

"Remember," Jerry always told his flight members, "no one in this war will be shot at as many times today as you. However, I have the biggest watch of any fighter pilot and I will get you through it."

Jerry would then smile and release the crews to go "suit out" and get to their aircraft. Today was no exception, Jerry made his statement, sent them to the equipment room to put on their flying gear and get ready for the mission. After the two crews were suited up for the mission, they were driven to their aircraft and went through the necessary checks of the aircraft and the weapons systems. Today's mission called for the F-4s to be loaded with 500-pound high drag bombs. Each F-4 could carry up to 18 of these bombs along with two external fuel tanks. This gave the F-4 plenty of firepower and enough fuel to spend needed time in the target area. The high drag bombs, with their extended tail fins, could be dropped very close to the target at a low altitude. This gave the pilots the ability to be extremely accurate at placing the bombs on target.

The two crews quickly readied their aircraft, started engines and taxied out to the end of the runway. The bombs were readied for the mission by the removal of all safety pins by the arming crew chief. Jerry made a call to the tower for permission for takeoff. The flight was cleared for takeoff. The two heavy F-4s completed their takeoffs, rejoined in formation and made a climbing turn toward the target area.

The flight time to the target area was approximately 35 minutes. As soon as the two-ship formation came within ten miles of the target, Jerry made a radio call to contact the FAC.

"Covey 1, Gunfighters 1 and 2 with you, how do you read me?" radioed Jerry.

"Gunfighter Flight, Covey 1, I read you loud and clear, how me?" responded Covey 1.

"We read you 5 by 5," radioed Jerry, "we have Mark 82 high drags today. Where do you want them?"

"I have a place to put them today," radioed Covey 1. "Heads up, we are experiencing some ground fire and have observed a lot of troop activity in the area. Be careful on your approach to the target. Gunfighter 1, do you have my smoke?"

"Roger the heads up and I do have your smoke," responded Jerry.

"Hit my smoke," directed Covey 1.

"Gunfighter 1 is turning final on the target," radioed Jerry. "Gunfighter 2 you come onto the target as soon as I am off."

"Wilco," radioed Thomas.

Gunfighter 1 turned final toward the target. The location of the smoke rocket that had been fired by Covey 1 was clearly identified. Jerry placed the target reticle of his weapons system directly on the target. He pushed the throttles full forward to get 100% military power. Down the heavy F-4 descended as it picked up airspeed. The airspeed indicator was moving above 500 knots as Gunfighter 1 reached the desired altitude of 150 feet above the ground. Thump, thump was the sound of two of the bombs departing the aircraft. Jerry pulled back on the control stick and moved the throttles outboard to ignite the afterburners. The F-4 responded rapidly to Jerry's commands. The G forces that Jerry had demanded with his upward control input, and the additional thrust from the afterburners propelled the F-4 skyward toward safety away from the target.

Gunfighter 2 was only seconds behind Gunfighter 1. The two 500 pound bombs from Lead's aircraft exploded at a safe distance in front of Gunfighter 2's aircraft. Thomas' eyes blinked at the sight of the flames from the explosions and the quaking of the jungle floor as it absorbed the fury of the half-ton of bombs from Lead's aircraft. Thomas was now over the release point for his bombs. Thump, thump, away with two of his Mark 82's. He also pulled on his control stick, banked back and forth to avoid enemy fire and ignited the afterburners of his aircraft. Up, up he escaped as his F-4 fought for altitude and safety.

"Gunfighters 1 and 2," radioed Covey 1, "good job, the initial target was hit and is burning. I believe it's wasted. There are also secondary explosions coming from the target. I want you to move to the south about two kilometers to an additional target location. I'm marking it now with a new smoke. Do you have the new target's location?"

"I have the new smoke," radioed Jerry, "am I cleared on the new target?"

"Gunfighter 1 and 2, you both are cleared to hit my smoke. I'm receiving a lot of ground fire and am moving to the east to escape it. Be careful, they're really lighting up the place. I think they have some heavy guns down there," radioed Covey 1.

"Gunfighter 1 is on final for the new target," radioed Jerry, "Gunfighter 2, change your run-in heading by thirty degrees. They're shooting like hell at me. We're taking fire from all quadrants."

"Wilco," responded Gunfighter 2.

"Gunfighter 2," radioed Jerry, "we've been hit. They hosed us good, we're off the target and turning to the east and climbing."

"Got you in sight," radioed Gunfighter 2, "we're off the target and coming to look you over. It looks from here like you have a fire."

"Yeah," radioed Jerry, " I have a Fire Light on both engines. The bird is climbing okay, we still have power."

Jerry's optimism was short lived. Bang! A loud explosion was heard in Gunfighter 1's aircraft followed by violent shaking of the bird. A stream of fire and smoke was coming from the rear of the aircraft. The nose of the injured F-4 pitched down as both engines began to lose power and started throwing parts through the sides of the fuselage. A loud grinding noise began coming from the engines. The Master Caution light was illuminated and the engine instruments and aircraft systems gauges began showing multiple failures.

"Damn it," called Jerry over the intercom, "Jim, I think we're going to have to eject. One engine just stopped and the other is producing a lot of flames. We'll hang on for a second or two, but it's not looking good. I show zero oil pressure on both engines and we have one hydraulic systems failure. I'm losing pitch control. I'd like to get us out of the target area before we eject and maybe even make the water."

"Confirm the engine damage Sir. I observe flames coming from the number two engine and number one has spooled down. I'm getting some smoke back here and am switching to 100% oxygen to breathe," responded James.

"That's it," called Jerry over the intercom, "the controls aren't responding. We're going to eject. Get ready Jim, I'll call it."

"Mayday! Mayday! Mayday!" radioed Jerry. "Gunfighter 1 is on fire and has lost pitch control of the aircraft. We're ejecting ten miles east of the target area."

The right side of the F-4 was burning a bright reddish-orange color as it started to roll starboard out of control.

"Let's get the hell out of here before she rolls inverted," instructed Jerry over the intercom. "I'll give the eject command. Straighten your back, lock your shoulder harness and pull your feet back to the seat."

"Eject! Eject! Eject!" Jerry yelled over the intercom.

As he completed the eject command, Jerry grabbed the two overhead hand loops for the ejection seat face curtain and pulled them with all his strength. For half a second nothing appeared to happen, then, all hell broke loose. There were flames and smoke from the rocket pack firing as the backseater's ejection seat blasted upward and out of the F-4. Almost instantly the front seat fired. The dynamite charge exploded and literally blew Jerry and his seat up the ejection rails and out of the aircraft. Immediately the ejection rocket motor ignited and propelled Jerry still higher above the burning F-4.

Until Jerry hit the ground everything that happened was a blur. His seat tumbled in 360-degree circles several times. His helmet and facemask were torn off by the windblast. His right arm was wrenched back hard against the seat causing intense pain. The Martin-Baker ejection seat worked as advertised and quickly the main chute was pulled from the seat separating Jerry from it. Jerry, partially dazed, realized he had a good chute and was descending safely to the ground. This gave Jerry strength and he soon began to collect his thoughts. The ground was coming up at him rapidly and he realized he wouldn't be in the chute for long. As he descended he observed men on the ground running toward him. They didn't have uniforms on but they were shooting at him with their AK-47 machine guns. Being suspended in the air and shot at by automatic weapons fire gave Jerry an extremely helpless feeling.

"I've got to get on the ground and shoot back at these bastards," Jerry thought as he continued to descend. The ground came up rapidly, too rapidly. Jerry didn't realize how close he was to the ground, but it soon became very clear.

He hit the ground hard and tumbled backwards as his head impacted the hardened soil. He was dazed for a moment but soon realized he had to act if he was to stay alive. He moved each leg and each arm to check if they had been broken. His right arm and shoulder hurt like hell. He thought that his right arm might be broken. Jerry slowly got to his feet and slipped painfully out of his parachute harness. He then defiantly pulled his 38-caliber revolver from its holster. *Damn these guys*! Jerry thought turning toward his attackers.

The Viet Cong were less than 100 yards away when Jerry opened up on them with his revolver. Jerry's gun was soon empty but the automatic fire from the Viet Cong's AK-47s kept coming loud and clear. Bullets were flying all around Jerry. They hit the ground around him and screamed past his head. Jerry rapidly realized that to try and shoot it out with these guys would be futile and just plain stupid. He understood he was out gunned.

Jerry hurriedly shoved his empty revolver back into its holster as he turned away from his attackers and ran like hell. He knew that his only chance was to find a hiding place and find it fast. He knew he had to hide and wait for help to arrive. As he ran he wondered what had happened to his GIB. The last time he saw him he was tumbling through the air in his ejection seat.

The fire from the AK-47s kept coming with the bullets spraying around him. He couldn't believe they hadn't hit him. Bullets were flying everywhere. Jerry looked to his left and then to his right for some cover and a place to hide. He noticed some tall grass only yards away. He headed for it running as fast as he could. He dove head long into the tall grass and began crawling deeper into the thicker parts.

Hide, he told himself.

"*Don't move,*" he remembered from his survival training. *"They can't see you if you don't move."*

Then all hell began to break loose. There was concentrated gunfire coming very close to him. He could feel the bullets as they hit the earth near his body. There were screams of men only yards from his location. He'd never heard the sounds of men dying let alone men being torn apart by high-powered automatic weapons fire. Only yards away he felt the vibrations of hundreds of rounds of gunfire pounding the earth. He was terrified by what he heard and felt.

He lifted his head out of the grass to see what was happening. As he turned he saw an Army helicopter gunship coming toward him. Out of the side door of the helicopter there was a gunner firing a machine gun at the Viet Cong. The Viet Cong were firing back at the helicopter but they were no match for the firepower of the Army chopper. The Viet Cong, realizing they were losing the battle, rapidly retreated and disappeared into the jungle 200 yards to the west.

Damn them! Jerry thought.

The Army chopper landed only yards from Jerry.

"Are you hurt Sir?" came a call from the chopper as two American soldiers came to help him.

"No, I'm okay," responded Jerry, "thanks to you guys. You saved my ass. Have you seen my backseater?" shouted Jerry through the noise of the helicopter.

"Yes Sir," replied one of the soldiers, "we picked him up a couple of minutes before we got you. He's in the chopper, a little banged up but nothing's broken."

Jerry ran and climbed into the chopper. James had been strapped against the bulkhead of the chopper by one of the chopper crewmen.

"Jim, are you okay?" asked Jerry.

"I'm fine Sir," James responded. "Just a little sore from the ejection sequence. Man what a ride, my back hurts like hell. I do have a question for you Sir," continued James. "How's your big watch?"

Both men smiled as the helicopter lifted off, climbed and turned toward Da Nang.

"I don't think it's as big as it was this morning," was Jerry's only reply.

Both men were delivered safely back to Da Nang and Jerry had yet another story to tell his fellow airmen about his flying adventures and his big watch.

12

Vertigo, Not Home Yet

The week was rough for the flying and maintenance crews at Phu Cat Air Base. At the start of the week, the battle plan for flying had switched over to flying mostly night missions. This caused a lot of fatigue and stress on the crews as they struggled to adjust to sleeping during the day and working through the night. The Air Force was good at preparing them for changes in the duty schedule. Even back in the world, the Air Force rotated flying schedules around so that all received extensive experience in working night shifts as well as day shifts. However it was still hard physiologically making the adjustments.

Recently promoted, Major Ron Kilmer, who was the ultimate professional Air Force officer, hated the switch to night flying. He would never make a big deal out of it to his fellow officers, but it was clear in the few remarks he made that he didn't like it. One of the main reasons for his dislike was the additional risk that it brought to flying. Flying a supersonic fighter like the F-4 in a combat environment had a ton of risk factors associated with it. These risk factors were multiplied many times over when you mixed night flying with them. They included reduced visibility, loss of depth perception, difficulty with situational awareness, inability to see terrain, and increased risk of vertigo.

Vertigo is a physiological condition that is caused, in part, by problems involving the inner ear. Movement of the aircraft or erratic movement of the pilot's head can cause the semicircular canals and inner ear to send false signals to the brain that the aircraft is moving in one direction when in fact it's moving in a counter direction. The eye normally corrects these false signals but in a situation of reduced or no visibility the eye has no reliable reference to make the needed corrections. These false signals in the pilot's brain can cause him to make mistaken corrections to the aircraft's attitude or flight path. In weather or in night conditions when the pilot's visibility is restricted this can cause the pilot to place the aircraft in an uncontrollable condition. If the pilot doesn't respond quickly and correctly, the aircraft and its crew can be lost. The only reliable source for proper attitude reference in flying is the aircraft's flight instruments. If the pilot can transition to them quickly and trust them, while at the same time disregard his physical senses, then he has a chance to save himself and the aircraft. The history of flight includes many stories where pilots experienced vertigo and had to fight to maintain aircraft control. Many pilots were unable to recover from the condition and thus lost their aircraft and their lives. Just turning one's head too quickly or leaning over to pick up an item dropped in the cockpit can bring on a vertigo episode while in conditions of reduced visibility. If a pilot was able to recover from a severe case of vertigo it usually left him nauseated and physically weak making the mission more difficult to safely complete. Knowing the dangers of vertigo, along with the fact that it can come on unpredictably at any time, pilots always have in the back of their minds the increased risk of flying in low visibility or night conditions.

However, it was going to be night missions for the next several weeks and the aircrews handled them like every other challenge they faced in Vietnam. They just did the mission, regardless of the dangers, difficulty, required flying skills or personal fears. The mission came first and everything else would just have to get in line. Aircrew members developed the ability to push their personal issues, including their doubts and fears, down deep within their souls. For many, they were pushed so deep that after the war it would take years to work through these issues, doubts and fears and to bring them to a satisfactory resolution.

Major Kilmer walked into the squadron building and immediately went into the target planning room. The other flight aircrew members were already in the room. This flight was not only going to be a night combat mission but was also going to be a night checkout for a new

Lead aircraft commander. It was common practice for a new aircraft commander to fly wingman with an experienced aircraft commander flying as Lead for the flight. After the wingman flew several missions in the number two position, he was given a checkout flight to see if he was ready to take on the role as Lead. He would have to plan, brief and lead a two or four ship flight in combat conditions. This training in the combat environment usually took ten to twenty flight sorties before the new aircraft commander was ready to lead a flight.

Major Kilmer would fly this night in the wingman position and evaluate if the new aircraft commander was ready to lead combat missions on his own. Kilmer's GIB for the mission was Captain Thomas Kern. Captain Kern had been a B-52 navigator for the last four years. He'd volunteered to transition to the F-4 and be trained as a weapon's officer. He'd grown tired of flying long missions in the B-52 and always landing back at the same airfield. He wanted a little more action and he was getting it. He'd already been shot down once in the F-4 and on another mission, after receiving battle damage over the target, had to make an emergency landing. His ejection, along with the frontseater, took place over Laos. Their F-4 had been hit by anti-aircraft fire during a bomb run on supply trucks moving down the Ho Chi Minh Trail. Their F-4, though badly damaged by the enemy ground fire, was able to take them several miles away from the target area before it became uncontrollable and required the two crewmembers to eject. The ejections with the Martin-Baker ejection seat went as advertised and both were able to parachute safely to the jungle floor. The rescue helicopter picked up Tom and his frontseater within 45 minutes. Tom had flown 176 combat missions in the F-4 in his nine months in country. His goal was to complete over 200 combat missions before he returned to the States. This was a goal that he was to accomplish.

The new aircraft Lead commander was Captain Randy R. Cutter III. Captain Cutter was an Air Force Academy graduate and had been a T-37 instructor pilot at Vance Air Force Base in Enid, Oklahoma for the last five years. He loved instructing in the T-37 and was good at it. The military training for Air Force pilots wasn't noted for its kind, friendly nature. In fact, the training was tough, fast, and matter of fact. A pilot trainee would either, keep the fast pace and make the grade, or they washed out. There were some limited make-up training opportunities for those who had trouble with the pace of the 53 weeks of training; however, they were limited.

Captain Cutter approached his training of T-37 pilots a little differently. He would take his students under his wing and work with them after hours to help them understand difficult concepts and overcome problems with their flying. His students appreciated his understanding and the extra time he would devote to them. As a result he gained the respect and admiration of his students. Many of them would keep in touch with him after they graduated and moved into their flying careers.

Captain Cutter was a good pilot and worked hard to be an excellent F-4 aircraft commander. Kilmer had little doubt that Cutter would get signed off this night as Lead.

Captain Cutter's backseater for the mission was Lieutenant Jose Gonzales. Lieutenant Gonzales was a recent graduate from pilot training and F-4 weapons school. Gonzales had been in country only two weeks and was still attempting to get settled at Phu Cat. He gave an immediate impression that he was a professional, levelheaded pilot and seemed to be making friends quickly. He was from Texas and never missed an opportunity to tell others this fact. He had, at this point in his combat tour, flown five combat missions. He was still wet behind the ears.

"Good evening Major, Jose, Tom," greeted Captain Cutter, "I'm glad to see you all came to the party."

"We wouldn't miss it for the world," answered Kilmer for the flight members. "What do we have going tonight Randy?"

"Well Sir, we have strikes planned on a suspected storage and truck staging area at Tchepone on the Trail. Intel is pretty damn sure that there are a lot of supplies and munitions parked there," responded Cutter. "Intel also predicts we will have a lot of enemy fire around Tchepone. It promises to be a big night with some challenges especially when you mix in the night and weather conditions."

Tchepone was a little village in northeastern Laos. The Ho Chi Minh Trail ran just to the east of Tchepone. It was one of the most highly defended areas in Laos. Crewmembers knew if they went there, they would probably have some real stories to tell.

"Roger that," responded Kilmer. "Tell us how you're going to handle this mission."

Cutter began to brief the crewmembers on his plan to get the mission accomplished successfully. It was soon obvious that Cutter had put a lot of thought and planning into the mission. He explained every detail of the mission and his expectations for all. When he'd completed explaining his plan for the successful completion of the mission he asked if there were any questions. There were no questions.

"Great briefing Randy," remarked Kilmer. "One of the best I've ever sat through."

"Yeah, great job," responded both Captain Kern and Lieutenant Gonzales.

"It was so good can we just stay home and say we did it," joked Kern.

Cutter just smiled at Kern and made no verbal response. It didn't need one.

"Let's call in the Intel and weather guys and get this thing done," remarked Kilmer.

"Yes Sir," responded Cutter, "I'll call them in right now to brief us."

The Intel and the weather officers came into the briefing room to give them the appropriate briefings. The Intel officer gave his briefing first.

"Gentlemen, you'll most likely have ground fire in the target area around Tchepone tonight. There has been 37 mm, automatic weapons and small arms fire reported in the local area for the last week. The enemy has something there that they don't want broken or destroyed. Let's break it and blow the hell out of it tonight. But be careful, we want you back in one piece."

"Damn straight," responded Cutter. "Remember the Big Picture, let's all go home when this is over."

The weatherman began his briefing. It wasn't really good news.

"Gentlemen," began the weather officer, "you're going to have layered clouds at several altitudes in the target area and the same for your return to base later tonight. The cloud layers will be scattered to broken through about nine thousand feet and will become an overcast layer at about twelve thousand feet extending upward to fifty thousand feet. At the flight levels you'll have possible icing conditions. That's the bad news. The good news is that I don't see any rain or thunderstorms in the forecast for now or later on during the evening. Oh! Just a little more bad news, with the thick overcast of the cloud layers, there will be no visible moon tonight, so it'll be black as hell out there with no visible horizon. Good luck and have a safe flight."

"Thanks gentlemen," responded Cutter to the Intel and weather officers, " we appreciate your help." The two officers left the briefing room.

"We won't take any unnecessary risks tonight on this mission," continued Cutter. "We have work to do to kill these trucks and destroy any weapons or ammo that might be in the storage area. There will more than likely be enemy fire directed at us. I don't want you to go too low just to kill a truck. Nor do I want you to make excessive passes on the target. Each extra run will bring an increased risk of being hit by ground fire. I want us to each plan on a maximum of two runs on the target unless the FAC directs otherwise. Nothing down there on the Trail is worth one of us. We need to be smart tonight. The weather will make it harder but let's stay together and get this damn thing in the logbooks. Any questions?" There were no questions.

"Okay, let's get suited up and get to our birds, the crew van will depart in one zero minutes," continued Cutter.

The crewmembers went to the equipment room and put on their flying gear and survival equipment. They made a last minute trip to the head and then boarded the crew van to head to their birds. The crews arrived at their aircraft and began the pre-flight of their respective F-4s with their bomb loads. Finding no significant problems, the crews climbed into their cockpits and strapped into their ejection seats. They completed their checklists and started their engines.

"Phu Cat Ground, Cobra 1 and 2 taxi," radioed Cutter.

"Cobra 1 and 2, taxi runway one-five, the wind is two-zero-zero degrees at five knots," responded Ground Control.

"Cobra 2, how do you read Cobra 1?" radioed Cutter.

"We read you loud and clear," answered Kilmer.

The two F-4Ds taxied to the end of the runway where their bombs were armed and the weapons crew chief gave them a ready signal.

"Cobra 2 go to Tower," radioed Cutter.

"Wilco, Cobra 2."

"Two, are you up?" radioed Cutter.

"Two is with you," answered Kilmer.

"Phu Cat Tower, Cobra 1 and 2 ready for takeoff, runway one-five," called Cutter.

"Cobra Flight cleared for takeoff, runway one-five have a good flight," responded the tower.

"Cobra Flight, cleared for takeoff."

The two F-4s taxied onto the runway and began their Before Takeoff checklists. The J-79s were exercised from idle to Mil power to make sure all the engine read outs were within proper range. Everything looked good. The flaps were positioned for takeoff and the checklists were completed. Cutter looked over at Kilmer's aircraft positioned on his right only a few feet back from the nose of Cutter's aircraft. He turned on, then off, his taxi light and Kilmer quickly flashed his taxi light, a signal that both F-4s were ready for takeoff. Cutter advanced the throttles to full military power and with a smooth continuous motion moved the throttles into afterburner position. Cutter's craft accelerated rapidly as it moved down the long runway. As soon as it hit rotation speed the nose of the F-4 started to bounce up and down trying to lift the heavy nose of the aircraft up into flying position. Cutter held the control stick full aft to get the nose of the aircraft off the ground as soon as possible and into climb attitude.

On the fourth bounce the F-4 made its move and its nose wheel came up off of the concrete runway. Cutter relaxed the backward stick pressure to catch and stop the nose at a ten degrees nose high attitude. Within seconds the heavy F-4 was airborne and climbing rapidly through scattered and broken layers of clouds. The sun had sat only minutes earlier so there was a little light that broke through the first layers of the thickening clouds. There was a sense of exhilaration and excitement as Cutter's climbing F-4 punched through layer after layer of clouds reaching for cruise altitude.

Kilmer followed and within a minute was on Cutter's wing in tight formation, only feet separated the two war birds. With every movement Cutter made, Kilmer was only a fraction of a second behind him. It seemed like the two birds were locked together with an invisible steel rod. Kilmer was a great pilot but he was an even better formation pilot. He could put his aircraft in position only feet away from the

Lead aircraft and never move from that location. There was no better formation pilot in the wing than Ron Kilmer.

The two F-4s climbed to their en route altitude of 29,000 feet. The clouds were thick and dark. The in-flight visibility was nearly zero. Kilmer could barely make out the outline of Lead's aircraft even though he was flying only feet away. He just kept the wingtip in the star.

The flight time to reach the target area in Laos seemed to pass especially quickly. Within 20 minutes after leveling off at altitude the two Cobras were approaching the target location a few miles below them.

"Cobra 2, go to the FAC's frequency now," called Cutter.

"We're on our way," responded Kilmer.

Both aircraft crews switched to the prearranged forward air controller's radio frequency.

"Cobra 2, are you on frequency?" Cutter continued.

"Roger that," answered Kilmer in response.

"Raven 1, Cobras 1 and 2 with you at Angels Two-Niner-Zero. Two F-4s with slick Mark-82s," radioed Cutter.

"Good evening Cobra Flight," answered Raven 1. "Come on down and join the fun. The bottom of the overcast layer is about ten thousand feet with only scattered clouds at nine thousand feet. In-flight visibility is good and the tops of the mountains in the area are no higher than six thousand feet MSL."

"Roger, we're on our way down," radioed Cutter.

The two F-4s began a descending left turn to lose altitude and get through the overcast layers of clouds. It was dark in the clouds with no reference at all to the horizon, the ground or sky. Descending through a dark, overcast sky at night into uncharted mountainous terrain is one of the most dangerous things that a fighter pilot can do. It takes a great amount of courage, faith and strength. It's the things of which nightmares are made. If an F-4 moving at 500 knots should hit the top of a mountain it would be all over in less than a second.

In what seemed a lifetime both F-4s broke out of the overcast clouds at 9,200 feet registered on their altimeters. They pulled up the noses of their birds to stop any further loss in altitude as they began to scan for the FAC.

"Cobra Flight, I have you at my 12 o'clock position about two miles.

Turn left ninety degrees and you'll be heading straight for me," radioed Raven 1. "The target is about one click at my 6 o'clock position. I'll fire a smoke rocket to pinpoint the target."

"Roger, we're turning toward you, and we do have you in sight," answered Cutter.

The FACs always liked it when the attacking aircraft called out that they were in sight. With several aircraft grouped together around a target and with the fighters traveling at high rates of speed it was good to know that visual contact was established.

"The smoke is away. When you have a visual on it, you're cleared onto the target," radioed Raven.

"We have your smoke and are turning to set up our run on the target," called Cutter.

"Damn, do you see that?" radioed Kilmer.

"I sure as hell do," radioed Cutter. "I'm aborting my run on the target and repositioning myself for a run with a different attack heading. I'll try a reposition about ninety degrees out."

The final approach to the target from Cutter's position had become alive with anti-aircraft fire. Flashes of bright light followed by black puffs of smoke peppered the darkening sky. There were hundreds of exploding anti-aircraft shells dancing along the northern approach to the target. The bursting shells laid a protective shield at least 2,000 feet thick.

"Ron, let's not fly through that crap, okay?" called Tom excitedly over the intercom.

"Don't worry Tom, we won't. That could ruin our whole day," responded Kilmer. "I'm going to adjust our heading into the target at least seventy degrees east to miss the fun stuff."

"I'm out of your way," radioed Raven 1. "Do whatever you need to do to kill the guns and get to the truck park. Good luck."

The two F-4s moved about 100 degrees from the original target heading before they could get a clear run to the target and stay out of the continuing pattern of ground fire. Cutter was first in with Kilmer tight on his tail, just far enough back to stay out of Lead's frag pattern. The first run on the target was good. After the first 500-pound bombs from the two F-4s exploded there were numerous secondary explosions in the target area.

"We're blowing the hell out of something down there," radioed Cutter.

"Yeah," responded Raven 1. "There are a lot of secondary explosions in the target area. It looks like you hit an ammo dump. A lot of crap is popping off. I also count at least three trucks burning. Come back again a little to the south. Maybe half a click."

"Wilco," responded Cutter. "We're in from the south. Two, are you behind me?"

"Roger, I'm on your ass, as close as I dare get," answered Kilmer.

The anti-aircraft fire began to be refocused. The enemy discovered that the F-4s were coming onto the target from a different heading so they began to circle the target with anti-aircraft fire. Bright flashes of light with black puffs of smoke began to surrounded the target. The two F-4s jinked from side to side to try and avoid the exploding flack that was protecting the target as they climbed to altitude to set up for another attack. While moving through the scattered layers of clouds, it was difficult to keep an eye on the target's location marked by burning trucks and exploding ammo. Both aircraft commanders worked hard to stay under the overcast cloud deck that was ragged with its base varying between nine and ten thousand feet. The unknown location of the invisible mountaintops in the area created additional concern among the crewmembers. It took total concentration to keep the aircraft properly oriented on the targets and stay away from the clouds, the mountainous terrain and the FAC.

The FAC requested repeated attacks on the target area as the F-4s were having phenomenal success at destroying multiple targets along the Trail. Each bombing pass brought new fires and secondary explosions. It was an exceptional evening of success for the attacking aircraft.

The Cobras decided to drop their bombs sparingly to continue to do as much damage as possible. The stress and fatigue of multiple attacks by the F-4s with the anti-aircraft fire and the dark, cloud-covered sky was wearing on the crewmembers. Still, not one had the thought of calling the attack off. Both crews willingly continued multiple attacks with great risk to themselves and their aircraft. Finally Lead, running short on ordnance, called an end to the attacks.

"Cobra 1 is on his last pass," radioed Cutter. "I only have two bombs left and I'll drop them on this run. What's your status Cobra 2?"

"Same, same, I'll be dry after this last pass," answered Kilmer. "I have you in sight and will join with you on climb out. Turn your beacon on when you're safe above the target so I can keep you in sight when we enter the soup."

"Roger, will do. Raven 1 we'll be off the target after this pass. Thanks for your help," radioed Cutter.

"Roger, Cobra Flight," called Raven 1. "Great job tonight. I'll report a BDA (bomb damage assessment) with at least eight trucks destroyed and six secondary explosions. You rained on somebody's parade tonight. Have a safe one home."

The last pass on the target was as bad as the others. The F-4s had to climb and dive and jink to stay clear of anti-aircraft fire, mountaintops and cloud bases. Their last attack caused more explosions and fires. It wasn't a good night for the bad guys.

Cutter was off the target and climbing for safety in full afterburner. It might not have been a good idea to be lit up with the burners going but it did give him separation from the ground and ground fire as quickly as possible. It also gave Kilmer a bright target on which to rejoin.

"Cobra 1, Cobra 2, give me a little power to catch up," radioed Kilmer.

"Roger, sorry about that," responded Cutter with a grin, "I'm so damn glad to get the hell out of that. I'm pulling it back to 97% power."

"I'll be joined with you in one," responded Kilmer.

Kilmer pulled up into tight wing formation, once again only feet separated the two aircraft.

"Let's go to en route freq," radioed Cutter.

"Roger, going now," responded Kilmer.

"You up Cobra 2?" called Cutter.

"Cobra 2 is with you."

The two F-4s were in black, thick clouds. There was no light from any source except the three small position lights on both aircraft. Kilmer had only the tiny wingtip light, along with the Air Force star painted on the F-4's fuselage to position himself on Cutter's F-4.

Then Kilmer began to struggle with flying his F-4. A strange feeling began to explode throughout his body. He felt like he, and his whole aircraft, were falling through the thick darkness. He had the sensation of rotating in space, now on his back falling through the dark sky. Fear gripped him. He thought, *what the hell is this?* A second, rapid visual check outside confirmed it; both F-4s had rotated onto their backs and were now falling inverted through the dark sky toward the ground. If correct action wasn't taken immediately, within seconds both aircraft would hit the ground inverted and both would be lost. How did this happen, how could both pilots have lost control so quickly?

Kilmer wanted to call for corrective action over the radio to Cutter but he couldn't pull his thoughts together rapidly enough to do it. He was still processing the information that was coming through his senses. His feelings were intense, as the uncontrollable falling through space on his back, started to bring on nausea. *Check your instruments! What do they say?* His thoughts screamed to him. This had been part of his training. *Trust your instruments and not your feelings.* He had heard it a thousand times before in his instrument training. He had repeated it many times to other pilots in their training. *Trust your instruments*!

Kilmer took his eyes off of the wingtip light and looked into his dimly lit cockpit with its reddish glow from his instrument lights. First he checked the attitude indicator (ADI) and then the vertical velocity indicator (VVI). Then his crosscheck went to the altimeter and airspeed indicator. All looked normal. They showed straight and level flight with normal air speed and attitude. What was happening? How can this be? Kilmer looked outside again at the wingtip and the star and the blackness. He was falling again. *"Oh God!"* he said to himself as he realized what was happening. His thoughts continued. *I've got vertigo and a bad case of it. I have to stay close to Lead to fly together in this soup, but when I look at Lead I begin to fall into the darkness.* Kilmer looked inside again to check his instruments. *Good, all is normal,* he thought, *we are not falling, we're okay, we're okay.*

Kilmer had no options. He had to fight through this. He had a bad case of vertigo but had to fly his F-4 on Lead's wing through this darkness. He got comfort looking at his instruments and being reassured that they were flying straight and level. When he looked outside the vertigo came back again and gave him the horrible sensations of falling and rotating. It was the most uncomfortable feeling he'd ever had in his life. He had experienced vertigo before, but not like this. He was nauseated and could hardly keep from throwing up in his oxygen mask. He reached for his oxygen regulator and flipped the switch to 100 % oxygen and pushed the pressure flow switch to deliver the oxygen under pressure. The cold 100% oxygen blowing in his mask and across his face helped. He spent the next ten to fifteen minutes fighting his feelings, dividing his time between keeping the wingtip light in the star and checking his instruments. Slowly he began to recover. He had shorter and shorter periods of the falling and rotating feelings. The nausea began to subside. By the time the two F-4s began their descent to land at Phu Cat, Kilmer was almost fully recovered from the vertigo. The falling and rotating sensations were gone. The two F-4s broke out of the clouds and could see the lights of the base. Kilmer made a call to Cutter.

"Cobra 1, Cobra 2, I'd like to request to land first if that's okay with you."

"Roger Cobra 2, you're cleared out of formation and cleared to go to tower," responded Cutter.

Kilmer broke out of formation and positioned his F-4 on initial for the pitchout to land. He called the tower for permission to land.

"Cobra 2, you're cleared to land runway one-five," radioed the tower.

"Roger," was Kilmer's only response as he made a normal pitchout and landing.

Cutter didn't ask Kilmer why he was in a hurry to land. Most thought it was just because he needed to hit the restroom. It would take a week before Kilmer was ready to talk about his vertigo experience and how it could have cost him and his backseater their lives. All who heard Kilmer's account of his experience listened and learned. They knew that if it could happen to a pilot of Kilmer's skills and experience, it could happen to them. When the horizon disappears and feelings provide a false path for action, it's important to trust the certainty of one's instruments for safe and steady guidance. There were so many ways to die in Vietnam.

13

Hung Bomb

It had been a long, hard day for the F-4 crews sitting alert at Phu Cat. The crew's alert duty day requirement was a twenty-four hour day with a maximum of three combat sorties flown. Lead aircraft commander Captain Larry Johnson, his backseater Lieutenant Jim Sour, the number two aircraft's commander, Captain Juan Webb, and his GIB, Lieutenant Dan Smith had already flown two combat missions today. The missions had been tough ones. Each had involved troops in contact (TIC), which meant that friendly forces were under attack from the bad guys. Both missions had been in support of isolated firebases that had come under attack by enemy forces. The enemy was good at picking opportune times for attack on these firebases. Usually they would pick times when the weather was bad and the cloud ceiling was low so that friendly attack aircraft found it hard, if not impossible, to provide relief by completing aerial attacks on enemy locations. Today was no exception. The weather conditions that allowed fighter support for these remote firebases had been questionable all day. However, today the F-4 crews had already scrambled twice to provide support to friendly forces under attack. The F-4 crews had made their way through the scud to help the friendlies. The combat mission requirements today, along with the stress of dealing with the bad weather, were taking their toll on the crewmembers. They had been on duty for 18 hours and had flown two difficult missions.

The crews wanted to sit out the rest of their duty day in the alert shack, grab a little rest and perhaps drink a cup of hot coffee.

Captain Johnson had the stress of his flying job, but he was also worried about the unknown medical condition of his wife. He received a letter from her, after a visit with their doctor, telling of a need for surgery. The doctor had discovered two small lumps in her right breast and believed it was best to remove the lumps surgically and have them biopsied. The operation was scheduled for the upcoming week and Captain Johnson was very concerned for his wife and the outcome of this procedure.

Like all military personal on remote tours of duty, personal feelings, fears and concerns had to be placed on the back burner of their minds. They had a job to do and the job, as cold as it may seem, had to come first. Communication with the outside world was difficult and usually took days. It was just a fact that feelings and concerns had to wait and be moved into the future for solution. This brought on added stress for military personnel but it was the way it was.

Johnson sat down in a chair in the alert shack and held his cup of coffee with both hands. In his mind, his thinking switched back and forth between the last two missions and the possible condition of his wife. He said a prayer that flying would be over for today. He was tired, unusually tired, and the coffee tasted so good. The warmth of it as it went down his throat sent a relaxing reaction through his body. He took another sip and put his head back on the chair's headrest as his body started to sink into the pillows of the chair.

"Ring. Ring." The alert phone rang loudly.

Oh God, thought Johnson as he dropped his coffee cup on the table with a loud bang.

"Alert shack, Captain Johnson," he answered as he picked up the phone.

"Yes Sir, we're on our way."

"It's a go guys," called Johnson to his fellow crewmembers. "Let's haul ass, we have TIC again."

The four crewmembers grabbed their flying gear as they ran through the door of the alert shack into the darkness and towards their F-4s. The sun had gone down a few minutes earlier and the moon was just rising about the eastern horizon. Within seconds they arrived at their awaiting aircraft with crew chiefs running around the F-4s getting them ready for engine start and for taxi. The crews hit the ladders of their aircraft in a dead run. Up the ladders they scrambled and crawled into their cockpits. The crew chiefs followed up the ladders to help the crewmembers strap on their F-4s.

Captain Johnson quickly gave the engine start hand signal to the crew chief and air was delivered to the number one J-79 for startup. With number one engine running Johnson gave the signal to light engine number two. In less than a minute both engines were running at idle power and Johnson called over the intercom.

"Jim is the INS ready and are your checks complete?"

"Roger Sir, the INS is up and I am ready to taxi," responded Sour.

Captain Johnson added power to the J-79 engines and taxied out of the concrete revetment and moved rapidly toward the runway.

"Phu Cat Tower, Cobra 1 and 2, scramble," radioed Johnson.

"Cobra 1 and 2, cleared to taxi runway three-three, call when ready for takeoff," radioed back the tower.

"Roger Tower, are you up Cobra 2?" continued Johnson.

"Number two is with you," responded Captain Webb.

Both F-4s taxied swiftly to the arming area at the end of runway three-three. The arming crews took little time pulling the safety pins from the ordnance under the wings of each F-4. The arming crew chief quickly gave the signal that both F-4s were armed and ready for takeoff.

Johnson started advancing power on both engines as he called the tower. "Phu Cat Tower, Cobra Flight ready for takeoff."

"Cobra 1 and 2, you are cleared for immediate takeoff," responded Tower.

"Roger, cleared for takeoff," radioed Johnson as he brought up both engines to Mil power and then into afterburner. The F-4 responded by immediately accelerating down the long dark runway and then broke ground and began its climb.

"Cobra 2, on the roll," radioed Webb.

Webb was airborne quickly and joined on Cobra 1's right wing. Both aircraft were airborne in less than three minutes from the time that they had received the alert.

Both F-4s were climbing through the darkness to altitude. Within minutes they were level at 30,000 feet or Angels Three-Zero-Zero and navigating toward their target location.

This was a good time for the crewmembers to look around their cockpits and check for any unaccomplished tasks they might have missed on the scrambled takeoff. It was rare but under the rush to get airborne crewmembers sometimes missed important items on their checklist. Some pilots even forgot to buckle their seat belts to the ejection seats. However, all looked good for both crews as they double-checked each checklist item.

The F-4s closed the distance to the target area and gave the forward air controller a radio call.

"Covey 1, Cobras 1 and 2 with you at Angels Three-Zero-Zero with hard bombs. How can we help tonight?" radioed Johnson.

"Cobra Flight, Covey 1, I have a special-forces base under attack by the NVA. The NVA have been on the attack all day and the firebase is taking a beating. I've pinpointed the location of the enemy artillery that's doing much of the damage. I need you to quiet it. I'll fire a smoke rocket near the artillery position and give you directions from there. Come on down through the overcast, the bottoms of the clouds are about nine thousand feet AGL and there are no high peaks in the area. High terrain isn't a factor."

"Copy that, we're on our way down," radioed Johnson.

From their positions both F-4s descended through the dark clouds. Down they both went through the darkness until they broke out of the clouds about 8,500 feet above the ground, just as advertised by Covey 1. It was always a good feeling to be able to see the ground when coming out of a cloud layer.

"I have you north of the target about five clicks," radioed Covey 1. "I'm rolling in now to fire the smoke rocket. Let me know when you see me and my marker."

"Roger," radioed Johnson, "we're turning south now and looking."

"I have you and the smoke," radioed Johnson. "Are we cleared onto the target?"

"A-firm, you're cleared in on the target. The target is one hundred meters southwest of my smoke. Kill those bastards and quiet their guns for good."

Both F-4s made repeated attacks on the artillery positions and continued dropping 750-pound bombs on the target location. After each attack the F-4s pulled up and off the target and tried to stay out of the overcast clouds. In the darkness, and with the F-4s moving so fast, both inadvertently climbed back into the clouds. This made their jobs more difficult as they had to keep track of their position relative to the target and then descend to get out of the dark clouds to make another run. They also had to try and keep track of the FAC flying below the clouds in the target area. It took a hell of a lot of concentration, flying skill and courage.

Finally the guns were stopped from firing on the special-forces compound.

"Good job, Cobra Flight," radioed Covey 1. "You've given the good guys a little relief tonight. Those guns that you just killed were pounding the hell out of them. They send you their sincere thanks."

"Send them our best wishes," responded Johnson. "Those ground pounders do one hell of a job."

"Will do," radioed Covey 1. "You both have a good flight home. You're cleared out of the target area."

"Roger," radioed Johnson. "Cobra 2, join on me. Let's go home."

"Wilco," responded Webb. "I'm on my way."

Webb rapidly gained altitude and initiated a rejoin on Cobra 1's right wing. As he pulled into position on Lead's right wing he made a call.

"Cobra 1, do you have a clean indication on your weapon's station lights?" radioed Webb. "If so you have a malfunction. You have a hung bomb on your number two station."

"I'm showing clean. You confirm I have a hung bomb?" responded Johnson.

"Roger, a 750-pounder is hung up. It looks like the back lug released but the front lug is holding fast. The bomb is jammed at about a 20 to 30 degree angle," continued Webb.

"Well, isn't that just friggin' great," responded Johnson. "I'll give a call and see if I can get a vector to an ordnance jettison area so I can try and get rid of this damn thing. Come up on 234.7."

"Roger, 234.7." responded Webb.

"Cobra 2, are you up?"

"Roger, Cobra 2 is on freq," responded Webb.

"Bongo Control," radioed Johnson. "Cobras 1 and 2 request."

"Cobras 1 and 2, Bongo Control, go ahead with your request," responded Bongo.

"Bongo Control," radioed Johnson, "Cobra 1 is six zero miles northwest of Phu Cat at Angels Two-Niner-Zero. I have a hung bomb. I'd like to have vectors to a safe location so I can try and get rid of the damn thing."

"Roger Cobra 1, fly heading one-five-zero degrees, Squawk 7321 and Ident. I'll vector you to the dump area. It's approximately four zero miles from you," radioed Bongo Control.

"Turning to one-five-zero degrees, Squawking 7321 and Ident," responded Johnson.

It seemed like the forty miles went very slowly but the two F-4s finally arrived in the ordnance dump area.

"Cobra 1, we have you in radar contact. You're in the dump area for the next one zero miles," radioed Bongo. "Do what you need to do to try and dislodge the bomb."

"Roger, thanks for the vectors," radioed Johnson.

"Cobra 2, stay well clear of me. I'm going to try pulling positive and negative Gs to get this thing loose. I don't want you to be close by."

"Will do," responded Webb. "I'm high above you and have moved well away."

Johnson yanked and banked and tried putting both positive and negative Gs on the F-4 to shake the bomb loose. He even tried jettisoning the whole bomb rack that held the bombs on the aircraft. Nothing worked, the bomb stayed hung on the underside of the right wing. After a few minutes in the ordnance jettison area fuel started to become a concern.

"Cobra 2, Cobra 1," radioed Johnson. "It's decision time. I need to either land with the hung bomb or we need to eject. I don't like either option. Come in closer and give me a look see, tell me the status of the bomb."

"Roger," responded Webb. "I'm moving in now to look you over."

In less than 30 seconds Webb was under Johnson's right wing looking at the hung bomb.

"It hasn't changed a bit. It looks exactly the same," radioed Webb.

"It's hung at the nose of the bomb at the same angle of about 30 degrees."

"Okay," responded Johnson. "We're going home and we're going to land with the damn thing. I want you to land first and clear the runway as quickly as you can. I'll land next and make as smooth a landing as I can. Go to tower frequency now so I can give them a heads up."

"Roger, going to tower now," radioed Webb.

"Phu Cat Tower, Cobras 1 and 2," radioed Johnson.

"Cobra Flight, Phu Cat Tower, go ahead," responded the tower.

"Phu Cat Tower, Cobra Flight is 20 minutes out. Cobra 1 has a hung bomb. I've tried repeatedly to shake it loose but it won't dislodge. Cobra 2 will land first and then Cobra 1 will land with the hung bomb. Please notify all appropriate groups including bomb disposal. I'm declaring an emergency."

"Roger," responded the tower, "I understand you're declaring an emergency and that you have a hung bomb. Cobra 2 will land first. I'll move all air traffic out of your way. Cobra 2 and Cobra 1 you're both cleared to land. Emergency and bomb disposal crews will be standing by. Good luck."

"Thanks," responded Johnson. "We're fifteen minutes out."

"Well Jim, never a damn dull moment," radioed Johnson over the intercom to Sour.

"Yes Sir," responded Lieutenant Sour. "You just can't make this kind of stuff up. If the bomb falls off when we land, do you think it might explode?"

"Who the hell knows? It's not supposed to without spin up on the nose fuse. But they're not supposed to hang up on delivery either. Both systems are advertised as fool proof. Well, we're about to write a new chapter in both books tonight."

"How about touching down real easy on this one? Easier than the first two landings you made today," continued Sour with a grin on his face and laugh in his voice.

"Thanks Jim," responded Johnson, "I needed that."

As both aircraft approached Phu Cat, Johnson made a call to Webb. "Cobra 2 you have the lead. Move ahead of me now. I'll join in loose trail about two minutes behind you. Remember to clear the runway as quickly as possible. I only want to have to make one pass over the field with this hung bomb."

"Roger," responded Webb, "Cobra 2 has the lead. Good luck Cobra 1."

"You have the lead," responded Johnson.

Cobra 2 pushed up the power on his J-79 engines to give additional separation from Cobra 1. Cobra 2 flew down initial and made a normal pitch out for landing. He made a quick downwind and turned a short base to final approach.

"Cobra 2 you're cleared to land runway one-five," radioed the tower.

"Roger, Cobra 2 cleared to land one-five," responded Webb.

Webb made a perfect landing and immediately deployed his drag chute, climbed on the brakes to slow down and cleared the runway as quickly as possible. He was swiftly off the runway and into the de-arming area. The emergency crews were lined up along the taxiway but away from the runway just in case the hung bomb might dislodge and explode. The fire trucks were standing by with their engines running and their lights flashing.

"Okay Jim, here we go, I'm going to land this damn thing," radioed Johnson over the intercom.

"Roger Sir, it'll go well," remarked Sour.

Just in case the bomb fell off, Cobra 1 made a long, wide downwind away from the base without the normal pitchout maneuver for landing. This required Johnson to pull the power back early to let the airspeed bleed off slowly so he could lower the landing gear. Johnson didn't want to put any unnecessary G load on the F-4 with the chance the bomb might fall onto the base. He stayed well clear of populated areas around the base.

Within a short time, Cobra 1 was on final approach and lined up in the middle of the runway. He flew a shallow final approach angle to the runway to achieve a minimum descent speed. He wanted this landing to be as smooth as possible.

"Cobra 1 you're cleared to land," radioed the tower.

"Roger," was Johnson's only reply.

The F-4 touched down smoothly with very little impact force with the runway. Then all hell broke loose! Showers of sparks began pouring over the wing of the F-4. It was like a comet had landed under the aircraft. The intensity of the sparks was so bright that Johnson couldn't see the runway lights on the right side of the aircraft. He looked down at the front of the wing and saw what was making the shower of sparks. It was the 750-pound bomb. It had broken loose from the lug that had been holding it so tightly. The bomb was skidding along the runway with its nose slightly in front of the right wing.

Johnson didn't know what to do. Several options rapidly ran through his head and none of them were good. *Do I try and stop and risk the bomb blowing up under us or do I attempt to takeoff and risk the bomb exploding just as we get airborne, blowing us out of the sky*? There wasn't time for deep reflection only reaction. Johnson climbed on the binders and deployed his drag chute. The nose of the F-4 sank down as maximum effort was used to stop the huge bird. Johnson and Sour could feel the anti-skid braking system working overtime to stop the F-4. The tires would repeatedly lock up, then release, then lock up. This cycling of the anti-skid system was constant and effective as it attempted to halt the forward movement of the aircraft.

Both the F-4 and the bomb began to decelerate. At first it seemed that they were doing so at the same rate. The bomb slid along the side of the F-4 with sparks filling the air around it. It had a strange beauty about it, a deadly beauty should the bomb explode. Slowly the decelerating F-4 began to open some distance between it and the bomb. The bomb made unpredictable turns and rolls as its fins were worn down. It continued down the runway as the F-4 made a complete stop. At once Johnson fully engaged the right brake, added full power to the left engine and turned the big war bird 180 degrees around on the runway. Then he brought up the power in both engines and quickly backtracked down the runway away from the bomb.

The emergency and bomb crews took immediate command of the situation, moved in, inspected and then defused the bomb. The safety mechanism of the bomb had worked as advertised and the bomb didn't explode.

Johnson and Sour taxied into the parking area and shut down the engines. Both were tired as hell but were very thankful to be climbing out of their aircraft in one piece. Neither spoke much about the incident that night other than to tell the facts to the Intel officers during the normal post-flight briefing.

The alert duty was now over and the four crewmembers of Cobras 1 and 2 went to the Officer's Club to celebrate that fact. They had a few drinks as the Cobra crews relived the details of this mission and the other two they'd flown earlier. Several of their flying buddies listened to the stories of the day's missions and helped celebrate their safe return to base.

After a couple of hours, Johnson and Sour left the Club and went to their BOQ rooms to try and get some sleep. However, these kinds of days weren't conducive to sleep. The events of the day including dropping tons of bombs on enemy artillery, aiding friendlies in trouble, dodging ground fire, navigating through bad weather, and flying home with a hung 750-pound bomb weren't the ingredients of a good night's sleep. Finally exhaustion won out and they drifted to sleep. However, their minds were filled with the thoughts and nightmares of this very busy day and what could've happened.

A week and a half later, Johnson received a letter from his mother reporting that the surgery had gone well. His wife was recovering nicely and the biopsy report was normal. He just filed it away in the depths of his soul to deal with some day in the distant future. He was thankful for the good news, but the new challenges each day of this tour demanded all of his strength, concentration and dedication. His emotions had to continue to be placed on hold. He had the rest of a year to complete and that demanded his total commitment to duty and mission.

14

The Trip Home

Because today was a scheduled non-flying day for Lieutenant Ben Stone, he was working duty as a squadron-scheduling officer. Pilots didn't fly air combat missions everyday. There were non-combat missions that might send them to pick up or deliver an F-4 to Taiwan for Inspection and Repair as Necessary (IRAN), or there were special missions to Thailand to deliver or pick up equipment needed back at the home base. When not assigned a flying mission, pilots were given other special duties in the squadron to make sure they always had a long duty day.

In 1969, most F-4 pilots flew between 200 and 220 combat missions during their year tour of duty in Vietnam. This meant that pilots would fly missions approximately two out of every three days. This would provide time during the typical Southeast Asia assignment for a crewmember to be provided a two-week Rest and Relaxation (R & R) time that could be taken at several locations. These could include either Hawaii or Australia.

Today Lieutenant Stone was working, along with two other lieutenants, on the flight schedule for the next two days. The two lieutenants were Jim Scott and Andy White. Scott was a pilot backseater from Montana and White was a navigator backseater from Kansas. Both had only been in Vietnam for two months.

At 0900 the Squadron Operations Officer, Lieutenant Colonel Terry Gibbs walked up to Stone and the other lieutenants.

"Good morning gentlemen, how's the scheduling going?"

"Going fine Sir," replied each of the young lieutenants.

"Hey Stone, you're a short timer aren't you?" questioned Gibbs.

"Yes Sir, I am," replied Stone. "I have twenty-nine days and a wakeup. I'm really ready to get back to the world."

Gibbs knew that Stone was due to rotate back to States at the end of the month of December. Gibbs had a motive behind his question. He was looking for some volunteers. He knew to get anyone to volunteer he'd have to offer something big in return. Getting short timers to volunteer for anything was almost impossible. When crewmembers got close to their rotation date back to the States, they became very careful about their missions and what they got involved in. They hadn't spent the last eleven months flying combat missions and working to stay alive just to be killed in the last two to three weeks of their tour. Some crewmembers even went so far as to have minor medical procedures done to take them off flying status for a few days. It wasn't uncommon for crewmembers to have their wisdom teeth pulled during the last few weeks of their tour. This would medically ground them for a week or so and consequently take them off the flying schedule. However, this wasn't for Stone. He'd decided to see it through to the end, whatever the assignments, but no volunteering!

All pilots and navigators heard stories about crewmembers that had been shot down and either killed or captured near the completion of their tour. This seemed like a double tragedy, given their rotation date. Many crewmembers became superstitious about their rotation date and events during their last month in country. This caused them to be very concerned and careful about even a normal mission.

"Stone, how'd you like to have two weeks taken off your tour and get back home in time for Christmas?" asked Gibbs.

"Wow," remarked Stone, "that sounds like a good thing. Just what are you thinking that could make this happen?"

"We need some volunteers to fly some older F-4C models back to the States," replied Gibbs. "It'd get you back home about two weeks earlier. Let me know if you're interested. I need to turn in the names to Wing by tomorrow."

"Yes Sir," replied Stone, "I'll let you know for sure by tomorrow. Do you have any more details about the mission?"

"The only other information I have," continued Gibbs, "is that you'd depart from Cam Ranh Bay on or about the fifteenth of the month and head home."

"Thank you Sir," replied Stone, "that helps a lot. I'll get back to you ASAP."

"Good," remarked Gibbs, "talk with you tomorrow. Gentlemen, thanks for doing a good job on the scheduling."

"Thank you Sir," replied the young lieutenants.

Gibbs left the three lieutenants and walked down the main hallway that led to his office area.

Stone turned to Lieutenants Scott and White with some obvious doubt expressed on his face concerning the information he just received.

"It'd be great to be home for Christmas," replied Stone, "but it'd also be nice to take the Freedom Flight home and let someone else do the flying."

The Freedom Flight was the name given by military personnel to the military contracted commercial flights back to the States. These flights were a time for great celebration for the veterans who were returning after a year away from their loved ones. Stone had looked forward to this flight back to the world for months.

"Yeah Stone," remarked Scott, "the Freedom Flight would be great but just think you'd be out of this place two weeks early. That's a good deal."

"Yes," replied Stone, "it sure beats getting my teeth pulled."

All three of the men laughed at the remark and the thought of pulling teeth to stay off the duty schedule.

Stone thought about his options carefully throughout the evening and the early part of the next morning. The more he thought of it, he really had no choice. He wanted to get home for Christmas even if that meant that he would have to fly an old F-4 home to get there. The Freedom Bird was great but the two weeks that would be saved seemed like a lifetime. Stone made his decision and he could hardly wait to tell Gibbs his answer. The next morning, as soon as he had finished breakfast he headed down to the squadron building and proceeded to Gibbs' office. As he approached, Gibbs looked up and saw Stone. Before

Stone could say a word he said, "Come on in Stone. I've been waiting for your answer."

"I'm in," responded Stone. "I want to be home for Christmas."

"Great," he replied, "I'll get the paperwork started today and I'll obtain more details about the flight as soon as I can. Whatever the case, we'll have a briefing on the details of the ferry flight mission within a couple of days. We'll hate to lose you here in the squadron but we'll see you again. The Air Force is family."

"Thank you Sir," answered Stone. "Thanks for the opportunity to get home early."

For the next couple of days no word was provided on the details of the mission to ferry home the older F-4Cs. Finally the word started filtering down the chain of command to the squadron. A briefing was called the next day at 1500 hours in the squadron briefing room. The time passed quickly and Stone was in the squadron briefing room early ready for the briefing. The room was only about a third filled when the briefing was scheduled to begin. As is military custom the room was called to attention as Gibbs entered the room.

"R-o-o-m A-t-t-e-n-t-i-o-n!" cried one of the officers in the room.

Everyone in the room stood and came to attention.

"Be seated gentlemen," replied Gibbs. "Let's get this meeting underway. I have the information you've been waiting to hear. You'll take a scheduled transport flight from here to Cam Ranh Bay on 16 December at 1300. You'll then RON (Remain Over Night) at Cam Ranh Bay with a scheduled departure for CONUS on 17 December. Any additional details will be provided to you at a 0500 hours briefing on the 17th. Are there any questions?"

There were no questions from the group. Everyone seemed stunned by the announcement.

"Gentlemen, seeing no questions, have a great day," finished Gibbs as he began to exit the room.

"R-o-o-m, A-t-t-e-n-t-i-o-n!" cried one of the captains in the room.

All of the men in the room stood and came to attention.

"Carry on," called the captain as Gibbs left the room.

It was a time of mixed emotions for all the men involved in this mission. They could hardly believe that the day they'd been praying for and had worked so hard for was now so close at hand. They would be completing their tour of duty in less than two weeks and would be heading home to their loved ones and to new assignments. However, they would also be leaving their buddies that they'd fought and trained with for the last few years. The thought of separation from some of these deep friendships was hard. There were thoughts of their buddies who would never be going home. These were friends lost in combat, many whose remains were lost in the jungles of Vietnam or Laos. These difficult thoughts were hardly ever discussed openly.

Surprisingly for Stone the next two weeks went by very fast. He flew five more combat missions in Laos and two more in country. Each mission seemed to have an additional load attached to it. There was an increasing anxiety that something might go wrong on each mission and he'd be lost or captured and not get to make that flight to Cam Ranh Bay on 16 December. However, nothing went wrong and that last flight came and was completed successfully on the 15th December.

The men who were to leave the next day each had a short celebration after their last mission flight. That night, they also had scheduled a last mission party at the Officer's Club. It was a wonderful time with all the squadron members present. There were congratulations from all of the men and a few speeches from commanding officers. The wine and liquor were present in abundance. It was a bittersweet time with a lot of joy and some sadness. It was a dream come true for the men who would be leaving the next day for Cam Ranh Bay.

The next day was business as usual in the squadron except for the flight crewmembers who were scheduled to depart for Cam Ranh Bay at 1300 hours. They were nervously hanging around the squadron waiting for their flight. They each had a small duffel bag packed with a clean flight suit, fresh change of underwear and basic toilet items. That's all they were allowed to carry with them. The rest of their belongings had been packed and were to be shipped back to the States. The F-4s they were to ferry home had limited space for carrying personal items.

Soon it was 1300 hours and a C-7 Caribou landed ready to take them to Cam Ranh Bay. The squadron commander and operations officer, along with several members of the squadron who weren't flying, came out to the tarmac to see their friends off. It was a joyous and meaningful time as good friends and faithful warriors departed and went their separate ways to continue their lives and their service to the nation.

The flight in the Caribou was uncomfortable. The Caribou didn't climb high and it was a hot humid afternoon. The F-4 pilots remarked to each other that this was a strange and certainly different type of flying. The flight was slow, hot, and bumpy, with no air conditioning for passenger comfort. All the passengers were glad when the flight was completed successfully at Cam Ranh Bay.

The arriving crewmembers for the F-4 ferry flight scheduled for the next morning were assigned crew-sleeping quarters for the night. Captain Lawson and Lieutenant Stone were assigned to the same building. The sleeping arrangements involved an assigned cot in a large dorm style room with community bath and restroom facilities. The large room wasn't air-conditioned but big screened windows let in the cool breeze that was almost always available from the nearby ocean beaches.

Stone had noticed the white open beaches at Cam Ranh Bay as they flew over them for landing. After he got settled in with his sleeping accommodations he walked the short distance from his quarters to the open shoreline. It was a miraculous sight. The white clean sandy beaches ran as far as the eye could see from north to south. The aqua blue ocean waves hit the white sand in rhythmic fashion. It was a beautiful sight. Stone wondered how long it would be before there were large American hotels built along these beautiful beaches to advance vacationing and tourism from the States. It was a thought that never became a reality; however, it was a beautiful area and Stone's memory of it would never be forgotten.

Stone walked back to the barracks and laid down on his cot for a short nap. What seemed like only a moment of rest ended when Lawson began shaking Stone's left shoulder.

"Hey Stone," yelled Lawson, "you going to sleep this war away? It's 1750 let's get something to eat before I starve."

"Okay, Captain A," replied Stone. "Man, I was really stacking the Z's. I didn't mean to sleep so long. I just laid down for a short nap. I guess I've been sleeping for a couple of hours."

Stone got up off the cot and both he and Captain America walked to the chow hall for dinner. There was nothing special about the mess chow; the food wasn't bad, but certainly not good either. Items offered included salisbury steak covered with a thick, dark brown greasy gravy, instant potatoes, canned green beans and canned stewed tomatoes. There was a very dry white cake for dessert. After dinner they both poured themselves cups of thick black coffee and sat down to talk about the upcoming mission the next morning.

"Do you think we'll fly all the way back to the States in one flight?" asked Stone.

"No, I think we'll have at least one stop-over and maybe two," answered Lawson. "It's a seven to eight thousand mile trip over the pond from here to the West Coast and that'd be just too many hours to sit in a fighter's small seat. Our butts would fall off when we landed in the States."

"Yeah, my butt gets numb on only a two hour mission," laughed Stone. "It'll be tough to sit six or seven hours on a single leg of the trip. However, it'll get us home for Christmas and that's a big deal."

The two men went back to their barracks and turned in early to get a good night's sleep before the big briefing and flight the next day. Both men slept well but the 0400 alert and the 0500 briefing came too early. The men proceeded to the community shower room hoping that a good shower would awaken them and help them be alert for the big day.

Lawson and Stone finished their showers, shaved and dressed in their flight suits for the morning briefing and the anticipated first leg of their flight to freedom. After getting dressed they made their way a few hundred yards down to the building where the briefing was to be held. They arrived about 15 minutes early and went into the briefing room. The room was already half-full of officers who would also be making the flights home. The briefing began at exactly 0500 hours.

"Gentlemen, keep your seats," began the full bird colonel that was clearly in charge of the briefing for the mission home. "First, congratulations to all of you who've completed your tour here in Vietnam. Your country and the Air Force both appreciate your sacrifice. Now let me give you the big picture of this planned mission to bring you and sixteen of our old F-4C models back to the States. These C models have served us well for many years and it's now time to take them back home to new assignments. Assisting us with this mission will be five KC-135 tanker aircraft. Will the crewmembers of the tankers please stand up? Thank you gentlemen for your assistance. Please be seated. Will the F-4 crewmembers please stand up? Thank you gentlemen.

"The overview of the mission is that at 0800 the five tankers will takeoff and turn to an easterly heading and space themselves about fifteen hundred feet apart. Four minutes later the F-4s will begin their takeoff rolls at thirty-second intervals. Each F-4 will begin joining on the tankers from left to right. Each tanker will have a maximum of four F-4s joined on it. The fifth tanker will serve as a spare. F-4s may also join on it. When a tanker has four F-4s, newly joining F-4s will move to another tanker. Each F-4 will stay with his tanker for the entire trip back to the States.

"The entire group of KC-135s and F-4s will make two stops and RON. The first stop will be Andersen AFB, Guam; the second will be Hickam AFB, Hawaii. After departing Hickam your destination will be George Air Force Base, Victorville, California. Upon landing at George you will be debriefed and dismissed to your new locations. Are there any questions?"

There were several questions about proper radio frequencies, abort and emergency procedures. The colonel gave short but clear answers to all the questions. He closed with the following remarks:

"Remember to keep your fuel tanks full at all times just in case there's a malfunction with the air to air refueling equipment. To accomplish this the fighters will cycle on and off the tankers at all times. Once an F-4 is topped off he will move to the outboard section of the tanker's wing. Then an inside F-4 will cycle onto the boom and top off his tanks, then move to the other outboard wing. This will keep your tanks as full as possible should you need to divert in an emergency. Remember there will still be times, even with full tanks, you won't be able to reach a landing field. You'll have to eject into the ocean. However, your full tanks will give us time to get a rescue ship headed your way and to vector you toward the ship. Let's don't have to go there.

"One more important point, if your aircraft should break for any reason during the trip and you can't make the takeoff time, you and your aircraft will be left behind. We have no idea how long you'll have to wait to continue the trip home. We've no plans at this point to bring home stragglers. In that situation you could be waiting a month to six weeks before tankers can get back to take you home. So make sure your bird is broken before you call it. Once you call it broken you'll be grounded. Is that clear?"

No one in the room said a word but everyone seemed to get the message. Don't call a broken aircraft unless it's really, really unsafe to fly.

With the colonel's briefing completed the Intel and weather briefings began. The Intel officer didn't have much to say since the mission was to leave Vietnam and any hot zones. The weather briefing was also short since the weather conditions were forecast to be good VFR for the first leg of the trip to Guam.

With the briefings completed the men were dismissed to get their flying gear and grab a quick cup of coffee and sweet roll before engine start up time.

Lawson and Stone soon found their way to their aircraft and started to look it over. It was clear from the physical appearance of the old C model that it had seen a lot of wear and tear. There was nothing about the bird that looked unsafe, but it just didn't seem to have the care and upkeep that both Lawson and Stone had been used to. The F-4D models that they'd flown the last year had seen excellent maintenance. However, this was the bird they'd been assigned and the one scheduled to take them home. It still looked good.

The aircraft's preflight was completed and both Captain America and Stone climbed into their cockpits to do their Starting Engines checklist. Soon all checklists were completed, engine start time arrived and Lawson called for air to start both the J-79s. Both engines started normally, engine instruments were in the green range and Lawson pulled out of the revetment that had housed the F-4. The aircraft's radios became alive with the tankers and F-4s checking in with the tower and the Flight Lead aircraft. The collection of five KC-135s and sixteen F-4s was quite a sight to behold as they moved down the taxiway toward the departure runway.

The plan for the departure sequence was for the KC-135s to depart before the F-4s. The first cell of KC-135s departed with only a one-minute spacing between each tanker. Then the second cell of two KC-135s departed three minutes later with one minute spacing between the tankers. The F-4s waited three minutes and then began departing at 30-second intervals. The F-4s joined on the tankers who were flying in loose formation. The F-4s took positions on the tankers filling positions from left to right with a maximum of four F-4s on each tanker. Once all the F-4s had joined with the tankers the entire group climbed as high as the tankers could fly and still off load fuel to the fighters. The fighters immediately began to cycle on and off the tankers to top off their fuel tanks.

Captain America and Lieutenant Stone were number eight in the F-4 sequence. As their F-4 broke ground and began to climb Lawson called to Stone over the intercom.

"Ben, I think we may have to eject from this thing," warned Lawson.

"Sure Captain America, our last flight in country and eject, nice joke," answered Stone.

"I'm not kidding, I can hardly control this thing in roll. I have full aileron trim to the left and it wants to roll right. It's taking both my hands to keep it from rolling. Take the stick and let me know what you think. I'm checking the gauges and I don't see anything out of limits. You have the aircraft," radioed Lawson.

"I have the aircraft," responded Stone. "Damn, I see what you mean. It does take both hands to keep it straight and level. I'll check circuit breakers back here for any electrical issues. Is the hydraulic pressure good?"

"Yeah, the pressures are all good," answered Lawson. "I have the aircraft back. Check the flight controls outside to see if you can see anything out of line."

"You have the aircraft," responded Stone as he shook the stick. This was a required call and physical signal for exchange of control from one pilot to the other.

Lawson responded, "I have the aircraft." He also shook the stick to show change of command of the aircraft. "Look back at the wings and check to see anything on the control surfaces or anything loose on the wings themselves."

"I think I see the problem," called Stone as he looked back to the trailing edge of both wings. "It looks like the ailerons may be out of rig. I have quite a droop on one side. I don't remember the limits but I've never seen this much difference in the alignment of the ailerons. The right flap also looks like it's not flush with the wing. I think we have an alignment problem, probably brought on from years of combat flying with a lot of stress on the aircraft. Do you think we can fly it home?"

As Lawson joined on the right wing of the number three tanker he continued his discussion with Stone.

"I think if we take turns holding this damn thing we can fly it home," continued Lawson. "I'm a little nervous about holding the bird in position during air refueling. It'll take a lot of strength and concentration to keep her in position for the boom to stick us and then to keep us plugged in. What do you want to do? Keep going or go back and declare an emergency and land? I'm willing to try it if you are."

"Damn, nothing like an easy decision here," answered Stone. "I sure as hell don't want to go back to Cam Ranh Bay and spend who knows how long getting home. However, I don't want to have to eject out over the Pacific Ocean and hope someone can pick us up in a week or two. I don't really care much for water. All the gauges still look good?"

"Yes, everything is in the green."

"Well, let's keep going then if you're okay with it," continued Stone. "Just when I thought the fun was about over, we get this. Oh well, it don't mean nothing."

For the next several hours, as the group of aircraft headed for Guam, Lawson and Stone took turns flying the bent F-4. Both pilots used their right knee and right arm between the stick and the wall of the cockpit to serve as a block to keep the aircraft from rolling to the right and becoming inverted. It took too much pressure for just the arm to keep the aircraft in level flight for any length of time. When it was their turn to refuel on the tanker they would switch control to the pilot who hadn't been flying for a while. The rested pilot, with great difficulty, would hold the F-4 in position to take on fuel. As soon as refueling was completed, the pilots would change control again, so that the refueling pilot could get a break.

The hours went by slowly as the distance began to narrow between the eastern shoreline of Vietnam and Guam, which was a tiny spot in the vast Pacific Ocean. Flying in the small, restricted cockpit of a fighter is very different than flying in the cabin of a modern jet airliner. There are no soft drinks, nuts or even music to listen to and more importantly not even the ability to stand up and stretch one's legs and go to the restroom. The only restroom available was what was affectionately called the piddle pack. It's a small plastic sack filled with absorbent granules. The crewmember, still sitting in his ejection seat, loosens his seat belt, unzips the lower section of his flight suit and makes an attempt to fill the plastic bag. It isn't great, but it provides much needed relief after flying for several hours. Now, where to store the plastic sack? There's no extra space in the cockpit of a modern fighter.

Finally, after a little over six hours of flying time and flying over 2,500 miles of ocean, Andersen Field at Guam came into view. The weather was clear and the F-4s pulled back from their tankers and joined into flights of three or four aircraft. The tankers landed first. Then each of the F-4s entered initial and pitched out and landed. This first leg of the flight home was about 2,500 miles. The next leg would be longer, flying from Andersen to Hickam Air Field, Hawaii was a distance of over 3,500 miles. For now it was nice for all the F-4 pilots to pull their tired, numb butts out of a very small cockpit and head for a good meal and rest for the next flight that would leave early in the morning.

The morning wake up call came very early. The engine start time was 0700 so all the crews were up at 0500 to get showered and dressed for the next leg of the flight home. The morning was beautiful with the temperature in the eighties with a gentle breeze blowing over the airfield. The F-4 crews were not overjoyed about climbing into their small cockpits again for a very long flight to Hickam. However, like all their flights for the last year, it was something that needed to get done and they were going to do it.

After a quick breakfast all aircrew members came together for a short briefing on how the flight from Guam to Hickam was planned. The briefing held nothing really new that hadn't been covered in the briefing flying out of Vietnam. It did include a reminder that if an F-4 broke, its two crewmembers would stay at Andersen for an undetermined amount of time until tanker arrangements could be scheduled. This might take at least a month to put in place. No one wanted to be in that group.

Lawson and Stone didn't say anything about the flight condition of their F-4. They were afraid that if they said anything, the bird would be grounded for repairs and they'd be stuck in Guam away from their families over the Christmas holidays. Instead they just went to their aircraft and gave it a normal pre-flight check. All looked good except for the out of rig flight control surfaces. Both knew what to expect from the tired old bird and believed that even if it were bent up a little, it would still fly them home.

They climbed into their cockpit areas and went through their Starting Engines checklist. With the engines started, Lawson double-checked all the instrument readings on the engines and operating systems. All looked good.

The takeoff was almost an exact repeat of the day before. Three KC-135s took off with one-minute separation between aircraft. After three minutes the remaining tankers took off with one-minute separation. Then the F-4s began their take off to join with the tankers. The flight Lead took off followed by all the remaining F-4s in thirty-second intervals. The F-4s joined on the same tankers that they'd joined on yesterday as the group climbed to FL220 and picked up a heading for Hickam. The F-4s could, of course, climb higher and fly faster than the KC-135s but they needed the gas from the tankers so they throttled back and flew at the tankers refueling altitude to always have access to the precious JP-4 that would allow them to make the long journey to the Hawaiian Islands. The flight would take a little over eight hours to complete and cover a distance of approximately 3,600 miles.

For Lawson and Stone the flight characteristics of their F-4 had not improved. Lawson struggled to keep it wings level for about 45 minutes before he turned it over to Stone for refueling.

"Hey Stone, it's our turn on the boom, will you take the bird to get the gas? My arm is cramping up," requested Lawson.

"Sure, not a problem. I have the aircraft," answered Stone as he shook the stick.

"You have the aircraft," responded Lawson. "Damn, my arm is cramping and my fingers are numb. I hope we can fly this thing for seven or so more hours. I don't feel like being fish food today."

"Yeah, the warm water down there with our blood in it will bring out the sharks," answered Stone with a laugh. "Don't worry, Captain America can fly this thing even if he has to use his feet to do so," continued Stone. "Captain America can do anything."

This brought a smile and a laugh from both the pilots.

Stone moved the F-4 off the wing of the tanker, positioned it behind the tanker, and started moving up an imaginary line toward the boom operator.

"Hold it right there," radioed the KC-135 boom operator. "I can stab you right there, open your refueling door."

"Refueling door coming open," reported Lawson as he flipped the air refueling door switch.

Within a second and a half the F-4 crewmembers felt a definite positive stick of the refueling boom against the refueling valve.

"We have connection and you are taking fuel," reported the boom operator.

"Roger, we're taking gas," confirmed Lawson.

Stone's right arm moved slightly but briskly as he tried to get more support from the lower wall of the cockpit to hold the control stick in proper position. This caused the F-4 to move up and then down on the boom line.

"Hold on there guys," radioed the boom master. "Keep it smooth and steady."

"Sorry about that," responded Stone. "I was just scratching my nose. All done with that now."

"Cool!" radioed the boom master. "My gauges show that you're full. You're cleared off the tanker. I'll see you again in a few miles."

"Roger," responded Stone. "Cleared off the boom and will be moving to your left wing. Thanks for the gas."

Stone pulled the throttles back slightly and lowered the nose of the F-4 to move down below the KC-135. He then put in a slight amount of aileron, added a little power and moved to the proper position on the tanker's left wing.

The process of flying formation on the tankers, and taking turns to take on gas, lasted for hours. Both pilots took turns positioning the F-4 in the proper location on the tanker to refuel. The two crewmembers talked very little about their time in Vietnam. They had flown several combat missions together but hadn't taken the time to talk about their flights. They did enjoy each other's company. Both men had a good sense of humor and enjoyed seeing the humorous side of an issue. Lawson and Stone were a good match for each other and for this long flight home.

After what seemed like forever, and the use of several piddle packs, the crews could see the Hawaiian Islands in the distance.

"The Islands at 12 o'clock low," came a call from one of the tankers.

"We have them in sight," responded the Lead F-4. "As briefed, all F-4s pull back from the tankers and join on your Lead. Flight Leads contact ARTCC (Air Route Traffic Control Center), and pick up a squawk for your flight and get landing instructions. I'll see you all on the ground."

The F-4s did exactly what was briefed. Each flight pulled away from their respective tankers and flew independently toward Hickam Field. Each flight of F-4s radioed the air traffic controllers requesting landing instructions. The tankers landed, then the flights of F-4s were cleared to enter the landing pattern.

As Lawson and Stone flew toward Oahu and Hickam Air Base they remarked that this must have been a very similar sight for the Japanese fighter-bombers that brought destruction and death to Hawaii just 28 years earlier. It was a strange feeling as they pitched out on initial to start their landing sequence.

Lawson taxied their F-4 to its parking place as directed by an airman. He went through the Engine Shutdown checklist and shut down both engines. They were very glad to be on the ground. Lawson and Stone opened their canopies to climb out of the aircraft. Lawson made it look easy but as Stone started to climb out there was no power in his legs and his back felt like it was paralyzed. Stone had experienced this condition before. It would come on without warning after a long mission or one in which he'd pulled a lot of sustained G force maneuvers. He'd even had it checked once in Vietnam but the X-rays showed nothing definitive.

"I'll be with you in a minute," yelled Stone down to Lawson. "I have to get my stuff together."

Stone used his arms and pulled his body up away from the ejection seat and onto the rails of the cockpit.

If I can just sit here a moment and get the blood flowing and my back working I can get down to the ground, he thought. Stone didn't indicate that anything was wrong and looked like he was just taking his time climbing out of the cockpit.

Strength rapidly started coming back into his legs. His back hurt like hell but at least there was feeling coming back. Stone had powerful arms and shoulders and he used them to swing his legs onto the ladder and with the assistance of his arms was able to slide to the ground in a standing position. It still hurt like hell but now he could walk and each step made his condition better. He moved to the debriefing location and joined Lawson to give maintenance the report on their F-4. They reported it was all good.

The Hawaiian Islands were absolutely beautiful. There's a reason they call them paradise. The temperatures seem to always be just right and the skies are mostly clear with just a few puffy clouds. Lawson and Stone, along with the other crews enjoyed their evening in paradise. They had a wonderful meal at the Officer's Club and for the first time started to talk about what had seemed impossible. They were going home. They were already in the States. They were back in the world. It was hard to believe.

Lawson and Stone were tired. They were tired from flying a damaged bird for so many hours but they were also tired from a year's worth of concern and worry about their duties in war, their families and getting home alive. They felt the weight of all of that starting to lift. However, it wasn't over quite yet, they had one more leg to go before they could start the recovery process.

Lawson and Stone checked into their housing arrangements for the night. They were assigned a room to share at the BOQ. It was a small but clean room. It had two twin beds and a shower. It was all that could be hoped for; a clean room and a soft bed with the chance for a good night's sleep.

After checking into their room they decided to take a walk on the base. It was a beautiful base with such a rich history. The flora that grows so naturally at Hickam is stunning. For those who had flown to Oahu, the beauty of Hickam Air Force Base is evident. Commercial air carriers that fly to Hawaii use the same runway as the military base. It's a joint use facility with Hickam on one side of the runway and commercial carriers on the other.

After their walk they decided that they needed to turn in to get as much rest as possible for the last leg of the flight tomorrow. The departure time had been set for 0800. The later departure time gave the flight crews a little more time to rest up for the last leg.

The morning wakeup call was given at 0600. This gave the flight crews enough time to get up and get dressed, have a little chow and get to their aircraft for the pre-flight check and departure at 0800.

Lawson and Stone made the wake up call, made it through the drill and to their F-4 by 0740. It felt like they were sleepwalking due to a heavy sense of fatigue. Their bodies were still operating on the local time in Vietnam. It was what is called jet lag today, but there was no name or even description for it in the late 60's. However, the desire to make it home and get this mission completed drove them to work through the fatigue. They completed the preflight of their F-4 and all looked the same. The aircraft still looked airworthy even if a little out of rig.

The time for departure came as the entire group of KC-135s and F-4Cs started engines and made their way to the end of the active runway. As they were taxiing out, one of the F-4s made a radio call to the F-4 Lead.

"Flight Lead, I believe I may have an intermittent radio problem," radioed the F-4 pilot who didn't give his call sign.

"No you don't," came a reply over the radio from an unidentified source.

There was a short period of silence, then a reply.

"I was mistaken, my radio is just fine," radioed the unnamed F-4 pilot.

The F-4 crew with the possible radio problems became aware that if they called the radio problem they would have to abort their departure and would be stranded in Hawaii until after Christmas.

The mixture of KC-135s and the F-4s were soon airborne without further difficulty. The tankers climbed to their best cruising altitude that would still allow them to refuel the fighters. The F-4Cs joined onto their tankers for the trip home. As before, the F-4s would cycle continuously on the tanker to keep their tanks as full as possible in case of a problem.

The trip home took longer than was forecast. The winds at altitude were against them. Instead of having a tailwind for the trip the group was experiencing a headwind of about 50 knots. This made the expected six and one half hour flight home about an hour longer, not really good news for the pilots sitting in the small confines of the F-4s. For the pilots who had a little extra coffee before the flights, the little piddle packs were worth their weight in gold.

The time zone of the West Coast is two hours ahead of Hawaii. With the extra time in flight, due to the headwinds, it became clear that the group of aircraft wouldn't be landing at George Air Force Base until about 1700 local time, just around sunset.

Lawson and Stone took turns flying the old bird and cycling on and off the tanker. They had a routine down now on how much time would pass before switching control of the aircraft for refueling. They found it important to give control to the rested pilot for refueling. The F-4 gets sensitive in pitch control when it takes on a full load of fuel at altitude. That made it a little difficult to fly in close formation with the tanker, especially with an out of rig aircraft.

As the time slowly went by and the west coast of the United States started to get nearer, the weather began to deteriorate. The clear skies gave way to an overcast condition with the visibility dropping to less than a mile. The tankers adjusted to this by getting separate clearances from ARTCC, called Center, for each aircraft. The F-4s just flew on the wing of their assigned tanker with their transponders turned to standby. As the group of tankers and F-4s arrived within 50 miles of George, Center decided for some reason to separate the F-4s and tankers from each other. Normally, this would be fine but Center gave instructions for the F-4s to separate from the tankers without giving each of the F-4s their own discrete transponder code for identification. It all happened so fast.

"All F-4s attached to your tankers please separate. You'll be given your transponder codes within three minutes," radioed Center.

With those instructions and before anyone realized what was going to happen, each F-4 separated from its tanker into the cloudy and now very crowded sky.

Lawson responded by reducing power on his craft and pushed the nose down to move away from the tanker. The tanker and all the other F-4s that had been flying on its wing disappeared into the darkening clouds.

"What the hell now Stone. We have airplanes all over the sky and we can't see a one of them. Keep your head moving and your eyes open. This is really bad."

"I'm looking but I can't see through this crap," responded Stone.

It took only a few seconds for Center to realize that it had made a big mistake.

The radios of all the F-4s came alive with each calling for its own transponder code and radar separation from all the aircraft around them. Center scrambled to correct the situation. It requested that only one F-4 call at a time and give its aircraft identification so an ID code could be assigned.

"Damn," commented Stone over the intercom, "we live through a year of combat only to get killed in a midair collision over our destination base in the States. That's just plain wonderful."

"I got some more good news for you," responded Lawson, "we just had generator failure on the number one engine."

"Oh, great news, it just keeps getting better and better," answered Stone. "I hope that's all we have, this could be the start of something big. I'll pull out the Emergency Procedures checklist and check it out"

A generator failure in the F-4 could mean several things. It could be just a generator failure and the number-two generator would pick up the load, or it could be the start of a hydraulic system failure or even an engine failure. In any case it was time to get this old bird on terra firma.

Lawson finally made contact with the Center and received a transponder squawk for identification. Their assigned call sign was Guardian 8 and their code was 4316.

"Guardian 8, radar contact two five zero miles west of George. Descend and maintain six thousand feet, turn to a heading of zero-four-five-degrees. This will be vectors to a GCA approach at George. The altimeter setting is three-zero-two-niner," radioed Center.

"Roger, descending to six thousand, heading zero-four-five-degrees with the meter at three-zero-two-niner," answered Lawson.

"Anything new on the generator problem?" requested Stone. "How are the pressures and temps looking up there?"

"So far, only the generator," responded Lawson, "everything else looks okay. However stay alert, we still may have to eject from this thing."

"Don't even talk that way," answered Stone. "Let's just get on the ground."

Center turned Guardian 8 over to George Approach Control and gave instructions to descend to a lower altitude, to turn on final approach and to contact the final GCA controller. Lawson gave the GCA controller a call.

"George GCA, Guardian 8 with you heading one seven zero degrees and descending to five thousand feet."

"Roger," responded the GCA controller, "I read you loud and clear."

As Lawson and Stone descended to 5,000 feet they broke through the clouds and could see George just a few miles ahead and slightly to their left. It was a wonderful sight. It's always a good thing for a pilot who's flying under instrument conditions to break out of the clouds and see the ground clearly.

"George GCA, Guardian 8," radioed Lawson. "We're canceling IFR and going to tower. We have the field in sight."

"Roger, Guardian 8," responded the GCA Controller. "Understand you have the field in sight and are canceling IFR. Cleared to tower frequency."

"Roger, going to tower," radioed Lawson as he started the Before Landing checklist.

"George Tower, Guardian 8 on a five mile GCA final, request clearance to land," radioed Lawson.

"Guardian 8," answered George Tower, "you are cleared to land runway two-one."

"Cleared to land, runway two-one," responded Lawson.

"Let's get this thing configured and on the ground," called Lawson over the intercom to Stone. "My butt's going to fall off."

"Mine has already fallen off," answered Stone. "I may never be able to walk again. Let's get on the ground now."

Lawson brought the F-4 over the end of the runway and made an almost perfect F-4 landing. To those not trained in F-4 landings it looks more like a controlled crash. The drag chute came out and the brakes applied. The rollout was normal and uneventful. Lawson taxied the F-4 off the runway, released his drag chute and, giving a little power, proceeded to his assigned parking spot identified by an airman lineman giving hand signals. They were lined up and parked right in front of the operations building.

Lawson quickly shut down the engines and both men went through their After Landing checklists. Swiftly they opened their canopies and began to crawl out of their cramped cockpits.

Indescribable feelings came over Stone as he made his way down the ladder to the ground below. They were unreal feelings. They were back! They were home safely after so many months of doubt and uncertainty. Stone slowly began walking away from the bent, tired F-4C that had so dependably brought its crew back safely. As Stone was about ten yards away he heard a loud swish and a draining sound. He turned back to the aircraft to see a large pool of red hydraulic fluid pouring out of the aircraft. The red fluid just kept pouring and pouring out of the bird.

Damn! Was that partial or total hydraulic failure? Stone thought. *What if that had happened on short final a few minutes earlier? Could we have taken care of it quickly enough? Would we have had to eject?*

Stone didn't want to think about it. He turned around toward the Operations building and lowered himself to the ground onto both knees. His head went down and he gave a prayer of thankfulness that today neither he, nor any of his flight members, died or were injured.

Stone got to his feet and went into the Operations building. He didn't know what to expect from the scheduled debrief, but whatever he'd thought it would be, it turned out to be much different. What was happening was a kind of busy, coordinated chaos.

There was a short line where all of the flight crews' gear was being checked in and a second line for schedules to be made on commercial flights out of LAX for their flights home. Stone's destination was Albuquerque, New Mexico where his wife was staying while he was in Vietnam.

There was a colonel in charge of what was going on and he was making it all happen and happen very quickly. Stone was through the first line within a minute and moved to the second line.

"Where are you going lieutenant?" asked the colonel.

"I need to get to Albuquerque, Sir," responded Stone.

The colonel quickly looked through his sheets of airline schedules.

"There's one more flight leaving tonight lieutenant. Get your ass outside and on the crew bus now. We'll be leaving here in five minutes for LAX. We'll get you on that flight."

Stone made a quick, and much needed, restroom stop and moved rapidly outside to the blue Air Force bus that was waiting with its engine running. Within a minute the colonel was on board and commanded that the bus make it to LAX as quickly as possible with their load. There were eight F-4 crewmembers on the bus each headed out to different locations in the States.

Stone had never seen such efficiency and desire as that shown by this colonel who was determined to get all these men on their flights home. It was a wonderful thing to see.

All of the men made it to LAX that night and all of them made their flights out. This was all due to the efforts of this forgotten colonel who made it his task to see this job done well and to get these men home for Christmas.

Stone's mind was on overload as he sat in his commercial aircraft heading toward Albuquerque. He'd only seen his wife once in the year he was in Vietnam and it had been six months since he'd last seen her. She didn't even know when to expect him home. All she knew was that he was going to try and make it home for Christmas. The flight time went swiftly as Stone switched back and forth from sleep to being wide awake. So many things were running through his mind. He was alive and going home. It was what he couldn't dare to dwell on while in combat. It was just too good to be real!

His commercial flight landed at Albuquerque a little after midnight. He quickly deplaned and went to a phone booth in the Sunport lobby and called his home number. His wife answered. Stone responded. "Honey, your husband is home. Will you come and pick me up?"

Epilogue

The author wants to thank those who have taken the opportunity to read this work. It isn't a traditional book with a plot or storyline. It wasn't designed to develop characters and carry them through the pages. It isn't a diary or a day-to-day description of a tour of duty.

What the author intended to do with the stories was to give a real and honest view of what aircrews experienced each day as they flew, fought, suffered or died to make an honorable contribution to the freedom of our country. The work wasn't designed to be dramatic or excessive in the descriptions of either the characters or their actions. The author wanted to describe the events as they were, no gloss, no color, just in black and white.

The heroes in our service echelons never carried out their missions for press or glory. They just worked to get the job done, without thought of the costs or consequences to themselves. They struggled to do their duty, to be true to those struggling equally at their side. The costs of these efforts became whatever the consequences revealed. Fate delivered its message in an instant. In one moment all was well and in the next, tragedy spread over all events, lives were changed forever.

The author expresses great confidence that the reader will understand and be able to pull together the messages delivered in each story. These are messages of personal courage, sometimes under fire, messages of personal efforts, struggles and sacrifices of our veterans and their families.

The F-4 Phantom II Fighter-Bomber

McDonnell Douglas F-4 Phantom II. (Photo Courtesy of National Museum of U.S. Air Force)

The F-4 Phantom II was first flown in 1958, and was developed by the U.S. Navy for fleet defense. The Air Force's first version, the F-4C made it first flight in 1963, and production deliveries began six months later.

Phantom II production ended in 1979 after over 5,000 had been built with more than 2,600 going to the Air Force.

In 1965 the USAF sent its first F-4Cs to Southeast Asia, where they flew air-to-air and air-to-ground missions.

In its air-to-ground role, the F-4C could carry twice the normal load of a WWII B-17 bomber. The armament loaded on the aircraft on display (National Museum of the USAF) is typical for an F-4C in 1967. It consists of four AIM-7E and four AIM-9B air-to-air missiles, and eight 750-pound Mk-117 bombs. The aircraft also carries two external fuel tanks on the outboard pylons and one electronic countermeasures (ECM) pod.

TECHNICAL NOTES:

Armament: Up to 16,000 lbs. of externally carried nuclear or conventional bombs, rockets, missiles, or 20 mm cannon pod.

Engines: Two General Electric J-79-GE-15s of 17,000 lbs. thrust each

Maximum speed: 1,400 mph

Cruising speed: 590 mph / 546 knots at 35,000 ft.

Range: 1,750 miles - 1528 nautical miles with one 600 gal and two 370 gal external tanks

Ceiling: 59,600 ft.

Span: 38 ft. 5 in. (27 ft. 6 in. folded)

Length: 58 ft. 2 in.

Height: 16 ft. 6 in.

Weight: 58,000 lbs. maximum designed takeoff weight

Crew: two

(Information Courtesy of National Museum of U.S. Air Force)

Made in the USA
Columbia, SC
07 November 2021

48479671R00138